Cassidy's Guide to Everyday Etiquette
(and Obfuscation)

Also by Sue Stauffacher

SUE STAUFFACHER

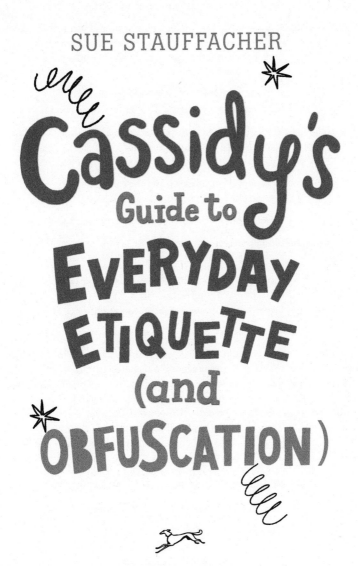

Cassidy's Guide to EVERYDAY ETIQUETTE (and OBFUSCATION)

ALFRED A. KNOPF

New York

THIS IS A BORZOI BOOK PUBLISHED BY ALFRED A. KNOPF

Visit us on the Web! randomhousekids.com

Educators and librarians, for a variety of teaching tools, visit us at
RHTeachersLibrarians.com

Library of Congress Cataloging-in-Publication Data
Stauffacher, Sue
Cassidy's guide to everyday etiquette (and obfuscation) / Sue Stauffacher.
—First edition.
pages   cm.
Summary: Eleven-year-old tomboy Cassidy is devastated to inherit a five-
week summer course at etiquette school, where even her classic epic pranks
cannot save her, and worse, her best friend, Jack, is more interested in their
new teenage neighbor than in Cassidy's woes.
ISBN 978-0-375-83097-6 (trade) — ISBN 978-0-375-93097-3 (lib. bdg.) —
ISBN 978-0-375-89899-0 (ebook)
[1. Etiquette—Fiction. 2. Friendship—Fiction. 3. Family life—Fiction.
4. Maturation (Psychology)—Fiction. 5. Practical jokes—Fiction.
6. Humorous stories—Fiction.] I. Title.
PZ7.S8055Cas 2015 [Fic]—dc23 2014035085

The text of this book is set in 11.5-point Horley Old Style.

Printed in the United States of America
June 2015
10 9 8 7 6 5 4 3 2 1

First Edition

For my longtime editor, Nancy Hinkel,
and agent, Wendy Schmalz,
with gratitude for helping me bring
so many wonderful characters to life

CHAPTER 1

Unwanted Gifts

"Of course there are worse things than being born a girl." Instead of kissing me good night, Mom was still trying to make her point.

"Name one."

"Well . . ." She smoothed my hair—the hair that just so happened to be sticking to my face because I'd been crying. Not baby tears. "No fair, life stinks, go jump off a bridge" tears. And all because stupid Great-Grandma Reed had died!

"You could have been born the hunchback of Notre Dame," Mom said.

I pushed my face further into the pillow. "He didn't have to go to school. *He* lived with bats."

"How do you expect me to understand what you're saying when your mouth is in that pillow? Should I draw some letters on your back?"

Now she was trying to distract me. I lifted my head. "Not unless they spell N-O."

"For heaven's sake, Cassidy, you can't say no. It's only a five-week course and it was her dying wish."

I rolled over and covered my mouth, faking a big yawn. "I'm tired."

"Nice try," Mom said. "You never cover your mouth when you yawn."

"I bet that's one of the lessons. Will you turn out the light, please?"

Mom tried to put her hand underneath me to reach my back.

"Not that one. Only Dad can turn that one off."

When he was home, Dad always stopped in before he went to bed to see if I was having trouble falling asleep. Then he'd rub my back a little, between my shoulder blades, before flipping off the switch. But tonight he was at a sales conference, learning all about vitamins. Dad manages the biggest grocery store in the Great Lakes Groceries chain.

After the news Mom delivered at dinner, I was pretty sure I'd lie awake even if he *was* home to turn off the light.

"Don't be so dramatic, Cassidy. Try to think of it as an opportunity. Your sister is."

"But it *is* an opportunity for Magda. She's going to forensic camp at Greer College!"

"Well, try to be more positive, then. It was my grandmother's dying wish."

My only answer was to squeeze my eyes shut and keep them that way until I heard the door close.

There was one person who would understand the unfolding tragedy that began yesterday, otherwise known as May twenty-second, when the box containing Great-Grandma Reed's will was dropped on our front porch. I'd been waiting for my copy of *Rolling Through Life: Hobos in America,* which Mom had let me order for one cent plus $3.99 shipping, so I saw the box straightaway. My excitement and anticipation quickly turned to horror after breakfast when Mom read us what was in the will.

Only Jack would understand. Jack, my fellow Knight of the Road, my comrade-in-arms, my best friend since kindergarten, when we learned that heavier objects travel faster and he could steer the sled and I could use my legs as a brake, which I hardly ever did, but was sometimes required to avoid a collision with the school Dumpster. Jack had been gone all day at his grandma Mimi's.

After Mom left, I crawled to the end of my bed to my stack of old-timey suitcases. Yanking open the top one, I sorted through my best junk for my slingshot. Mostly, I put tinfoil golf balls in it and shoot them at the crane mobile my sister, Magda, made for me the year Mom forced us to exchange homemade Christmas presents.

No slingshot. But I did find a sugar-candy skull left over from Halloween and made a mental note in case Mom decided to torture us with another broccoli-and-mushroom casserole. Next, I mined for my slingshot in the Lego tub next to my bed, kicked around in my favorite clothes pile (Detroit Tigers hoodie, patched Levis, red flannel underwear that doubled for pajamas) and finally found it in the hollowed-out stump Dad let me cart to my room to use as a stool. Now all I needed was my metal lunch box full of skipping stones, which I kept at arm's reach under my bed in the event that I woke up and surprised an intruder.

Opening the window and propping it with the book I'd also inherited from Great-Grandma Reed, I loaded the slingshot and let one fly.

As soon as Jack pulled back the curtain, I shone my flashlight—*dot dot dot dash dash dash dot dot dot*. SOS. Only to be used in cases of extreme emergency. Shivering, I zipped my hoodie over my pajamas. Even in May, it was still cold after the sun went down, and I wanted to watch Jack's progress.

It took him a minute to get his gear, but soon enough he was lowering himself from his bedroom window with a rope tied to the grappling hook the Taylors kept in their bathroom as part of their emergency fire-escape plan. Then he tossed the hook into our oak tree, hauled himself up until he was over our sunporch and dropped down onto the roof as easily as a cat. From there, all he had to do was grab the drainpipe and pull himself up to my window ledge. I once heard my dad tell my mom he'd anchored that drainpipe to the side of the house with industrial screws so Jack didn't kill himself.

"Of course I don't like that he does it," he told her. "But I can't stay awake all night to prevent it."

"Impressive, huh?" Panting, Jack kissed the grappling hook and held it up like it was a trophy.

"Maybe." I wasn't in the mood to be impressed. I jumped back onto my bed. "How do you feel about running away?"

"Bad timing. Dad's helping me make the harness I need to practice falling out of buildings."

Jack's goal in life is to be a stunt man for the movies. His fallback: escape artist. If there's a fear gene, he got shorted, and he has the broken bones to prove it.

"What's up, Cass? When I saw the SOS, I figured—"

"Great-Grandma Reed died."

"Oh. Sorry."

"Well, I'm not! She had chin hair and she snored."

Jack put his hand over my mouth. "Quiet down, will you? I don't want to get caught again. Wasn't she the one you visited last summer? You disconnected her oxygen tube or something?"

"I was *trying* to wheel her outside to show her the squirrel tail I'd found. It still had some blood on it!"

"Hard to appreciate squirrel tails if you can't breathe." Pulling my arms until they stuck straight out in front of me, Jack used them as guides to rewrap his rope. Why he needed to do this when he was just going to use the rope again on the trip home I didn't understand; Jack is picky about his tools. I held still, my arms exactly twelve inches apart.

"Besides, it was only for a few seconds."

"I thought you said she turned blue."

"A minute, tops. You're not helping, Jack."

He finished wrapping and set the loop of rope on the floor with the grappling hook in the middle. "You probably shouldn't talk trash about her, either, seeing she's dead. It's bad for your karma."

Jack's mom, Janae (that's *juh-NYE*), is a yoga instructor. She was always reminding us about our karma. "So that's what the SOS was for? Great-Grandma Reed?"

"Yes. No! I mean, I didn't want her to die but she was headed in that direction. Even *she* said so. It's what I inherited."

"Wow. There was a will? Did you have to put on a suit and go to a lawyer's office? Were people weeping?" Jack jumped onto my bed and let his head hang over the side. Like me, he couldn't sit still for long. I climbed up next to him.

"She lived in Tennessee, remember? Last I checked, this was Michigan. We got it in the mail. What are you doing?"

"Gotta practice hanging upside down . . . you know, keeping my wits about me when my head is full of blood. Can I see the will? Does it have a bunch of official stamps on it? Did she have loads of money under her mattress?"

I had to lean way out to look him in the eye. I wanted to see his expression when I told him. "Check out what's propping open the window."

Jack followed my gaze. "The dictionary?"

"Sort of . . . dictionary of politeness, maybe."

"Sorry. Not following."

"That book is by a lady named Emily Post. That book and etiquette lessons are what I scored when my rich great-grandma died, Jack Taylor. A boring book the size of a lunch box and ten sessions with some stuffy lady in a hat and gloves teaching me what fork to use."

"Ten weeks of summer school?"

"No! Geez . . . five weeks is bad enough. It's every Monday and Wednesday, from June fourteenth to July fourteenth. You're turning red, by the way."

"How long was that, do you think? Sixty seconds?"

"Jack!" I grabbed his leg and attempted a Polish hammer, one of the moves I'm famous for when we wrestle.

"Hey! Cassidy!"

"Shhhh! We're supposed to be quiet, remember? Go on . . . say it, then."

Jack wriggled free. "You know I'm not going to say it."

I knew. I was just trying to distract myself. In all the time I'd known him, Jack had never said "uncle." The word was not in his vocabulary. He wouldn't even call his uncle Bob "uncle."

Jack reached up to massage his leg. "Don't tell me you're gonna miss the Fourth of July picnic."

"No, I get that Monday off, but we have to make it up with an extra class. You okay?"

Putting his hands on the floor, Jack flipped his legs over his head and rolled himself into a sitting position again. "What about Magda?" Reaching over to the window, he yanked out my manners book.

"She got *Cause of Death: Forensic Files of a Medical Examiner,* and a week at sleepover camp studying dead bodies. Where is the justice?"

Riffling through the pages, Jack said, "You got the short end of it, Cass. Wow, you can learn how to do anything the polite way in here—I never knew there was a right way and a wrong way to open presents at a birthday party."

"It's only because I stepped on her tube." It was so unfair! "Well, that and her precious sand dollars from the Florida Keys. How was I supposed to know they weren't coasters?"

"Didn't you say there was an accident at her swanky club?"

The mad tears threatened to make a showing for Jack. "She said I needed instructions in the rules of polite society or else I'd be the death of my parents."

"She was probably still sore about you cutting off her oxygen."

"Cassidy?" Mom knocked on the door. "Janae is on the phone requesting that her son return home via normal human conveyance . . . otherwise known as the stairs. Tomorrow's a school day, after all."

"So busted." Jack handed me the book and looped his rope and grappling hook over his shoulder. "You never could talk in a normal voice about your great-grandma."

After he left, I got back under my covers, wondering if he was right about the karma thing. Was karma what made you a boy or a girl?

There were worse things than being born a girl. There had to be. I could be buried in a fish tank full of worms like they did to that lady on *Fear Factor,* for example.

Manners lessons only made sense if my goal was to become a princess or a movie star or something wacko like that, but I think I made it quite clear to my great-grandma that I planned to be a Knight of the Road. What did hobos need to know about etiquette? Or pirates, for that matter—my fallback. I mean, she remembered Magda wanted to be a scientist. Why couldn't I go to a camp that taught me how to jump off a speeding train without losing any limbs? Or to sleep in an alley without getting my shoes stolen?

"Cass?" Now it was my older sister knocking.

I covered myself in blankets. "I'm hibernating," I said from my burrow.

"I'm coming in anyway." I felt Magda take a seat on my bed. "You're reading this already?" I heard the sound of riffling pages. "Interesting. If you're divorced, there are rules for who gets to go to the spring concert. And, here's how to tell someone you don't want to go to their party after all. Hey . . ." Magda must have remembered she had a sister, because she added, "You're going to suffocate under there."

"Good. Then you can stuff me and put me in a dress and send me to my etiquette class."

"A point of clarity, Cass. Forensic science is not about embalming. It's about the mystery of decomposition."

I poked my head out of the covers. "Even embalming's better than solving the mystery of how to curtsy."

"For me, maybe, but not for you." Magda's glasses were so heavy she had to push them up her nose at least four times during a normal conversation. Even her new "rimless" glasses, which Mom swore made her look much less like an egghead, required repositioning. "You could never be around dead bodies. You hate the smell of rotting and you'd freak if you saw a maggot."

"Magda!"

"What? No one else can hear us."

It's a little-known secret that bugs, especially squirmy, scuttly ones, creep me out—in a big way. Little-known, as in Jack . . . and Magda. And, okay, Mom and Dad. My future occupation and *all* my fallbacks—pirate, mutineer, voodoo doctor, etc.—involved bugs, and plenty of them. When I'm a hobo, I'll have to deal with bugs in my bedroll, bugs in my hair, bugs in my soup. I knew I had to get over this problem, but that's what high school is for, isn't it? The hard stuff?

Magda kept going with her list. "Did I mention larvae,

which are by nature squirmy? It is a well-known fact that dead bodies are an ideal host site for—"

"Okay, okay! Thanks, Mag. I feel loads better!" I fell back on my pillows and started to snore.

"You're not the only one who has to deal with onerous tasks," Magda said, pushing back on my legs as I tried to inch her off the bed. "Mom says I have to introduce myself to our new neighbors."

"What? The new people moved in already? The Fensters just left. I was going to practice breaking into their house." The Fensters' house was directly behind ours and kitty-corner to the Taylors'.

"Yup." Magda was chewing her thumbnail, something I'm pretty sure you get executed for in etiquette class. "I watched the movers bringing in suitcases this afternoon. It all matches and it's all—"

"Don't tell me. Pink."

"Worse. Pink plaid. Mom went right over, of course, and interrogated them. They have a daughter my age. Her name is Sabrina. She's flying in on Friday."

"Sabrina?"

"Yup. She competes in beauty contests. She was Miss Runner-Up Teen Decatur last year."

"And she's your age, right? So she wouldn't want anything to do with a runt like me."

"But you could come with me and drive her crazy so she gets the idea that being friends with me wouldn't be so fantastic."

I thought about it for a minute. Driving people crazy *is* one of my hobbies. "Nope. But I will let you borrow my book. I'm sure there's a whole chapter on meeting the new neighbors."

Magda couldn't resist. She turned to the index. "Let's see what *Emily Post's Etiquette* has to say. Neighbors, neighbors . . . borrowing from neighbors, pets, noise issues . . . wait. Here it is: new neighbors." She proceeded to read: "When strangers move into an established neighborhood, it is courteous and friendly of the residents nearby to call on them. The newcomers wait for present residents to issue the first formal invitation—"

She slammed the book shut. "Ugh. Mom was right. *Please* come with me, Cassidy."

You'd have to know Magda to know why something as simple as introducing herself was such a hardship. Magda is like a big floating head. When she gets into her decomposition zone, she doesn't think about anything else: eating, sleeping, going to the bathroom. According to Mom, she has no interest in what most fifteen-year-old girls like—boys, music, boys, dressing up, boys. Mom figures if Magda ever does get interested, she'll get married in her lab coat to a boy version of herself. They won't dare have any babies because they'd forget where they put them on a regular basis.

"I hope you two are de-escalating," Mom said, pushing her head through the door. Without knocking first. "Why haven't you dimmed the lights, Cassidy?"

After eight-thirty, I wasn't supposed to have any bright lights on in my room. Magda stepped on the dimmer switch. "Mom. This is private."

"Just checking in to make sure you haven't let any more boys through your window."

"It was Jack, Mom."

She closed the door and Magda started in on her thumbnail again.

"Say, Mag. What is karma, exactly? Is it like luck? That reminds me . . . I gotta find my lucky rabbit's foot." I did a couple of scissors kicks under the covers, just in case the foot had worked its way to the bottom of the bed.

"About that rabbit's foot . . ."

"Did you decompose it? Are you kidding me? I won that at Niagara Falls! They don't even sell colored ones in Grand River."

"I just needed a little bit." Magda stared off into space. "I couldn't figure out how they dehydrated it . . . there had to be a chemical involved. . . ."

I grabbed my sister's hand and squeezed.

"Let go, Cassidy! I'll tell you everything I know about karma." Magda has a very low pain threshold.

"Which is?"

"Well . . . wait a minute while I revive." She massaged her hand as if I'd done real damage. "Karma is . . . I guess you could say karma is 'you get what you deserve.'"

"Seriously?"

"Yep. If you do bad things, bad things get done to you. And if you do good things, like let your sister have a tiny patch of rabbit fur, then good things get done to you."

I fell back on my pillows. "That's not karma, Magda. That's blackmail."

"Well, there you have it. Now, I have to go to bed and get my beauty rest. I'll have to sleep all week to get ready to meet Sabrina the beauty queen."

"Anything's gotta be better than the Fensters."

"I don't know. I liked them."

"That's because they donated their dead canary's body to

12

science." (Which means Mr. Fenster gave it to Magda so she could watch it decompose.) The real truth was the Fensters were ancient and their house smelled like cabbage. I tried a couple of times to train Percy, their yappy little dog, with treats so he would let me jump over the fence to get back all the balls and tin cans that accidentally got into their yard. I used quality stuff—pepperoni-and-cheese beef jerky—but the little mongrel bit me every time. He'd wait until I poked my finger through the fence, bite me and make me watch him eat the jerky I'd dropped on his side.

Percy did things on his terms, Jack said. He was full of admiration for that dog.

After Magda left, I buried myself alive under my covers again, and thought hard about what possible good could come from a beauty queen living next door. Maybe *she* would want my etiquette lessons! Nah. She probably already knew that stuff. *Maybe* I could skip half the lessons due to an unexplainable and highly contagious disease and she could tutor me.

There were a lot of possibilities to think over. Could one of them be that Magda was right? No, I decided. Anything had to be better than Mr. Fenster with his smelly cigars and his hairy shoulders, leaning over the fence giving *me* advice about how to fix my Rollerblades.

Mr. Fenster had sided with Magda. "Just remember, Cassidy," he'd said when he informed me that he and Mrs. Fenster were moving to Sunny Pointe Senior Center. "There are worse things than living behind a couple of old farts."

CHAPTER 2

Understanding the Feelings of Children

"Hungry?" I asked Jack after school the next day.

"Starving."

"Your house or mine?"

"No question. Didn't you look at the calendar? It's the fourth Monday of the month."

I smacked my forehead. My mom was so sly she hadn't said a thing that morning. On the fourth Monday of every month, Mom and her friend Mrs. Pearce drove an hour east to the Lansing Garibaldi's Import/Export Store to stock up on essentials, like meatless meatballs, navy-bean hummus and spinach-and-kale dip. It's probably obvious from that list that Mom and Mrs. Pearce are health nuts. After years of lobbying,

Magda and I got one more item onto the essentials list—cookie butter!—which if you've never heard of it means you live in a one-horse town like Grand River, with no Garibaldi's.

Eating cookie butter is like mainlining a gingerbread house. They take a million gingersnaps and grind them into a paste. What a brilliant and efficient way to get more of my favorite food group—dessert.

"Hi, sweeties." Mom kissed the top of my head. Then Jack's. I looked around. Everything had been put away: the fabric bags, her insulated Garibaldi's cooler.

Cool as a cucumber, she said, "You two hungry? I could make you a smoothie."

Jack looked at me and shrugged. "You hungry?"

I could hear his stomach growling. "Nah. You?"

"Not really."

I turned to Mom. "Those fish sticks and that irradiated apple they gave us at lunch really hit the spot."

"I would have been happy to pack you a lunch, Cassidy, but you said you'd rather take your chances with the slop they serve at school."

Jack and I just stared at my mom without blinking.

"That's a direct quote."

We didn't respond because, without even agreeing to it beforehand, we'd become iridium. You see, Jack and I have a number of superpowers that drive our parents crazy. Tops on the list has to be density. When we don't like what's happening—or we've just done something that other people won't like, such as one of our famous pranks—Jack and I become osmium and iridium. I can never remember which metal is denser, but since they are both considered thicker than anything else, it doesn't

15

really matter. I like the word "iridium" better, so I usually call that.

"Very funny, you two. I know exactly what you're doing, but all the obfuscation in the world will not get you to your goal." Grabbing her sweater and her cell phone, she continued, "I'm assuming Janae is home, Jack. There's something I need to talk to her about."

I wondered if Jack would emerge from his density to grill Mom. When there's "something she needs to talk about" with Janae, it usually has to do with an improvement project, like getting us to watch less TV or volunteering us to pick up the trash after the May Day parade.

But Jack stayed in position. He's a real pro.

"Fine." Tugging on her sweater, she added, "You'll never find it."

As soon as we heard the front door close, Jack sat down at the kitchen table and said, "What's that mean, anyway? Obfuscation?"

"Not a hundred percent sure; she only says it when she's annoyed."

We stopped talking and concentrated on the problem. Hunger really helps you focus.

"All we have to do is think like your mom."

"I'm becoming her right now." I froze. When I started moving again, I was in character: "Jack and Cassidy will never think to look where I keep the peanut butter. They don't think I'm clever enough to hide it in plain sight."

We both made a grab for the cupboard, but Jack was faster. I curled my arms around his chest. Normally, I could lift him a few inches off the floor to mess with his footing, but he wasn't budging. It's like his feet were made of iron all of a sudden; so I put him in a choke hold. In seconds, he had me down on the floor, my choking arm behind my back.

"No more wrestling in the kitchen, remember? Your mom's soap dish?"

"You've been practicing that move."

"No I haven't." Jack stuck out his hand and pulled me up before moving aside all the jars anywhere near the peanut butter.

Nothing.

"I've got it!" I snapped my fingers. I was now in the character of a TV detective. "Remember the time she hid it in her sock drawer?"

We raced into the hallway. Jack caught my ankle on the stairs and stepped right over me. By the time I got to my parents' bedroom, he was holding up a sticky note. "Give your mother a little more credit than that," it said.

Jumping onto my parents' bed, Jack lay back and crossed his ankles and his arms in his best thinking position. "Maybe we should channel the cookie butter."

I lay down next to him and did the double cross, too. We could generate some good electricity between our two brains that way. For a whole minute, Cassidy Corcoran and Jack Taylor were completely still. And silent. Which might have been the first time in recorded history.

It's also what helped us crack the case.

"Did I hear Magda's door close?" I asked Jack.

"You mean the same Magda who programs her phone to alert her to your mom's Garibaldi runs?"

Holding our breath, we spider-crawled down the hall. "She's opening a package of crackers," Jack said, his ear to the door.

Despite the sign on the door that warned NOXIOUS FUMES PRESENT. DO NOT ENTER UNLESS DRESSED IN A FULL HAZMAT SUIT AND A RIOT MASK, we burst in anyway.

"Magda Corcoran. I am arresting you on suspicion of stealing the cookie butter and eating it in your room. Officer Taylor, where are the handcuffs?"

"Obviously, I'm eating in my room, but I didn't steal the cookie butter." Magda held up the disgusting jar of soy-nut butter that Mom tried to sneak by us during her most recent evil campaign to get us to eat health food.

Jack rubbed his chin, TV detective–style. "Something's not adding up here."

Magda tried to look at us without blinking—as dense as iridium—but her cheek was twitching and she couldn't maintain eye contact.

"We'll need to bag that as evidence." I held out my hand for the soy stuff.

"You will not. I'm . . . conducting an experiment."

"Really." Now I double-triple knew something was fishy. Mom just bought that stuff a week or so ago. It wasn't even near to rotting! "And what kind of an experiment would that be, Professor Corcoran?"

I glanced over at Jack, who nodded to show he understood my plan. I'd distract. He'd swipe the jar.

"It's an experiment about . . ." Magda tried to pinch the rim of her glasses and look all scholarly, but, as I think I mentioned, her new glasses didn't have rims.

"Magda, are you sweating?"

"No! I'm . . . it's an experiment about . . . aflatoxins and, uh, how they accelerate the rate of— Jack!"

Jack had accomplished a clean lift of the jar and was now sitting on Magda's dresser, swinging his legs. "Don't you find it interesting, Officer Corcoran"—he held out the jar to me—"that this jar of soy-nut butter smells suspiciously like ginger-bread?"

"How can that be, Officer Taylor . . . ?" I almost fainted from hunger after taking a big sniff. "The label clearly says healthy, disgusting soy-nut butter." Giving my sister's shoulder a push, I said, "Spill it, Mags, and we'll put in a good word for you down at the station."

"I almost got away with it. If only Mom and Dad would let me put that dead bolt on my door!"

"We'll share," Jack said. "C'mon. Hand over the knife. How'd you find it?"

"Two key pieces of evidence. Remember when Mom hid the cookie-butter jar so well even she couldn't find it?"

"Of course I remember. Mr. Fenster brought Percy over to see if he could sniff it out and he wee-weed on my bedpost!"

"He was marking his territory," Magda explained.

"You don't see me hopping the fence to do that on his doggy lounger, do you?"

"Stay on task, Officer." Jack handed me a graham cracker.

"We remember," I said. "That jar has never been recovered."

"To your knowledge." Magda licked her fingers. She'd already been indulging. "Dad's insulated lunch bag did have traces. Anyway, I heard her tell Dad she had to make the jar easier to find. Then, when I came home today, I found this on the counter." Magda held up one of the single-use superglue tubes we go through by the dozen in the Corcoran household.

"Sooo . . . she soaked off the soy label and put it on the cookie butter. Brilliant. Really." I took half of Jack's graham cracker and bit down. "I don't give Mom enough credit."

"You're spraying crumbs, Cassidy."

"Didn't I tell you, Jack? Hidden in plain sight."

My stomach went from growling to purring as we finished off two packets of graham crackers and half a jar of cookie butter.

"We'd better stop," Magda said. "Dad told me if the jar was empty when he got home, I should prepare to see a grown man cry."

"So why do you think Mom wants to talk to Janae?"

"Probably some do-gooder idea she picked up from the bulletin board at Garibaldi's."

"Well, I'm not going in on it. I'll generate enough do-goodness for one hundred eleven-year-olds by going to etiquette class."

Just *thinking* about etiquette class made me want to lick the rest of the cookie butter off my fingers.

"Maybe we can eavesdrop. Wanna go through the window?" Jack asked.

It might not seem like it, but there *are* differences between Jack and me. He likes having a lot of air between his feet and the ground. I'm not so into that.

"I'll wait until you reach the porch roof and then I'll sprint. Better vacuum in here, Mags," I said as Jack took off for my bedroom window. "Destroy the evidence."

"Cassidy, haven't I taught you anything over the years? There is *always* residue."

As I dashed through the kitchen, I couldn't resist screeching to a stop in front of my startled mom and huffing a big breath of cookie butter in her face. "Nice try, Mom."

It didn't really matter if there was no one to eavesdrop on now that Mom was back at our house; something was always happening at Jack's house. Mr. Taylor pulled up just as I arrived. "Look what I discovered at Liquidation Station," he said, hopping out of the cab of his old Ford pickup and planting a kiss on the hood—which he did every time it successfully got him back home.

Jack jumped into the back of the truck and tore into one of the boxes. He held up the wooden U, framing his face. "Toilet seats?"

"Yep. They're cracked."

"Dad? What's exciting about this?"

"Use your imagination, Jack-o."

Mr. Taylor leaned down and whispered in my ear. "Think heat." He smelled like sawdust and paint and something else you smell in hardware stores that I couldn't put my finger on— maybe engine oil. If they sold that smell, I'd buy a bottle and give it to my dad for Christmas.

"A hobo would burn them," I said. "If they're cracked, that means they're dried out."

"Precisely. I will burn them in my woodstove in the shop this winter. If you and Jack want to pull out the hardware, we can sell the metal and I'll let you have what's left over from purchasing the lot."

It was just the sort of thing a 'bo would do, take something other people think is trash and find use in it. Jack tossed me a toilet seat. "Let's get the tools and see if this is worth making a deal."

I followed Jack to their garage, which the Taylors converted into a workshop for Jack's dad. He went to the back wall and switched on an overhead light, illuminating Mr. Taylor's pegboard filled with tools: hammers, wrenches, screwdrivers, mallets. There was always something in the vise grip on the edge of the long bench, always wood shavings on the floor. It was from Jack and his dad that I learned about things like miter boxes, planes and rasps. As Mr. Taylor pointed out, knowing how to put something together would come in handy on the road—even if just to barter for a night in a farmer's barn.

"What's your dad got going now?" I asked, running my hand along a smooth post with a big ball of wood on top.

"He's making my mom a garden gate. See?" Jack held up a pair of old iron hinges. "He got these from a house they salvaged in Wayland. There was so much rust, it took me forever to loosen the screws and fasteners. I finally got them free with some cutting oil. I almost used the propane torch, but Dad saved the garage from going up in flames when he reminded me that propane and oil don't mix."

Jack went on, talking about flexible sanding sponges and wire wheels and all that elbow grease that made him better than me at push-ups; listening to the sound of his voice was hypnotizing me . . . I wanted to lie down in the sawdust and fall asleep.

If it wasn't for the stupid fly that had to bumble right into a spiderweb!

"Jack, get him out!" I shouted, pointing at the fly while

keeping my eyes covered, which did not block out the pathetic buzzing.

"But it's not fair, Cassidy. That'd be like swiping the spider's dinner."

"I know! I just . . . I can't watch it struggle. Ugh." I jumped off the bench and wrapped my arms around my head. There was nothing wrong with it, I told myself. Flies are *supposed* to be spider food. "Please, Jack. Do something."

Jack grabbed needle-nose pliers and snagged one of the dead flies on the windowsill. "Here, I'll give him a couple, in case they're a little dry." After he finished with the dead ones, he took the one that was still alive and pulled it off by nipping the web strings with his pliers. It wiggled around on its back.

I stood on the workbench and traced my finger around some routers and a hacksaw, something Mr. Taylor taught me to do after he saw me freak out over a desperate earwig.

"By the time you finish tracing, you'll be back to your old self. It's what I do after work when the interns we hire at the plant mess up the machinery."

Now that the fly was safe, I felt better.

"You okay, Cass?"

"I gotta get a handle on this."

"You will. Don't worry." Jack patted me on the shoulder.

"Seriously, Jack."

"I am serious. Why don't you start over? Trace the drill bits this time."

CHAPTER 3

Arriving at the Door

Saturday morning, I woke up clawing my way out from under the covers. I dreamed I jumped off a speeding train car to avoid the Pinkerton detectives and landed in Magda's compost pile. It's a mystery how Magda's compost pile got in the Western territories, where I'd been searching for new poisonous plants for a rich and eccentric Chicago collector—but that's a dream for you. Since it *was* Magda's compost, which she prides herself on being the healthiest environment for decomposition anywhere, it was teeming with slimy bugs!

I sat up in bed only to find her—my evil sister—sitting at the end of it.

"Will you go with me, Cass? Over to the Bensons'? You know how bad I am at this stuff."

"Sorry, Mag. I have plans."

"Really? You can't spare fifteen minutes?"

"Don't give me that." Swishing my arm under the covers, I found my hoodie. My sweats were down there, too. "These visits never wind up in less than four hours."

"Come downstairs. You'll be in a better mood after you have some pumpkin pancakes."

I looked out the window. It was a perfect Saturday in May. Mother Nature was practically dumping buckets of green paint over everything. I was not going to sit at some beauty queen's house making small talk—no matter how many ancient Indian artifacts Magda promised to buy me on eBay.

I had goals. Jack and I were searching for a big flat rock that we could chisel hieroglyphs in and plant in the new housing development. Then we'd "discover" it and pretend it was a valuable artifact. It's something we saw on the History channel.

"So," Mom said as she slid a couple of steaming cakes onto my plate. "Magda tells me you can't spare a half hour to go meet our new neighbors."

Dousing my pancakes with maple syrup, I whispered to Magda, "See? Now it's a half hour."

"Sorry, Mom." I filled my mouth with pancakes. "Big plans today."

"Big plans. And those would include . . ."

Didn't Mom know it was impolite to talk with your mouth full? I pointed to my chipmunk cheeks. *Who besides me could use some etiquette lessons?*

She pinched my fork and held it hostage until I swallowed.

"Mom! Didn't anybody ever teach you not to touch other people's stuff?"

"This fork happens to be *my* stuff, young lady. I'd like you to elaborate on your plans, please."

"But my pancakes will get cold!"

She waited. I hated it when she had me over a barrel. "Okay. Me and Jack are going for a bike ride."

"Jack and *I* are going for a bike ride."

"No you're not, because he's busy going on a bike ride with me."

Mom didn't find this funny. "And what is your final destination?"

"Um . . . the gravel pit."

"The gravel pit? The one down by the recycling facility? That has to be five miles."

"So?"

"So, I've never given you permission to ride your bike that far."

I looked at Mom and blinked slowly. Once. After which I became as dense as iridium. My look was saying "Your point is . . . ," but it wasn't any fun because my pancakes were getting cold. Pretty soon, they'd be decomposing.

"The recycling facility is a regular stop for homeless people, Cass. You and Jack are not going down there by yourselves."

Magda reached over me to snag the butter. " 'Homeless people' is such a pejorative term, Mom. It's better to call them itinerant wanderers." She spread some butter on her plate, which she is sure is the correct way to get butter on every inch of pancake; then she reached over me *again* for the serving plate of pancakes.

26

I slapped her arm. *Who could use some etiquette lessons?*

I was about to suggest the term "hobos," but remembered I was being dense, so all I did was assume my zombie stare while Magda made sure the steam from her very hot pancakes wafted in my direction.

"They're not going by themselves, Mom. I'm going with them. Right after Cassie and I meet our new neighbors." She put another pat of butter on top of her stack. "Isn't that right, Cassidy?"

I'm melting, I thought.

"Right," I said, before tearing off a piece of pancake the size of a slice of pizza and stuffing it into my mouth.

After Mom had pulled my hair with a comb and made me brush my teeth, I said to my sister, "All right. You got me, but I'm holding you to that bike ride."

"I know." Magda never did any exercise unless she absolutely had to. When Dad pulled our bikes out of the garage last year, hers had a mouse nest in the seat.

"Just don't go on and on about something disgusting," I warned her as she held my arm with one hand and rang the doorbell with the other. "Like slime."

"I won't if you won't."

I didn't have time to think about any nondisgusting subjects of conversation because the door was flung open almost immediately by a lady in long curly hair and a polka-dot headband who looked like she was expecting good news.

"Sabrina, come and see," she said. "I'm guessin' these are our new neighbors."

Sabrina's head appeared over her mother's shoulder. Same hair, same headband, same smile slapped on her face.

My first thought was *Jack got his wish—these two are from the circus.* I waited for Magda to take control of the situation, but all she could do was push her glasses up her nose and study her shoes.

"Well, howdy, neighbors," I said in my best Southern accent. "This here's Magda and I'd be Calamity Cassidy." I shook the mother's hand powerful-like.

Magda yanked on my other arm.

"What?" Turning to my sister, I whispered, "It's polite to speak to people in their native tongue."

"Oh, that's all right, Magda." Sabrina's mom reached out and took Magda's hand, pulling her inside. "Everyone practices their Southern accent on us. We don't mind, do we, Sabrina?" The polka-dot headbands bobbed in unison.

"But I should tell you, Miss Calamity, we speak proper English in this house."

"That is a disappointment, Mrs. . . ."

"Benson. Sabrina and Olive Ann Benson."

"I was hoping to learn a new language."

"Oh, there are some differences, region to region. In the South, all we have is coke. Even Pepsi is coke. And the other day, I asked the lady at the grocery store where they kept the buggies and she looked at me cross-eyed. I guess what I wanted was a shopping cart, but they're buggies in Decatur."

The Bensons found this funny enough to laugh out loud. Even Magda managed a smile.

"Magda, do you want to see my room?" Sabrina asked her. "I love those glasses, by the way."

"You do?" Magda pinched the stems and repositioned them. "I wanted to try the rimless kind."

Sabrina waited for Magda to say something more, but my sister had exhausted that topic of conversation and was now at a loss for words.

"I've still got some sugar cookies from the best bakery in Atlanta, Miss Calamity. I could make some sweet tea and we could chat here in the kitchen. Do you know what sweet tea is?"

Magda was throwing me desperate "don't you dare desert me" looks over her shoulder, but I wasn't much in the mood to rescue her.

Taking Magda's arm, Sabrina persuaded her toward the stairs. "My friends call me Bree. Do you like decorating, Magda? Jack might be finished hanging my curtains by now."

I froze. "Jack?" And speak of the devil, there he came, clanking down the stairs with an old leather tool belt strapped around his waist. It looked ancient, worn and scratched, with loops for all the old-timey-looking tools. It was sweeter than all the sugar cookies and sweet tea in Atlanta.

Normally, my first question would be "What in the Billy blue blazes are you doing here, Jack Taylor?" But that tool belt cast a spell on me.

"Where'd you get that?" was all I managed.

"Hey there, Cass. Magda." I think it's fair to say Jack swaggered a little as he came into the kitchen, clanking his old-timey tools for my benefit. It made me feel the same way that that darn Percy did, right before he gobbled down my pepperoni-cheese jerky.

"These tools belonged to my daddy. Funny thing. Everything else in the world has changed, but tools don't change that much. Glenn—he's my husband—can't cinch this belt around his waist anymore, so there's no harm in lettin' Jack use them.

Especially since we're employing him to help us out around the house until Glenn gets back from Switzerland." She patted Jack on the shoulder. "Mr. Fenster told us all about Jack's talents at the closing."

"He's learning about security techniques over there," Jack piped in. "Mr. Benson is."

"Is he a spy?" Maybe things were finally looking up for me.

"No. Nothing like that," Mrs. Benson said. "He's been hired by a law firm here. File security is his specialty."

While we'd been discussing this fascinating subject, Sabrina had whisked Magda upstairs. I felt bad for a flea's breath, then decided she'd have to learn to fend for herself someday. Might as well start now.

"Can I see them?" I held out my hand for the tool belt, but all Jack did was jut out one hip. He wasn't taking that belt off.

Mrs. Benson held up a box that read VOTED BEST SUGAR COOKIES IN ATLANTA SINCE 2006. "I need a scissors to cut the tape on this box. I think I left them on the dining-room table. If you two will excuse me for just a minute."

After she disappeared through the doorway, I moved closer to Jack. "What are you doing here?" I whispered. "We're supposed to go to the gravel pit."

Jack shrugged. "They needed a strong man to help out with things." He was wearing his plaid shirt; it was, hands down, his favorite.

"Why do you smell funny?"

Clearing his throat, Jack said, "It's aftershave. Don't make a big deal out of it."

"Now, there's a puzzle. I thought you put on aftershave *after you shave*."

"Jack?" Sabrina's voice came from above us somewhere. "I need you to hang one more album. Magda's convinced me that symmetrical is the way to go."

Jack bounded up the stairs, losing screws at every step. You had to run differently with an old tool belt on. The way Jack lifted his knees did make him look a little like a circus clown. If we were at my house, I might have run up behind and tackled him just to see how it sounded to have a hundred or so screws ping down the stairs at one time.

But there was Sabrina at the top of the steps, smiling, waiting for him.

"Here we go." Mrs. Benson ruffled my hair as she passed by me. "And lookin' for the scissors, I found my cookie tray."

"Well, saints be praised," I said.

"Mr. Fenster was mum about your talents, Cass—do you prefer Calamity or Cassidy?" Mrs. Benson asked as she piled cookies on the tray.

"It's Cassidy. Calamity is my road name."

"Road name. Is that like . . . a trucker's handle? Where is the box with the tea glasses?" Mrs. Benson held out her arms as if she could make the glasses jump out of one of the dozens of boxes stacked in the kitchen.

"Sort of." I wasn't sure what a trucker's handle was and I didn't want Mrs. Benson to know. "But not exactly."

She gave up on the glasses and handed me a coffee mug full of cold tea.

"Well, park yourself on this stool, Miss Cassidy, and have a cookie. It'll sweeten up that pretty face of yours."

It was a rare occurrence for someone to remark on my face. *Wipe that smile off your face* was as close as I could remember.

I bit into a cookie that had a snowdrift of frosting on it. All that sugar would power my legs to the gravel pit and back.

"Your mama tells me you're signed up for etiquette lessons. I believe I was about your age when I had my first course."

"Doesn't sound like much fun to me."

"I can see that by the way your shoulders are sagging. Well . . ." Mrs. Benson licked blue frosting off her fingers, something I'm pretty sure you face a firing squad for in etiquette class. "Maybe if you think of it as a story . . . the unfolding story of your life. You like spies, don't you, Cassidy?"

I nodded. I did like spies.

"Well, say you were hunting a spy in Buckingham Palace— that's where the queen of England lives. Better than that, let's make it an assassination plot on the queen herself. It's your job to protect her, but you have to be undercover and follow her everywhere. What do queens do but go to big fancy dinners and such? If you didn't know which glass to drink from or where the crease of your napkin goes, they'd see right off you were an imposter. You'd be out on your tush, and later on that night they'd be mopping the queen of England off the floor."

Mrs. Benson's face came closer and closer as she told her story; I even forgot to eat my cookie thinking about the poor queen of England.

She had a point.

"You're not eating all the cookies, are you? Magda and I want to take some upstairs." Sabrina had arrived, breathless, back in the kitchen, followed by my sister and clackety-clack Jack. I looked carefully at Magda to study the effects of spending time in a beauty queen's bedroom. She didn't look ill or anything.

"Magda has a way to clean those old album covers of Daddy's . . . the ones I want on the wall." Sabrina turned to me to explain. "I love the pictures, but they're so nasty and Daddy won't let me wash them."

"You need to clean off that mold," Magda said. "Or it will digest the paper. I observed some other forms of fungi, too."

Sabrina put her arm around my sister. "I'm taking the whole pile over to Magda's laboratory. Can I bring the record player, too, Mama, so we can listen?"

"Of course you can. But not for a few hours. I've got a whole list of pictures I want Jack to hang and I need your help. He won't be able to do it on a school day."

"Jack?" I stared at him.

Jack blinked.

I couldn't believe it. He was doing osmium. On me!

Shrugging, he said, "It's real money, Cass."

"Yes it is. Now, you have another sugar cookie, Cassidy. I need them out of this house or I will eat every single one."

start

33

CHAPTER 4

Informal Greetings

Magda unwrapped the sandwich Mom had packed for the bike-ride-that-never-happened and took a bite. "They're really nice . . . the Bensons."

I flicked my finger at the wax paper. "Not hungry." I was going to tell Mom that Mrs. Benson fed me a bunch of junk food, but I didn't have the energy to say something mean about her. If Jack hadn't paraded down the stairs, clanking tool belt and all, I might even have agreed with Magda. About Mrs. Benson, anyway. She had a good imagination.

Instead, I pout-slouched—something I'm pretty sure they put you in the penalty box for in etiquette class.

"Cassidy, what's wrong?" Mom asked me.

"She's mad because Jack took the handyman job at the Bensons' instead of going with her to the gravel pit," Magda said, picking olives out of her cream-cheese spread and wiping them on her plate. Definitely a penalty-box offense.

"I offered to take her myself, but we have to make it quick. Sabrina's coming over at two." Magda set her sandwich down and got that dreamy chemistry look she's so famous for. "Album covers aren't like regular paperboard, you know. They're covered with a veneer. If you try to clean them with soap or—even worse—vinyl-record cleaner, it removes the ink and makes them bubble. So the challenge is how to keep mold from eating the paper. *And* if there's paste glue in the seam, there might be silverfish, too. Silverfish love starch . . ." She stopped talking and sat there with her mouth open, hypnotized.

If Sabrina hadn't been trying to hang those old album covers, she would have thought Magda was a total zero. But Magda had better karma than me!

"Does your karma make you a boy or a girl?" I asked Mom.

"What a strange question, Cassidy. I don't know. I'm not as informed about karma as Janae. I always thought the boy-girl thing was about chromosomes, and karma was more like . . . what goes around comes around."

"I agree. I couldn't have done anything that bad before I was even born!"

"I'm not following you, honey."

"If I was a boy, Great-Grandma Reed wouldn't have left me etiquette lessons, and Mrs. Benson would have asked *me* to hang her pictures and wear her husband's tool be—"

"Pretty sure karma takes into account your previous

lifetimes," Magda said, reaching for an apple from the bowl in the middle of the table.

"Well, how am I supposed to do anything about those?"

"You call yourself Calamity. You love hobos and you dream of outrunning railroad cops. Maybe you have outlaw karma." Magda rubbed the apple on her shirt and took a bite. On another day, it might be exciting to think about the possibility of having outlaw karma. But not today.

"I'm going back to bed," I announced, leaving the room and making clomping noises on the stairs. The same stair, to be exact. It always worked on Mom and Magda, who thought my clomping on the stairs meant I was out of range.

MOM: "Poor Cassidy. She really wanted to go on a bike ride."

MAGDA: "You should have seen Jack. He followed Sabrina around like a baby bird."

MOM: "Do you think he has a crush on her?"

MAGDA: "Well, it's hard not to. She's so interested in you . . . like learning to fall out of buildings and preserving record albums are the most fascinating things she could think of."

MOM: "Maybe she's being polite."

MAGDA: "Maybe. But she asks good questions, too. And she's coming here in a couple of hours to see my lab and then over to Jack's to see the setup in his garage."

MOM: "I guess it's time . . . for Jack, I mean. Remember, Janae kept him back in Young Fives. He is a year older. Didn't you notice the other day . . . when he wore shorts . . . how hairy his legs have gotten?"

MAGDA: "But Sabrina's my age, Mom."

MOM: "Oh, Magda, you don't choose your first crush. My first crush was my sixth-grade math teacher. He was brand-spanking-new to teaching, and the way he'd run in from the parking lot with his tie plastered to his face . . . or use his pencil and his fist to make an exclamation point when you got the right answer—adorable!"

That was enough listening for me. TMI! Of course Jack didn't have a crush on Sabrina. Jack and I were not at all interested in . . . that. You had to be totally focused when you were flapping in to the top of a speeding railway car or balancing on a telephone wire. If Jack let his head fill up with thoughts of high school girls in polka-dot headbands, he'd be a pavement tattoo before he was thirteen.

When I got to my room, I threw open the window and crawled under my bed so if Mom and Magda came looking they'd think I'd finally decided to run away. If I really was Calamity Cassidy in a previous lifetime, that would explain my present circumstances. I wasn't the sort of girl to shoot innocent bystanders, but who knows? In a heated gunfight, with outlaws behind every saloon door, maybe a stray bullet of mine had zinged the town librarian.

That's when I decided to start improving my karma. With the kind of weird dreams and fears I had—geez, maybe I'd plugged half a dozen charity workers or members of the church choir. So, starting Tuesday morning, I would give out *better* than I got. When Jack came over to walk with me to school, I wouldn't ream him out for throwing me over. I'd say, "How was church? Good eats?"

"So . . . how was church? Good eats?"

"Mimi brought potato knishes and babka. My cousin

Reggie from Toledo showed us these sweet parkour video clips from the movie *District B13*. I want to be David Belle when I grow up." Jack was so excited about the stunts he'd seen on the video clip, he didn't notice how polite I was being.

We were almost to school before he said, "Hey, Cass. How come you're so quiet? You still cheesed off that I worked at the Bensons' instead of going to the gravel pit with you?"

"Me? Nooo. I forgot about that."

Jack put his hand on my forehead. "You're not running a fever, are you?"

"No, but thank you for inquiring."

"C'mon, Cass. Tell me what's eating you. You know you can't hold it inside. It'll pop out sometime today."

I swallowed. "Fine weather we're having."

"Okay, be that way. Two can play that game. Look, there's Delton. Let's practice being nice to him."

Jack!

Being nice to Delton Bean was like going to the karma World Series two days after you got bumped up from the minors. I'd be willing to bet that, at eleven, Delton Bean had a brain even bigger than Magda's. Every chance he got, he had to show it off, too.

"Good morning, Jack. Good morning, Cassidy."

"Good morning, Delton. Did you have a nice holiday weekend?"

Delton looked at me all suspicious, like he didn't know the rules of this extremely boring game we were playing called "chitchat."

"Yes, I did," he said, finally. "My dad took me back to the Third Coast Transportation Museum in Marshfield. We have a membership. I was interested in their traveling exhibit of World War II fighter planes. The combustion engines of planes manufactured in the United States during that time were the very first made out of silicone."

I yawned, but I covered my mouth first, which is the correct order. "You don't say."

I was beginning to wonder if all this goodness was worth it. I mean, I was already a girl.

In class, Mrs. Parsons was handing back our final paper. "I know the weather feels like summer vacation, but we still have important work to do here. Your writing portfolios will be forwarded to your middle-school language-arts teachers. Some of them are ready to go, but some of you"—she paused at our table and dropped my portfolio folder in front of me— "seem to have intentionally misunderstood the assignment. As you recall, you were supposed to research a field of interest, some occupation you could see yourself holding in the future. I'd like those of you whose portfolios are finished to work on peer evaluations with those whose papers still need polishing. So, Hayley, you will work with Mary; Jack, you pair up with Graham; and, Delton, I think you will be very helpful to . . . Calamity here."

"Calamity?" Graham piped up. "When I read your rough draft, it was Catastrophe."

It doesn't take much for our class to go on a laughing jag. Magda warned me not to use my road name, but Mrs. Parsons said she wanted colorful language. And I spent a lot of time picking out that name. Catastrophe Cassidy was my first runner-up.

I told myself that the laughing didn't matter. I'd been nice to Delton before school. Now Delton would be nice to me so I could finish my paper. And more importantly, fifth grade.

Delton read the title of my paper. "Your occupation of interest is . . . hobo?"

"She told us to pick something interesting." I crossed out the word "hobo" and replaced it with "Knight of the Road." If I changed every "hobo" to "Knight of the Road," I might meet the minimum word count. "What'd you pick?"

"Aeronautical engineer, of course. Like my dad." Delton scanned the first page of my paper before reaching into his backpack for his red pen.

"Cassidy, we were supposed to cover contemporary issues in the field—job security, earning potential, regional—"

"I did. Look here."

Delton made clicking noises with his tongue as he read. "Sooo . . . hobos live off the goodwill of others, they have each other's backs, and your dad says with rising gas prices more people than ever are riding the Amtrak, making you confident that we'll add more train lines? You used your dad as your main source?"

"Well, it's hard to pin down a real hobo."

"Possibly because they are extinct? You know very well there are no classified ads for hobos." Delton uncapped his pen and put it in hover mode over my paper. "Where to begin . . . ?"

Then he stopped talking to me and started talking to my paper. "Setting aside the logical fallacy that hobos exist . . . I would argue with this transition between 'hobo hash' and barter arrangements. . . . Can you really be a hobo and not know when the steam engine was invented?"

As his pen scooted over the pages, I concentrated on scraping a blob of one hundred percent fruit preserves off my shirt.

"Maybe you should change your stage name to Rambling Rose," he muttered, handing back my paper.

"It's my road name, thank you very much." I scanned all the pen marks. "That's it?" Delton had messed up my paper so bad I'd have to retype the whole thing. "I thought you were supposed to fix it."

"The purpose of peer evaluation, Cassidy, is to give feedback to the author of the paper, not to *fix* it. You and I both know you are perfectly capable of doing it yourself—if you choose to. I've seen your standardized test scores. You were almost as high as me in expository writing."

I grabbed the sheets of paper and started to fold them. Whenever I didn't like something, I tried to make it disappear. In second grade, I'd taught myself to fold papers with bad grades into packages so small I could slip them into my shoe. But papers get longer in fifth grade, and no matter how I folded, I couldn't conceal this mess.

"Thanks for nothing, Delton. You've got a lot of nerve saying those things about my honest efforts."

Delton pinched the tip of his nose, which was just one of his many nervous habits. "Was I too forthcoming? My mother says I need to work on my social cues. She says being blunt isn't a leading-edge technique in the workplace and that the reason my father doesn't advance is his lack of understanding in the area of social cues." He moved from the tip of his nose to his earlobe. "How should I have handled it, Cassidy? Should I have said it was a good paper even if it wasn't?"

41

"I guess not." I managed to make my paper small enough to sit on it with no corners showing. "Then you'd just be a phony."

"Like you were to me this morning when you asked about my weekend?"

"Can't a girl be nice without raising suspicions?"

"Well . . . no. Not you, anyway."

"Say, Delton, you're a smart guy. What do you know about karma?"

"Karma?"

"Yeah, you know. The old 'what goes around comes around' thing."

"Are you asking me for the definition?" Delton slipped his cell phone from his pocket and consulted the Internet.

"I guess. It's just that, lately, I feel like maybe I have . . . I don't know . . . rotten karma. And I'm wondering if I can turn it around before . . . hmmm, let's just say before June fourteenth."

"What's special about June fourteenth?"

"None of your beeswax."

"I don't know, Cassidy. It says here that karma is built up over lifetimes. I'm not sure being nice to me this morning is enough to turn that around."

"Delton, I hope you are using your handheld device for academic purposes . . . otherwise, I'll have to confiscate it."

The sudden appearance of our teacher made Delton switch from pinching his earlobe to folding a pleat in his lower lip. "We were talking about karma, Mrs. Parsons, and I was looking up the definition."

"What does karma have to do with—where is your paper, Cassidy?"

"Um . . ." I shuffled my hands around in my backpack and looked on either side of the table as if I'd dropped it.

"She's sitting on it, Mrs. Parsons. Isn't it time to transition to social studies? I can't really count the last twenty minutes as instructional time. In fact, I've noticed that student time-on-task has taken a huge dive since Field Games Day."

As Mrs. Parsons walked away, I whispered, "I may have rotten karma, but you have snitch karma, Delton, and that is much worse."

"All I did was tell the truth."

"She didn't even ask you. You should have kept quiet. You would make a lousy hobo."

There's a big difference between a catastrophe and a calamity. Getting hit by a train is a catastrophe. Going over Niagara Falls in a barrel is a calamity. The way I figure it, you get a fighting chance with a calamity. Things don't look too pretty, but people have survived a barrel ride over the falls. Get hit by a train and you've got a one-way ticket to that great cattle car in the sky. It takes brains, ingenuity and nerves of steel to survive a calamity.

I knew that, according to my own definition, etiquette lessons were only a calamity, something to survive and do my best to forget. Then why did they feel like such a catastrophe? Was it because every Monday and Wednesday from June 14 through July 14 (aka *the best part of summer vacation*), I would be imprisoned in a stuffy classroom?

If the other great Calamity in history—Calamity Jane— was telling this story, she'd skip the boring junk about how I revised my paper to focus on being part of the transportation industry, and how I finished up my social-studies poster about the Incas. (For Family Night, Mrs. Parsons made me cover the part where they sacrificed their babies.)

I *might* tell the story of how in retaliation for being forced to wear a dress and curl my hair for the fifth-grade graduation ceremony, I wore my sister's tap shoes to cross the stage and palmed Principal Janescko a note that read "See you later, alligator" when he shook my hand.

But no, I think Calamity Jane would skip ahead—straight to the moment when, on a beautiful summer morning only three days out of fifth grade, I stood in front of Miss Starr Melton-Mowry's School of Poise and Purpose.

ready for next plate

CHAPTER 5

What to Call Whom

The sign was painted on a glass door, wedged between Bliss in a Glass Juice Bar and Olde Worlde Tailors Alteration Shop.

"Scoot, Miss Cassidy," Mom said, rolling up the car window so I couldn't complain. I looked up at the perfectly blue sky and wondered what Jack and I might do on a morning like this. Ride our bikes to Riverside Park and go fishing? Maybe play Frisbee golf or mess with the squirrels by feeding them the clay peanuts I made in art class?

I started to curse Great-Grandma Reed again but remembered my karma and yanked open the door, making the bells jingle—multiple times. I have a little palsy in my right arm every time I open a door with bells.

"Miss . . . ?"

"Cassidy."

"Corcoran. Miss Corcoran."

I gave Miss Melton-Mowry the once-over. She kind of figured to be an etiquette teacher, with hair as stiff as cotton candy that moved exactly when her head did and lines around her mouth and eyes that seemed to keep them in marching order.

"We'll cover promptness in Wednesday's class. For now, see if you can find a seat . . . quietly, please."

At breakfast, Magda and I decided I wouldn't know anyone in my etiquette class because one, it was on the posh side of town, and two, what normal kid would be caught dead in a place like this? Now, as I rolled up on my tiptoes to get a look over her shoulder, I saw a dozen students sitting at fancy tables set up with enough glasses and plates and silverware for dinner with the queen of England. Either a lot of great-grandmas had a twisted dying wish or there was something funny in the drinking water here on the east side. Who in their right mind would waste their precious summer vacation on this?

"Hello, Cassidy. I saved you a seat."

"Delton? What are you doing here?"

"Freeze."

The other kids, who'd been whispering to one another, froze instantly. Even I did. Maybe we were playing statues.

The tables were set up in the shape of a U just like small-group time back at Stocking Elementary. Miss Melton-Mowry walked into the middle of the U and said, "Good morning, Mr. Bean. What a pleasure to see you."

Those magic words broke the spell and all the kids could

move again. "When I want to insert the preferred way of behaving," she explained to me, "I ask the class to freeze. . . . Well done, class."

"What's with the stiff?" I pointed to the table at the front of the room. There were only two seats and one was occupied by a dummy like you see in department stores, only she was dressed in the exact same suit as Miss Melton-Mowry. Same cotton-candy hair combed to her shoulders. Even the same scarf.

"Freeze." One more time, the whole class froze. I contorted my face like I was frozen under ice—it's a look I'm famous for in freeze tag.

Miss Melton-Mowry pinched my pointer finger. "I'd be delighted if you would introduce me to your companion, Miss Melton-Mowry."

I stayed frozen, but I squeaked out, "Wait a minute. I thought *you* were Miss Melton-Mowry."

"I am. And she is my assistant. Be seated, Miss Corcoran, and I will explain."

I took the only seat available to a girl with rotten karma—next to Delton and some girl wearing a headband just like Sabrina Benson's.

"Now that we are all assembled, we will begin. Again. Welcome, students. I am Miss Starr Melton-Mowry, international poise, etiquette and communication consultant. Every summer, I return here to teach my renowned finishing classes for genteel young men and women. Over the winter, you will find me in Dubai or Tokyo. During polite conversation, I will share my hobbies and other details about my life."

I couldn't figure out why she talked so slow, but even I knew it wasn't polite to ask if she was a recovering stutter-holic or something.

"Allow me to introduce you to my assistant, Miss Information." Miss Melton-Mowry waved her hand in the direction of the dummy. "That is a gesture, Miss Corcoran. In polite society, a slight gesture can indicate positioning. It is the preferred method to pointing."

Even though Miss Melton-Mowry hadn't told us to, I froze as I watched six of the twelve kids write down what she said on their notepads.

"Miss Information is a gift from Sheikh Jaaved of the Dubai High Council. In some cultures, it is considered humiliating to be singled out as a bad example, so the sheikh had this replica made of me. While she purports to be full of information, she demonstrates the incorrect way to do things, thus the double meaning of her name."

More scribbling by the brownnosers. Could there really be a test on all this malarkey?

"Now." Miss Melton-Mowry smoothed her skirt, which was already straight as a ruler. "I'd like you all to stand behind your chairs."

We did. Miss Melton-Mowry unbent Miss Information and stood her up so that they faced each other. "Note her excellent posture. The head is in line with her shoulders, her back is straight, her arms are not crossed but hanging loosely at her sides. Her torso . . ."

Miss Melton-Mowry went on. We learned there was even a right way to point your feet—straight ahead.

"This is the posture we will take when standing to greet

someone. So, first I'll demonstrate and then you'll have a chance to practice with one another. We want to make sure we're at the correct distance from a person when we introduce ourselves. This automatically puts everyone at ease. The distance varies from culture to culture. Here in the United States, we're most comfortable about an arm's length away." Touching Miss Information on the shoulder, Miss Melton-Mowry got in position.

I raised my hand. "In WWE, it's called the neutral stance, but your knees should be bent in case of a surprise attack."

Rubbing her brow, Miss Melton-Mowry asked, "WWE?"

"World Wrestling Entertainment, Miss Melton-Mowry," Delton said. "Cassidy's a big fan."

"Well, in this class, we will be *introducing*, not wrestling, so while that information might be useful in other contexts, let's try to focus on introducing ourselves this morning." Miss Melton-Mowry straightened up—again—practically locking her knees; I could have knocked her over with a feather.

"To continue . . . when greeting one another, extend your right hand, look the person you are about to meet in the eye and say your name. 'I'm Miss Melton-Mowry,' followed by 'It's very nice to meet you.' Your grip should not be limp or tight, but firm."

It took a bit of work to get Miss Information's arm in the right position, during which time I noticed Miss Melton-Mowry lost her perfect smile.

I wondered if we were going to cover any of the handshake variations, like the missing-hand handshake, the funny freeze, the tickling finger, the knuckle-knocker or the one I used on Principal Janescko, the surprise-in-the-palm.

But I guess polite people don't have a sense of humor. They just grab hands and let go. Why we had to spend time practicing this basic move was beyond me.

"I'm Calamity Cassidy," I said to the girl next to me. "Nice to meet you."

"And I'm Miss Parker," she said without blinking. "It's very nice to meet you, too."

Wow. That was dull.

"Very nice, Miss Parker. Now, everyone, turn to the student on your other side."

Delton got what he deserved—the tickler. That's where you rub your finger up and down the other person's palm. It makes them either laugh or yank their hand away because it's so creepy.

"Look me in the eye," I reminded Delton as he tried to yank his hand out of mine. "It's so nice to make your acquaintance, Mr. Bean."

Delton bit his lip. "It's . . . so . . . hard to meet you, Miss Corcoran."

I leaned in so only Delton could hear. "You think that's hard? I'm not letting go." We stood there, smiles tattooed on our faces.

I was having my first etiquette showdown.

"I think this is the perfect segue to *polite* conversation time," Miss Melton-Mopey said, staring straight at me. And when we're finished, we'll have Miss Corcoran and Miss Information exchange seats.

"What?" I squinted at our teacher until I could see her double—a little trick I can accomplish without crossing my eyes.

"Would someone with superior hearing like to repeat what I just said?"

Twelve hands went up, including Delton's.

After that, we got a long boring lecture about the things polite people did and did not say. Basically, you can talk about the weather; the décor, whatever that is; the traffic this morning; and how nice everyone looks. You can't talk about anything that causes an argument, or anything that makes the other person feel bad, uncomfortable, stupid or snort with laughter.

"How are you enjoying the class so far, Miss Corcoran?" Delton asked me when we'd been given the go-ahead to actually talk.

I figured there was plenty of time to be polite *after* I interrogated him. "What do you think you're doing here?"

Delton's eyes darted over to Miss Melton-Mowry. I pictured his big brain working overtime trying to decide whether to play by my rules and answer the question or to keep talking polite nonsense.

"I am so enjoying etiquette class," he said. "When our mothers chatted about it at the fifth-grade graduation ceremony, mine thought it was a perfect chance for me to practice learning the social graces."

I had to give it to Delton. He was answering my question in high-society code. I could play at that, too. "That is sparkling, Delton, but your manners are so good already. Wouldn't you rather be at airplane camp?"

"I couldn't agree with you more, Miss Corcoran. However, to quote my mother, Mrs. Bean, 'To be in Cassidy's company will give you some backbone, Delton. Not all learning takes place in a book. Cassidy has the kind of derring-do necessary to succeed in today's workplace.'"

Miss Melton-Mowry came over to me and Delton. "Don't let me interrupt," she said, putting her hand on Delton's shoulder.

I didn't. "Well, give my regards to your mother, Mr. Bean. She is a very intelligent woman. Next time we meet, I'll tell her about my other class. It's on public speaking. At the community college. The auditorium there holds five hundred seats."

I smiled like a beauty queen in the May Day parade as Delton's fingers started working away at his collarbone. It is a well-known fact that Delton has a serious case of performance anxiety. He practically needs to be medicated to give an oral report. He can talk just fine from his seat, but make him stand up and have everyone be quiet—it's like he's been set in front of a firing squad.

He opened his mouth to respond, but no words came out.

"Mr. Bean. Are you all right, Mr. Bean?" Miss Melton-Mowry asked.

Delton nodded, still in shock.

"You do have a way of surprising people, Miss Corcoran," Miss Melton-Mowry said to me. "I look forward to chatting with you further."

The further the better!

If you ever get a bad case of insomnia, the cure is to take an etiquette class in a room with no air-conditioning. Just when I thought I couldn't keep my eyes open for another long lecture about how to sit, stand and stick your arm out, our teacher decided we'd had enough for one day.

Hallelujah!

Just my luck. By the time we got out, it was raining, which

meant that Jack and I had to hunker down in my bedroom to figure out what to do.

"Let's go outside anyway," I said, knee-bouncing on my bed to keep Mom from delivering a bottom-of-the-stairs lecture about the ceiling caving in again. "I'm like a puppy. I need exercise every day or I start chewing slippers."

"You were out all day yesterday! We practically wore out our bicycle pedals."

"Still . . ." I grabbed my stuffed bunny and tied his ears in a knot. "Maybe we should play Pound the Bunny."

My uncle Oscar, who has zero kids, so he doesn't know any better, gave me a giant stuffed version of Pat the Bunny for my eighth birthday. At first, I thought it was the worst present ever, until Jack showed me what a great stand-in the bunny could be for a WWE opponent.

"Bad idea. Remember what your mom said she'd do if she had to resort to using the air horn again to bust us up?"

"True." I did *not* want to be a volunteer pooper-scooper at Riverside Park. Bouncing just high enough to land on my feet, I hopped over to the dresser and set the bobblehead dolls on the edge. "Let's play Bobblehead Suicide Leap." This involved doing carefully timed jumping jacks to make the dresser vibrate until at least six bobblehead Tigers lost their lives in a three-drawer fall.

"We should play a prank on Magda."

Jack and I are legendary for our pranks at Stocking Elementary . . . to anyone who knows us, really. We're very particular about them and very strict about the rules. One, they have to be funny. Two, they have to involve danger. Three, you can't leave behind any evidence. Four, no permanent damage. Five, no hurting anybody. Six, when confronted, become iridium. Seven, if—heaven forbid—you're caught red-handed, confess and take your punishment like a man (woman).

"Magda's so boring. All she'll do is tell Mom— I know! We can play a prank on Sabrina Benson."

"Bree? We just met her."

"So? That's even better." I threw myself back on the bed, crossing my arms and legs. "This could be good . . . something with her makeup."

Jack did not join me on the bed the way he was supposed to. I pushed myself up on my elbows. "What's wrong?"

Unknotting Pat the Bunny's ears, Jack tossed him to me. "I'd rather wrestle. I can't pull a prank on . . . my employer!"

"Why not? We did that one on Percy. Remember when we tied his favorite squeaky toy to a bungee cord and hung it just out of reach?"

"That was different."

"No it wasn't. You shoveled their walk when Mr. Fenster threw his back out."

"I just . . . think Magda's a better target."

"Skip the pranks," I said. "I say we go outside."

"It's still raining."

"So?"

"I know," Jack said. "Let's see how many push-ups we can do."

"Boring." We both knew Jack had passed me on push-ups last year; the gap was growing.

"Okay. I'll balance you on my feet."

"Deal, but if I fall on you and perform a cobra clutch, don't scream out loud, okay?"

CHAPTER 6

Giving Your Undivided Attention

Why does time speed up when you're riding bikes, playing Frisbee or fishing, and slow down when you're in etiquette class? I tried to focus as Miss Melton-Mowry taught the lesson on how to sit at the table, something I'd been doing since I was, oh, two and a half.

"For example, at the moment, Miss Information's posture is not one we like to see in a dining situation. Does anyone know what is objectionable here?"

Looking her over, I noted that Miss Information seemed as bored as I was, but she wasn't breaking any laws. The girl next to me in the headband knew better. She raised her hand.

"Miss Parker?"

"She's got her elbows on the table."

"Precisely."

"My dad always says, 'Donna, Donna, sweet and able, get your elbows off the table. This is not a horse's stable.'"

"Is that how horses eat?" I asked. "I didn't even know they had elbows."

"How quaint, Miss Parker. Miss Corcoran, in polite society young people refrain from speaking unless spoken to."

I gave Miss Melton-Mopey my zombie stare and pushed up on my tiptoes, tilting back in my chair. I'd like to visit this polite society sometime and show them a few tricks.

"What we say here, Miss Parker, is . . . *never.*" Miss Melton-Mowry touched Miss Information's illegal elbows before lifting the dummy's arms until they were about an inch over the table. "*Sometimes.*" With some trouble, she bent Miss Information's arms so they fit under the table. "*Always.*"

I thought about raising my hand and informing Miss Melton-Mowry that a lot of funny business could happen under the table, but I changed my mind. Let her find that out for herself.

"Note her excellent posture. She does not lean back; she does not make any quick side-to-side moves that might interfere with the dinner service. Miss Corcoran, are you taking note of this?"

I sat up straight as a general, smacking my feet flat on the floor before raising my hand. "Does her stomach growl? All this getting ready is making me hungry."

"It states very clearly in your brochure that we will not eat until our final reception with the parents."

"But that's four weeks from now!" I looked down the line

of kids, hoping to get a little mutiny going. "No food for four weeks is torture according to the international human rights convention."

"I'm sure they'd be happy to expedite your case in the World Court, Miss Corcoran; but until then I'm going to have to request—or rather, insist—that you refrain from speaking until this lesson is over. We are on a very tight schedule."

"I'll say it's tight," I mumbled. "Not even a graham cracker? Delton, you got any mints? Gum?"

Delton looked at me wide-eyed. His back was straight, his hands were at "always" and he wasn't going to say a word, not even if I offered him a ten-spot.

Our teacher took her seat next to Miss Information. "At an elegant lunch or dinner, we can always infer what will be served by the dishes and cutlery before us. For example, we know by the size of the napkin that this table is set for lunch. A dinner napkin is much larger. The very first dish in front of us is a soup bowl; beneath that we have a service plate. The purpose of the service plate will be to catch any drips from the soup; it will be cleared after the course is finished, leaving a clean space for the next dish to be served. Moving on to the cutlery, the smaller fork on our outside left is the salad fork; next to that we have our luncheon fork and our dessert fork. These will be easy to remember because you use them in order from the outside in."

I kept a yawn from escaping my mouth by pressing my lips together. All those forks made me think of Mrs. Benson and her Buckingham Palace story. They must have giant dishwashers in that place. Probably everybody got patted down on the way in, so a would-be assassin would have to use something on the table here. Where were the sharp knives, I wondered. Didn't they use sharp knives to carve up the wild boar or the roast pig or whatever these fancy-schmancy people ate?

I figured a trained assassin could accomplish the job with one of these salad forks. With everybody's hands under the table, I'd have to keep a sharp eye out to see if he slipped any forks up his sleeve. Then I'd shadow him as he snuck up behind the prince of High Falutinbury and readied his fork to strike. My first move would be to blind him with my dinner napkin. Then we'd have a good old-fashioned rumble with me throwing in a few WWE holds—maybe a bulldog or a Harlem hangover—to make it a good show. The queen's china would have to be sacrificed for the greater good of the country as I knocked out the evil assassin with the first thing that came to hand . . . a big soup bowl or possibly a platter of cold cuts.

"To review, Miss Corcoran, can you tell me what the letters *b* and *d* stand for?" Our teacher was holding up her hands, each one forming a letter with her fingers. I felt like it was first grade again!

I gave the answer under my breath. "Boring and dull?"

"Never mumble, Miss Corcoran. If you don't know the answer, either say so or remain silent and shake your head no."

Miss Melton-Mowry proceeded to shake her head no. What a fountain of information she was.

I shook my head no.

"Mr. Bean?"

"The *b*," Delton said, putting his left hand an inch from the table, "stands for bread plate, and the *d* stands for drinking glass. He put his right arm out to reach for the glass in front of him. "It helps you to remember which dish or glass is meant for you. The bread plate is always to the left of your plate and your water glass is always to your right."

"Oh, oh!" I stretched my arm high. "Penalty! Delton's sleeve touched the table."

"My, but you are entertaining, Miss Corcoran. I hope to hear more of your etiquette insights during the review sessions I hold after class when we don't have time to get through our scheduled material. Have you noticed we don't have air-conditioning? By noon, it gets quite stuffy in here. I'm used to it, having spent many a summer in desert countries, but you might not enjoy it quite as much. No matter. As soon as your parents find out my private hourly rate, I'm sure they will see the advantage in helping you to remember the points of order regarding the question-and-answer format."

She pressed her palms together and said to her table partner, "I do wonder how teachers manage these days, Miss Information."

"Mrs. Parsons said she'd be only too happy to see the back of Cassidy . . . er, Miss Corcoran," Delton said.

I smiled at Delton in the politest way possible. Him and his snitch karma!

"What? It's hardly a secret. She said it in front of the whole class."

"The difference between school and etiquette class is that all of you—including Miss Corcoran—choose to be here. Your interest in improving yourselves during your summer break will pay off when you can navigate any formal lunch or dinner with ease."

"I just want to navigate the pond on the ninth tee at Frisbee golf," I said into my napkin. If this lesson didn't wrap up soon,

I was in danger of having one of those seizures I'm so famous for at the all-school no-smoking assembly.

"Mr. Bean, Miss Parker, please help me stack the dishes and silver while the rest of you create your own place settings to review."

"Even Miss Information?" I asked.

"How thoughtful of you to see that Miss Information needs assistance, Miss Corcoran. Why don't you set hers as well?"

I gave myself a knuckle-knocker handshake under the table. *Why don't you shut your mouth, Miss Corcoran?*

Looking over the jumble of forks, knives and spoons, I asked myself who could be bothered to remember all this stuff. Wasn't it enough to know what was used for what? If only Miss Melton-Mowry would let me pace the halls the way Mrs. Parsons did so I could calm down and concentrate. There weren't even any halls in this joint!

"Cassidy," Delton whispered. "Your forks are in the wrong place."

"No they're not. They're pointing up. And the business ends of my knives point toward the plate." (I may be watching out for assassins someday; I paid attention when Miss Melton-Mowry talked about the knives.)

Pinching the fork on the far side of my plate, Delton said, "But that's your dessert fork."

"She said we put our forks in the order they are used, Mr. Bean. It just so happens that I eat dessert first."

After Miss Information got corrected about the difference between a water glass and a wineglass—hello, hobos drink from the bottle!—and how her butter knife was supposed to be on the bread plate and not next to its mother by the lunch plate, and about a million other things I was sure to forget as soon as the blinding sun knocked them out of my brain, class was over.

Like a dog who has to pee something fierce, I was the first at the door. I managed to leave a nose print before Miss Melton-Mowry called me back. "I only release students to their parents, Miss Corcoran. Unless your mother comes in here, you'll have to wait."

Of course, it makes sense that my rotten outlaw karma would kick in and *my* mother would be late.

Plenty of mothers came and went, but mine was AWOL. Miss M&M sat across from me with her arms folded. "Since we have a moment, tell me, why are you in this class, Miss Corcoran?"

"It's like this," I said, trying to figure out how to politely say I almost offed my great-grandma and this was her revenge. "I . . . inherited it."

"From your great-grandmother. I understand it wasn't your first choice for how to spend your summer vacation."

I shook my head.

"I'm going to let you in on a little secret. It's not mine, either."

Was that a sigh that came out of my manners teacher's mouth?

"It's called work, Miss Corcoran. It's what you do when you're a grown-up. I enjoy my work, but there are moments"— Miss Melton-Mowry paused and looked at me—"when I wonder if there might have been a better choice, long-term."

"Maybe you could teach Frisbee golf. Or fishing. I know lots of things in the normal world you'd like."

"I have decided to stick it out for the duration; so shall we agree to make the best of this? There really are advantages to learning how to be polite."

The phone rang in her office, which was probably a good thing because it kept me from asking her to name a single one.

Looking at her watch, Miss Melton-Mowry said, "Where is your mother, I wonder? That will be London calling. I have a phone con—"

"I say we call the police," I offered. "And make a missing-person report."

"Why don't you sit here—quietly—and review your place settings. Knock on the door when she arrives. If I'm still on the phone, just have her leave a note on the table." With that, she disappeared behind the door with her name on it.

I did what I was told—my way. First I practiced slouching with my arms at "never." Then I threw my knees so far apart the king of England could've seen my underwear if I'd been wearing a fancy dress. Next I pulled my chair over to Miss Information and had a staring contest; the deck was stacked against me there.

I bent her arms until her elbows were on the table. Which took some doing, I can tell you.

"Cassidy, what are you doing?"

Delton Bean again!

"No, Delton. What are *you* doing?"

"I forgot my spring jacket. I always do that when the weather changes." Delton went to the coat closet in the back of the room and took his jacket off the hanger.

"Well, since you're here, I'm going to give you your first lesson."

"Excuse me?"

"You know, the kind full of do-daring."

"My mom's waiting. Maybe we can set up a playdate or something?"

"Sit down, Delton. It's called a prank. All you have to do is put Miss Information's wig in Miss Parker's soup bowl."

Delton's head swung back and forth between me and the door. He did not sit down.

"Just pick it off—it's a wig. And drop it in the bowl. This is rank-beginner stuff. Here, I'll hold her steady." I grabbed Miss Information's shoulders. "Go on."

Delton put his hand out and touched the dummy's wig. "I don't think—"

"Delton! Don't you want to get a backbone?"

Delton pressed his lips together and yanked.

Nothing.

"Pull a little harder. There must be some glue."

He tugged.

"Geez, Delton. Put some muscle into it." Being a teacher was harder than I thought. "Trade places with me."

"My mom—"

"This is exactly what your mom wants you to do. It's called a prank—it's harmless fun. Don't worry. No one gets hurt."

Delton exchanged places with me. It's possible by this time I was trying to show off a little or maybe it was the pent-up energy caused by all that sitting still; I grabbed a handful of Miss Information's hair and yanked as hard as I could. Sometimes I don't know my own strength. There was an awful scraping noise, and then Miss I's head came right off her shoulders and landed facedown in her soup bowl.

CHAPTER 7

Respect
for Others'
Property

"Oh my goodness. Oh my goodness," Delton kept repeating, squeezing his hands until his fingers were white.

"Delton, pull yourself together. When a prank goes wrong, it's like . . . a plane going into a nosedive. You just get back to where you started, put it back the way it was." I picked up the head and examined it. There was a screw poking out of Miss Information's neck. I stuck it into the hole between her shoulders, where her neck would fit, and spun her head around. Every time I thought I'd got it in, the head wobbled and fell out again.

"You broke it when you yanked on it, Cassidy! Those shavings are from her neck. You stripped the screw and it won't hold anymore."

"When *we* yanked on it, Delton. Calm down. Your cheeks are twitching."

"This was her present from Sheikh Jaaved! It's priceless."

"I'm going to wrap her scarf around *your* neck, if you don't shut it. I need to think."

"This isn't a prank in a nosedive. This is a prank in a death spiral!"

I crossed my arms and tried to generate some thoughts, but it was impossible with Delton making those squeaking noises.

"Look, just go. I'll figure this out. And don't tell your mom or your snitch karma will follow you through the next five lifetimes."

"Sorry we're late, Cass." Magda burst through the door, breathless. "There was a ginormous line at Family Fare and then the lady in front of us was one of those coupon collectors who made the clerk so upset insisting he use her expired coupons he had to call the mana— What's this?"

"It's a head. What's it look like? Now scat, Delton!"

Delton transferred his squeezy energy to his jacket, wringing it like a washrag. He tried to say something to Magda, but I think he was officially in shock.

"I mean it. Not a word."

He ran out.

"What have you done now? Where's your teacher?"

"She's talking to London. In there." I pointed to Miss Melton-Mowry's office door. "Help me put this back on, Magda. Hurry!"

But Magda wasn't any better at it than I was; turns out, she's only good at watching things fall apart. "What should I do? I can't just leave her head lying here. She'll know it was me."

"Maybe not. The door's open. Maybe it happened after you left."

For the record, Magda would make a very bad criminal. My fingerprints were all over this. "We're going to have to make her disappear," I said.

"You mean . . . kidnap her?"

"No! Disappear. Just until Monday. Delton said the screw is stripped, so if I get a bigger screw . . ."

That was it. I had it! Stuffing Miss Information's head into my backpack, I gave Magda the plan. "I'll get a bigger screw from Jack and put her head back on before class on Monday. I'll come early and do it while she's not looking."

"Not a good plan, Cassidy. She's sure to notice the missing head."

"That's why I need *you* to help me hide the body."

"What?"

"Just for a few days."

One of the great truths of a prank is that, most times, people won't notice when something is missing as much as they notice when something's messed up. Miss Melton-Mowry might not notice Miss Information was gone from the room; but if she walked out and Miss Information had been beheaded . . . well . . . if there was an etiquette purgatory, I'd be sure to end up there.

"Here, help me straighten her legs."

Magda did what I told her to do, but not without a running

commentary. "There are so many holes in this plan I don't know where to begin. Wow, she even has stockings on."

When we'd stretched Miss Information out straight as a board, I started for the back of the room—to the closet.

"You can't be serious. Her raincoat's in here."

"I have eyes, Magda." I shut the door—a little too loudly for someone who was trying to dispose of a body. "What is wrong with these places? There's nowhere to hide."

Magda nodded her head in the direction of the back door. "I can't believe I'm helping you do this," she said as I shouldered my way through the door and into the alley.

We stood there, blinking in the sunshine. The alley didn't look much better—who knew alleys could be so clean? This one was almost empty, with only a trash can and a recycling bin to separate it from the perfectly mowed grass on the other side.

"You can't leave her back here. It might rain. Someone might steal her."

"Miss Information is not a 'her,' Magda. She's an 'it.' And I do think we could put *it* in here . . . just until Monday."

"The recycling bin?"

"Sure. It says they pick up on Tuesdays—I'll be back Monday. And look. It's almost empty. How much recycling can one tailor have?"

"Cassidy, I . . ."

But I'd made up my mind; after dragging an empty milk crate over to the bin, I flipped the top open. With the extra height, I could just about shove Miss Information inside. "Help me out, Magda. Make sure the feet go into that empty box. Here, take off her heels."

"This doesn't feel right, Cassidy." Magda bleated about it, but she did what she was told. "Wouldn't it be easier if you just told her?"

"Told her I messed with the big doll she got from the sheikh of Arabique—and broke it? No, Magda. It would not be easier. After her call, Miss Melton-Mowry will turn off the lights and leave. She won't be back until the next class and I can get this fixed before then. You have to fix it and put it back. Then it's like it never happened."

Back home, I sat in my room, my stomach feeling the way Delton's jacket must have felt—wrung out. I remembered what my dad said after I'd convinced Magda to help me find the sandbar in Lake Michigan and we almost drowned in the undertow: "When in doubt, Cassidy, Magda's seniority wins. Promise me that from now on!"

I'd promised. And since this wasn't a life-or-death situation, I felt it was okay to make Magda go along with my plan. But, if Miss Melton-Mowry found out what I did, it might *become* a life-or-death situation.

"So how was Manners 'R' Us, Cass?" Jack asked, pushing open my bedroom door. He was holding one of his stunt-performer catalogs. "Whoa! I haven't seen that look since you thought a can of spray paint was artificial snow and you dusted your mom's car."

"I need help." I grabbed my backpack from under my bed and pulled out Miss Information. Well, her head.

"You beheaded your teacher? On the second day of class?"

It took a while, with Jack interrupting me every ten seconds, to get the story out.

"So you hid the body and swiped the head. Why didn't you confess and take your punishment?"

"Because I wasn't caught red-handed! And . . . it's not very polite, is it? To break somebody's stuff? Especially stuff like this you can't replace. It would have been such a great prank to have her wig in Donna's soup bowl."

"Would have been." Jack sat down next to me. I could see he'd been marking his catalog with Post-its. "But that's not what happened."

"No, that's not what happened. Because of my outlaw karma."

"I hate to tell you this, Cass, but I think you've got it worse than outlaw karma. This ranks right up there with"—Jack riffled the pages of his catalog, thinking—"maybe *Titanic* karma. You remember the *Titanic,* don't you?"

I nodded. No one at Stocking Elementary could forget the *Titanic.* Our librarian, Mr. Pinter, had an ashtray from the worst shipwreck in history. Every year on April 15, the day the ocean liner went down, he set up a display in the media center with the ashtray in a fishbowl.

"I was just trying to do Delton a favor and show him some do-daring!"

"The fact that Delton followed you to manners class means he's got a thing for you, Cass. It's probably not fair to use that to get him to break the law."

"I wasn't trying to get him to break—"

"Hey, do you think your parents would pay me to mow your

lawn? Because if I can get three more lawns, I might be able to buy . . . um . . . a crash pad." He held up the catalog, his finger pointing to the picture.

"Since when do you use a crash pad? And why would they hire you when they have slave labor to do it? You gotta help me fix her, Jack. Maybe we could ride our bikes over and reattach her to the body. That's it! Break in, and—"

"Didn't you say this place was on the other side of the river? Our moms would never let us ride that far. Besides, I have some handyman work to do over at the Bensons'. Sabrina needs a hook for everything. She's got a makeup mirror, a hair dryer, a little cabinet for her—"

"Talk about a thing. You've got a thing for Sabrina Benson."

"Why would you say that? I need money, is all. I've got goals."

"You didn't used to need money. Last summer, remember how we made hobo stew in the fire pit with those old coffee cans—that didn't cost anything."

"That's called playing, Cass. There are no Knights of the Road anymore and you know it."

"But we'll bring 'em back. They're putting in a new high-speed train to Chicago. By the time we're fifteen—"

"Cass, wanting to be a stunt performer is crazy enough; at least I can join a circus or be in a Wild West show. But being a hobo?"

"I can't believe this. We've been planning our whole lives for this."

"I guess—if you count from five to eleven. Let me see that head again."

Jack held up Miss Information by the hair and peered into the hole in her neck.

"Delton says we stripped the screw."

"Yep. You need a special headless screw for this."

"Very funny."

"No, I mean it. It's got two thread ends and no head. I might have one in my workshop."

"Well, let's go get one."

Jack handed me back the head. "Maybe you should put this in a pillowcase . . . to keep my mom from asking questions."

Janae was in the kitchen making something spicy. Because his mom's from India, Jack eats spicy-hot things at breakfast, lunch and dinner—that is, unless Mimi comes around and saves him with some potato knishes. Jack likes to eat at our house to get a boring old plate of spaghetti every once in a while.

"Mom, cheer up Cassidy, would you? I have to find something in the workshop."

"Cassidy. It seems like I never see you anymore. How's your elocution class going?"

Maybe elocution is what they call it in India. I let it pass. "Hi, Janae. Okay," I said. Janae insisted we call her by her first name, which I'm pretty sure we'd lose a finger for in etiquette class.

"When I went to boarding school in England, it was one of my favorite classes. We recited poetry and learned the importance of posture . . . come to think of it, maybe that's one of the reasons I became a yoga instructor. So many of us slouch our way through life, Cassidy."

"Fine by me," I mumbled, but I sat up straighter and took my elbows off the counter. "Janae, I think I need a karma transplant. Or at least I need to trade up."

Janae laughed. Janae's laugh sounds like the wind chimes the Fensters had in their backyard. "Oh, Cassidy, karma is something uniquely yours. It's like . . . your eyes or your heart. You wouldn't wish to trade them away, would you?"

"Well, no. But Jack says I have *Titanic* karma. I'm just a kid. It doesn't seem fair."

"You mustn't worry about what Jack says, Cassidy. He has a flair for the dramatic. I do believe that your thoughts create your reality, however. If you truly believe you have *Titanic* karma and you tell yourself that, then that could become your destiny."

I folded my arms and burrowed my head inside. My karma was in the toilet and now Janae was telling me *I* made it that way?

"Don't look so discouraged. You should come to my Yoga for Teens class."

"Except I'm not a teen, Janae."

"Yes, you are, dear. You're eleven-teen. It's happening to Jack, too. Can't you feel it? Last summer all he wanted to do was ride his bike and fish and play Frisbee golf, and this year he's mowing lawns and doing odd jobs. You used to look at me double when I talked to you about karma and now you're asking me about it."

"You can tell when I'm looking at you double?"

"Of course I can. Your eyes aren't crossed, but you get a very odd look on your face. Seven years of elocution taught me a great deal about reading others' body language."

Seven years? Janae was nice to everybody. What could she possibly have done to get a seven-year sentence?

"Hey." Jack poked me with something sharp and pointy.

"Sorry it took so long. I didn't get the exact right thing, but this might work."

"What might work?" Janae asked.

"Cassidy's fixing one of her teacher's dolls and she needs a special screw."

"There you are, Cassidy. When our thoughts and actions are of a good nature, we create good karma for ourselves. That was the subject of my dharma talk in class today. You should come. I think you would feel better."

"Oh, yeah, Mom. Bree wants to come, too."

"Bree?"

"Sabrina Benson. From next door. Her friends call her Bree."

"What's wrong with her karma?" I asked, hoping it was something big.

"Nothing. She read that dancers use yoga to stay in shape. That's her talent . . . in the beauty competitions. Jazz dance. I'm going, too."

"But you said yoga was for girls."

"That's what I used to think, but Bree's dance teacher recommends it for balance, and I thought, if it helps me with my wind torque . . ."

Janae cupped Jack's head in her hands. "I have been telling you that for years, Jack Taylor."

"I know, Mom, but when Bree said it, it just clicked. You should go, too, Cass. You know, for the trains."

I sank back into slouch mode. Was there a shipwreck worse than the *Titanic*? Jack said *I* should do it for the trains, not *we*. And Janae thought *I* should go to Yoga for Teens in order to get some better karma. But if I did, I'd have to watch Jack be all googly-eyed about Sabrina instead of helping me figure out how to wedge our bodies through the vent in a coal car. What exactly did Janae mean when she said *last summer* all Jack wanted to do was fish and play Frisbee golf? We'd barely started *this* summer!

"I gotta go," I said, taking my backpack and tossing it over my shoulder.

"Good luck with that," Jack said. "Oh, and you're welcome."

pause

CHAPTER 8

When in Doubt, Ask for Help

Can one—not even real—severed head cause a lump to grow in your throat? There was no way I could look at Miss Information's unblinking eyes all weekend, so I stowed her in the biggest of my old-timey suitcases. But every time I passed by the foot of my bed and saw the suitcase, my throat started to swell up like the time I had tonsillitis.

Mom would call it my conscience. More than anything, I just wanted to go back to Wednesday and get a do-over. I would spit-swear to be very, very, *very* good for the rest of my life. But I couldn't go back. I had to go forward.

On Sunday night, I got the courage to open up the suitcase

and pull her out. She'd survived all the jostling, except one little patch where her eyelashes had fallen out. I searched the bottom of the suitcase with my spyglass. No eyelashes. Next I searched my backpack—the first place I'd hidden her away. Nope.

If I put her back like this, Miss Melton-Mowry was sure to know something was up! I needed help and I needed it fast.

"That smell is disgusting, Magda. You're not cremating moths in the halogen bulb in there, are you?"

"Is it that obvious from the hall? Dad will kill me."

Dad wasn't due back from his buying trip until tomorrow, but Magda had learned from experience that the smell of charred remains lingers.

I went in, pinching my nose. "You're supposed to put a wet towel in the door crack. Why don't you ever listen to me? You're hopeless at being a sneak."

Magda opened the window. "I'm burning samples of hair I collected from our carpet. I want to take them with me to Greer College to see if I can still recover DNA. Cass, they have a scanning electron microscope there! Do you have any idea what those things cost? We're allowed to bring as many samples as we want. . . ." Magda stared out the window, no doubt imagining a magnifying lens as big as her bed. "I plan to put that thing to good use."

"You're not going until August."

"So? I bought a three-ring binder with ten vinyl sleeves for microscope slides and enough mounting medium to bring seventy-two samples."

"You didn't find any of her hair, did you?" I produced Miss

Information's head from behind my back. "Once I get this back on her shoulders, I don't want any evidence linking me to her abduction."

"You mean *its* abduction," Magda corrected me. "I agree with you. We should practice calling her 'it' in the event of a court case. No, I didn't, but when I was looking for my old mounting slides in the basement, I found this." Magda pulled open her top dresser drawer and handed me a fuzzy black-and-white photo of a woman with a spear in her hand; she was bending over a dead elephant; its tusks had been cut off. The back of the photo read: "Hunting poachers . . . too late!"

"Who's she?" I asked.

"I'm pretty sure it's Great-Grandma Reed. The dates fit, and remember she had all that stuff from Africa in her apartment?"

"Great-Grandma Reed hunted poachers and she sends me to etiquette school! Where's the sense in that?"

"Search me." Magda reached over and pulled out a single strand of Miss Information's hair. "Maybe that's why it smells so bad in here. Maybe I did burn some of this hair; inorganic material gives off a stronger smell. Whoa. Wait a minute, Cassidy. Hand me that magnifying lens. I think . . . this is real hair!"

"*What?*"

"What?" Jack's voice echoed mine as he pulled himself through Magda's bedroom window. "Open window. Three heads? Sorry. I couldn't resist."

"Miss Information has real hair," I told him. "They must have scalped somebody for it!"

Magda had Miss Information's head wedged under her arm like a football; pulling out one strand at a time, she examined each hair under her lens.

"They probably just bought someone's hair, Cassidy." Magda examined something on her finger before sticking it in my face. "Do you realize that she's losing eyelashes, too?"

"That's what I came in here for. Please don't tell me those are real, too. Oh, man. I have the worst luck! If I find them, can you glue them back on with your slide stuff?"

"Mounting gel? No. That won't hold them permanently. I'd check the bottom of your backpack if I were you."

Magda's one eye behind geek glasses *and* a magnifying lens stared at me in accusation.

"Seriously, Magda? Don't you think I checked there already?"

"You could always buy some," she suggested. "I'm sure they're fake."

"No problem, Mags." I took the head from my sister. "I'll just go borrow Mom's car!"

"I know who has fake ones," Jack said. "Bree."

Magda nodded. "Jack's right. She has lots of makeup stuff."

"Oh, and I'm supposed to go knock on her door at eight o'clock at night and say, 'Excuse me, Mrs. Benson. I have this creepy head *with real hair* and missing eyelashes and I'm wondering if Bree could loan us some of her fake ones to replace them'?"

"Not loan," my sister corrected me. "She'd have to give them to us."

"I'll take it. I'll go through her window. Pass it here." Jack cupped his hands at his breadbasket, like I was going to toss him a football.

"You . . . go through Bree's window?" If I didn't like to talk so much, I'd be speechless.

"Just once. She told me she wanted to learn how to get out in case of a fire. But I think she likes the idea of sneaking out herself."

Five minutes later, we were standing outside, looking up at Bree's window. "Wait a minute. Doesn't sneaking out of the house net you some bad karma?"

Jack shrugged. "You know the rules better than I do." He tossed a couple of pebbles at Bree's window. Nothing happened.

"Maybe she's not home," I said. "We could use a little of Miss Information's hair to make our own eyelashes."

"She probably has her headphones on."

"Well . . . try this." I handed Jack a rock the size of an ostrich egg.

"That might break it."

"Gee, you think?" I got some karma amnesia and hurled it up there myself, missing the window by inches.

The window flew open and Bree's leg was dangling in midair before Jack could say "We'll come up!"

"I need the practice." I watched Bree lower herself like Catwoman with . . . was that one of Jack's Manila climbing ropes?

"Phew. How'd I do?"

"Faster than green grass through a goose," Jack said, patting her on the shoulder.

"Uh . . . ?"

"I'm teaching Jack some Southern sayings," Bree explained. "That one's my aunt's favorite. It's like . . . faster than greased lightning."

How much of a beating can one karma take?

"Now, how can I help you two?" Bree pulled her long hair out of the back of her shirt, the same thing Jack had taught me to do so hair didn't get caught in the rope on the way down.

Jack held out Miss Information's head.

"Well, look at this pretty thing. Where's the rest of her?"

"In a recycling bin," Jack said.

"That's not . . . true, is it?"

"Don't worry," I said. "It's just cardboard and they don't pick up until the day after tomorrow. I'll get her back by then."

"We need to know if you've got some fake eyelashes. She's missing a few."

"I can do more than that." Bree turned the head this way and that, admiring it from all angles. "I would love this head to practice my hairstyles. What I can't figure . . ." She held Miss Information up so she could see her better in the porch light. "Why would they give blue eye shadow to a blue-eyed lady?"

"What difference does it make?" I asked Bree. "Can you do it?"

"Of course I can do it. If you promise to tell me the story of how you got her. I love a good story."

"I can't tell you tonight. My mom will be up to say good night any minute."

"Can I fix her up and give her back to you tomorrow?" Bree asked, petting her hair.

"We have to go early."

"You say when and she'll be ready."

"How will you get back up there holding on to her?" Jack wondered. It was the sort of puzzle he liked to figure out.

"I can still slip in the back door. Mama hasn't locked up yet."

"Deal." Flicking the rope, Jack made the grappling hook come loose, caught it and started rolling up his rope. "Eight o'clock sharp. Right, Cass?" He handed the rope to Bree. "I owe you one."

Putting the rope over her shoulder with the hook at her back, Bree said, "You don't owe me anything, Jack Taylor. It's because of you that we're almost unpacked and settled."

After Bree left, I sat down on the ground. "All this for nothing. It's a not-prank."

"Think of it this way," Jack said, sitting down beside me. "You're still sharpening your skills. Boy, what a night. Look at the bats in the streetlight."

"Can't." I covered my eyes. I couldn't think about anything but getting that head back on its shoulders. "Now I have to convince Magda to go in early with me. I'll have to promise her something."

"You want me to help you find a dead squirrel?"

"No. She's got three in the garage freezer. Maybe a cracked bird's egg. She likes stuff that really stinks."

The next morning, after I promised Magda three DO NOT DISTURB cards, a cracked egg *and* a dead baby bird, she said to Mom, "Hey, Mom. I've got these burning questions about the right way to sign the emails I'm sending my camp professors. I never know whether I should say 'sincerely,' or 'best wishes,' or even . . . 'in gratitude.' Do you think we could go early to Cassidy's class so I can ask Miss Melton-Mopey?"

"It's Melton-Mowry," I corrected her.

"I thought you called her Melton-Mopey."

"Not to her face," I whispered, hoping my enormous cereal pour would cover the sound of my voice. For the record, Magda is the worst liar in the history of . . . well, pretty much recorded history.

"I had no idea you were struggling with this, Magda. Hmmm . . ." Mom consulted the calendar. "And I guess your sister can't help you because in week two it seems you are still practicing your table manners."

Even though Mom was talking to Magda, she looked straight at me after she'd finished with the calendar.

Time to get dense as iridium.

"Well . . ." She put her hand on my forehead. Mom swears she can tell by my temperature when I've been up to no good. "I guess Miss Melton-Mowry wouldn't mind a quick question, and I do need a new cell-phone battery. Okay. How about we leave in fifteen minutes?"

I looked down at my bowl, imagining all that mush in my stomach. "I better go find my backpack," I said. "We have to take a lot of notes in etiquette class."

I shouldn't have added the part about the notes because I'm not really known for caring about those. But I was getting all fluttery inside! This was starting to feel like one of those bank jobs on TV where the cops are waiting for the robbers in an empty vault.

Slipping out the back door, I ran over to Bree's, where I found her sitting on the porch with the head in her lap.

Instead of just shoving the head in my backpack, Bree held it up for the whole neighborhood to see. "Take out these pin curlers right before you put her head back on. And tuck a few strands of hair behind her left ear. That's her best side."

"Thanks, Bree." I reached out for Miss Information, but Bree took the backpack instead, unzipped it completely and laid the head inside like it was a present.

"Hold it like this," she instructed me, cradling the backpack like a baby. "And no jostling. I used cement glue. It needs a full twenty-four hours to cure."

Whatever.

"That's a powerful amount of paper you need to take notes with," Mom said as I got into the car. Mom really should have gone into police work. She knew I'd done something already. Once, I heard her say to Dad that the only way to get me to straighten up and fly right was to let me suffer the consequences of my actions.

Delton was right about this being a prank in a death spiral. "Anybody got a paper bag?" I asked.

"Feeling sick, dear?"

When we arrived at the School of Poise and Purpose, we said good-bye to Mom and waited for her to pull out of the parking lot before hightailing it around to the back alley.

"Quick, get the rest of her out of there." I found the empty milk crate for Magda.

"*It,* remember. Get the rest of *it.*"

"This is no time for a grammar lesson, Magda. Fish her out."

Magda lifted up the lid. "Oooh, it stinks in here."

I think I have provided sufficient evidence to demonstrate that when Magda says it stinks, it really, really stinks.

"It was perfectly clean last Wednesday."

"Well, it *is* a recycling bin! I told you leaving her in here for so long was risky. There's been a big dump of something . . . get me a stick."

I found a broom wedged between the recycling bin and the trash bin and handed it to Magda.

As Magda stirred up the boxes with the handle of the broom, she added, "And when will you learn, Cassidy? There is no such thing as 'perfectly clean.' There's always residue. Boost me up, will you? I can't see." Holding Magda's foot in my hand, I tried to stay steady as she rooted through the bin.

"Nope. Sorry, Cass. She's not in there."

"But it says right here . . . no pickup until—"

"They didn't pick up. The boxes are still there. I guess . . . somebody must have found her."

"It, Magda. It! You're the one who keeps telling me!" I sat down on the ground. "Who steals a dummy with no head from a recycling bin?"

"We better go in and tell your teacher," Magda said. "Before Mom gets back."

I would have followed Magda, but I had to sit down and feel my stomach to make sure my organs were still in the right place. Being responsible for the disappearance of the teacher's special mannequin seemed certain to earn me a failing grade in etiquette school.

Not to mention the criminal charges.

Spending time in jail would be good experience for an aspiring hobo like me; but would I still have to take etiquette lessons upon my release? Would Mom and Dad get a refund for the class to apply toward my bail? Would Great-Grandma Reed turn over in her grave? I wasn't sure what that meant, exactly—but somehow I knew that, if at all possible, the old bat would haunt me.

"Cassidy?" Bending over, Magda put her hand on my knee.

84

"I shouldn't always assume the worst, should I, Magda? Janae says we create our own reality. Maybe we can find Miss Information's body around here somewhere."

"Cassidy, I found her. You better come look."

We stood behind a big cement pillar, staring into the School of Poise and Purpose. There sat a headless Miss Information. Her skirt was torn and there were red smudges on her blouse. She looked a little worse for wear, as they say.

Across from her sat a police officer!

"Magda, is there a shipwreck worse than the *Titanic*?"

"No, Cassidy, there isn't."

"The jig's up, then. Time to take my punishment."

I walked through the door and placed my backpack at the officer's feet. "Let's get this over with," I said, holding out my arms.

excellent

CHAPTER 9

Reprimands

The officer looked at my hands. "It's the right one," he said. "You shake with the right."

"Aren't you going to clink the cuffs on me? I've got the head in this bag."

I guess they don't make police officers as smart as they used to; all he did was rub his chin and look up at me. "That doesn't seem very polite . . . especially right before class."

Miss Melton-Mowry came out of her office. "Sounds like someone has a confession to make." She crossed her arms and waited. I resisted the urge to say it was all Delton's fault and looked at my shoes while I figured out my next move.

The officer reached into the backpack.

"Hold it." Stepping in, Magda took the head from him and unclipped the curlers. "Which ear?" she asked me.

"Left. It's her best side," I explained to Miss Melton-Mowry as Magda fitted the head back on the mannequin and spun it around a time or two until it was tight enough to stay on, even if a little crooked.

It was time for me to say something. "If you want the whole truth and nothing but, I have to tell you, it isn't pretty, Miss Melton-Mowry. The fact of the matter is this was all Delton's idea."

"You don't say."

"I'm Cassidy." I shook hands with the police officer, nice and firm. "Uh, sorry. Miss Corcoran."

"And I'm Officer Weston."

I kept on shaking, hoping Miss Melton-Mowry was taking note of how good I was at introducing myself. "And that's my sister, Mag—Miss Corcoran, the second."

Magda didn't answer because she was hyperfocused on Miss Information's blouse, using her library card to scrape some of the red stuff into her palm.

"That's not"—I broke off for dramatic effect and pressed the back of my hand to my mouth—"blood, is it?"

Magda sniffed her fingers. "Pizza sauce, I think."

Officer Weston took a finger full and sniffed it, too. "Yep. When I hauled her out, she was covered in pizza boxes."

"But you're not allowed to recycle pizza boxes in Grand River!"

"There's been a rash of illegal dumping since the city started charging for trash by the pound," Officer Weston added.

"None of this explains how she got there in the first place,

Miss Corcoran, and obfuscation is not the way to handle this issue."

Miss Melton-Mowry's body language—crossed arms, narrowed eyes, one tapping foot, frown—was looking suspiciously like Corcoran-family sign language for "cut the crap and move it along."

"How can I obfooskate if I don't know what it is?" I asked.

"It means to confuse the issue," she said. "Or skirt around it."

Really? I had no idea there was a word for the very thing I'm genius at!

I put my feet together and straightened my shoulders. "I agree completely, Miss Melton-Mowry. Speaking of skirts, I'm guessing Magda here would be happy to donate one of hers to Miss Information. She has a whole closet full that she never wears. Isn't that right, Magda?"

I had to poke her before she nodded.

Miss Melton-Mowry's arms stayed crossed. "I'm waiting, Miss Corcoran."

"The thing of it is, we felt Miss Information needed a . . . makeover. We had a real beauty queen to do it."

"And the 'we' is you and Delton?"

The other students were coming in, even though there was still five minutes before class started. Is everyone who takes etiquette lessons a suck-up?

Delton Bean almost fainted when he saw Officer Weston. "You're not . . . arresting Cassidy, are you?"

I put my hands on Delton's shoulders. "No, Delton. He's arresting *you* on the charge of gross bodily harm and fleeing the scene of a crime. I hope you brought along a change of clothes."

Delton looked like he did the day he got an 89 percent on his math test. Or like the day he dropped his graphing calculator in the mud.

"I'm not here to arrest anyone," Officer Weston said. "I'm here for class."

"But you're a grown-up."

"My fiancée says I'm an uncivilized clod and if I don't get some manners by July and her big family reunion, she's not going through with the wedding."

"So?" I asked him. "What's the problem?"

Which is how Officer Weston and I became friends, because he didn't see the problem with it, either. Well, with being an uncivilized clod. Then and there we made a pact to see this manners thing through to the bitter end.

Of course, what remained was the issue of taking responsibility for vandalizing Miss Information. I favored an "all's well that ends well" approach, but as I have discovered in my eleven years on this planet, grown-ups are big on responsibility.

After she'd interrogated me and Delton enough times to be satisfied—and had a long conference with Mom and Mrs. Bean—Miss Melton-Mowry asked for time to think about how best we could serve out our sentence. I felt etiquette class was punishment enough, but I knew the drill. She wanted us to stew.

As we were leaving, Miss Melton-Mowry pulled me aside. "Though I am not as familiar with WEE holds as you are, you will find me a formidable opponent, Miss Corcoran. How would you say that in wrestling terminology? I think it's . . . you're on the ropes."

"WWE, Miss Melton-Mowry." I didn't give her the satisfaction of telling her I wasn't just on the ropes. I was down for the count.

Dad got home late that night; I couldn't fall asleep, thinking of him, tired from making grocery shoppers happy all day, having to hear about my latest mess-up.

Right on time, he showed up at my door. "I understand you've been very busy, Miss Cassidy."

"Dad!" I untangled myself from the covers and reached out to him.

Bear hug. We both growled.

"So . . . kidnapping, destruction of private property." Sitting down on the edge of my bed, Dad added, "I thought you aspired to a life on the road, not a life of crime."

"It wasn't kidnapping, Dad, it was more like . . . hide-and-seek. And it was all Delton's fault, really. His mom wanted him to learn some do-daring, and I—"

"Delton Bean? The one who turns his back to the audience during the Christmas concert?"

"Mrs. Parsons called it the worst case of performance anxiety she's ever seen."

"I'm beginning to think *you* have the worst case of good-behavior anxiety I've ever seen. Did Delton really force you to behead Miss Information? As counsel for the defendant, I need to know everything."

When my dad puts his hand on my head and looks into my eyes, it's like being forced to drink truth serum from a voodoo doctor. "No. It was my idea to put her hair in the soup bowl. I just figured she had a wig. I didn't know it was attached to her head, like . . . real hair."

"Yes, hair has a way of being attached to the head. You do understand how wrong that was."

"Yep. And two wrongs don't make a right." I hoped to hurry the lecture part of this conversation to an end. "I should have told Miss Melton-Mopey—Mowry—what I'd done."

Taking my hand, Dad started massaging my palm, going under each knuckle and pressing. It was one of his strategies for helping me relax so I could fall asleep. "What continues to surprise me about you, Miss Cassidy, is that given two courses of action, you almost always choose the most difficult one. Why is that?"

I shrugged. "I'm an overachiever?" I could tell by the look on his face that this answer didn't satisfy him. "Search me, Dad."

Before he got his second wind about how, despite my above-average intelligence, I could be a real knucklehead, I tried to change the subject to what was really bugging me. "Dad, why does Jack all of a sudden have goals like saving money? And why does he want to hang around Sabrina Benson instead of hanging out with me?"

"By Sabrina Benson, you mean new-neighbor Bensons, 'sweet tea have a sugar cookie' Sabrina and Mrs. Benson?"

"Yep."

"You're not moving us from the intricacies of the law to the eternal mysteries of the heart, are you?" Dad put my left hand under the covers and started pressing the palm of my right.

"No! I just want to know why he'd rather be with her than with me."

"Well, since I haven't observed Jack and Sabrina together, I couldn't say. Sabrina seems like a very nice girl. A little old for Jack, maybe, but then your mom and I are three years apart."

"Uck. Dad, I'm not talking about that."

"What, then, pray tell, are you talking about?"

"I don't know. That's why I asked you."

Lifting the sheet, Dad put my hand back down by my side before kissing the top of my head. "You're going to have to let me ponder that one, Miss Cassidy. Your question is . . . complicated. Now, regarding the matter of your sentencing, which we will skip to since you've already confessed to the crime, your mom and I will be joining you and Miss Melton-Mowry after Wednesday's class to discuss the matter."

"That's okay, Dad. You don't have to come. I know how busy you are saving the grocery store from disaster."

"True, but I wish to be present at my client's sentencing, so instead of taking a walk in the park and feeding the ducks on my lunch hour, I think I will eat my sandwich at my desk and drive across town so that I can spend that time with you at the Bright Corners strip mall."

I scrunched my eyes closed to avoid Dad launching into the "your actions affect other people" speech. "I'm practically asleep, Dad. Can we save the rest for another time?"

Before Wednesday's class, Delton tried to go through the door to the School of Poise and Porpoise before me. "Hey, watch your manners." I pulled him back by the shoulder. "Ladies first. Geez."

"Sorry, Cassidy. I'm just trying to be punctual."

"I am impressed with your almost-lateness. Try harder

next week." Everyone was pretty much seated by the time we got in. Donna was polishing her silverware with some special cloth she'd brought from home. Ryan was tugging wrinkles out of the tablecloth. It was like a meeting of the after-school teacher's-pet club.

"Mr. Bean. Miss Corcoran. You may take your seats on either side of Officer Weston."

"Yes, Miss Melton-Mowry." Delton took his eyes off the floor only as long as it required him to see the way to his chair.

Donna raised her hand. "Is this our new Miss Information?"

All eyes went to the seat previously occupied by the world's biggest doll, where a lady in a raincoat sat holding so tight to the oversized handbag in her lap, you'd have thought this was the meeting of the after-school purse-snatchers club.

"Miss Information"—Miss Melton-Mowry paused, letting her eyes rest on me—"is undergoing some . . . renovation. But allow me to introduce you to Miss Glennon. Miss Glennon is the granddaughter of Private Reserve Academy founder Eudora Glennon, who has been, over the years, a personal mentor of mine. Miss Glennon is with us today on a very special assignment."

Another meaningful look at me.

Miss Glennon swallowed and squeezed the top of her purse like it was a stress ball; her eyes darted around the room, avoiding eye contact. If we were in Cassidy Corcoran's Executive School for Spies and Counterintelligence Agents, I would have taught her about iridium. Sure as my keister was glued to that plastic seat, the lady was hiding something.

"Miss Glennon was just about to demonstrate the proper placement of one's purse." Miss Melton-Mowry proceeded to pinch the purse as if it was a used Kleenex. "On the floor, just next to the chair leg."

"No, please. I need that." As Miss Melton-Mowry lifted and Miss Glennon tugged back, the purse squealed. Before you could say "time for recess," out popped a furry head, its eyes darting around just like Miss Glennon's had, looking for an escape route. The critter chose to dive under the flap of Miss Glennon's raincoat.

Donna forgot to raise her hand. "Oooh," she squealed. "That's a rat! My disgusting brother has one just like it."

"We have a strict no-dander policy here at the school, Miss Glennon. I must ask you to remove that animal immediately."

Grabbing her lapels to prevent another escape, Miss Glennon tried to explain: "I couldn't leave her in the car—by the end of class, it would be too hot! It's her annual physical today; appointments are very hard to make with Dr. Schoen. Only two veterinarians specialize in long-tailed rodents in Grand River and I would never take Feathers to Dr.—"

At this point, Miss Glennon was interrupted by a head popping out of the neck of her coat, just under her chin. What Feathers saw must have frightened her enough to go back the way she came. The next glimpse we got was of the rat's nose through a torn seam in the arm of Miss Glennon's coat. At this point, Miss Peabody, one of a half-dozen wimpy girls in our class, announced that she was going to faint.

"Put your head between your legs," Officer Weston instructed, not taking his eyes off the incredible bulging raincoat.

Feathers managed to poke her head out between two buttons on Miss Glennon's lap, the raincoat belt draped over her head like one of those scarves old ladies wear to protect their hairdos.

All the fancy-pants manners went out the window as Miss Glennon struggled to keep Feathers in her coat and we watched the bulge move to the tune of girls screaming their heads off. Clutching herself here and there, our visitor gave the impression that she was possessed by aliens.

Officer Weston elbowed me. "Wow, manners class is better than I thought."

do not like ✗

CHAPTER 10

The Lunch Table

The first five minutes, maybe. But after the rat was corralled and delivered to Miss Glennon's car—which had been moved to the shade—it was business as usual. The only difference was that Miss Glennon sat in her wrinkly raincoat in the seat normally occupied by Miss Information, nodding in enthusiastic agreement to all the rules we needed to learn that day about what to pass and where to pass it and put it down and wait for everyone to be served. Do polite people ever eat anything hot, I wondered.

When eleven o'clock finally rolled around, I had my knees pointed in the direction of the exit until I remembered the conference after class. Miss Melton-Mowry stood at the door so the students could practice egressing or whatever fancy word she had for making a clean getaway.

Officer Weston didn't seem to be in any hurry. "Who knew there were so many ways to put food in your mouth," he said, eyeing all the silverware on the table. "Hey, I can see my reflection." He picked up his dinner plate and admired himself.

"Look at me." I stretched my lips over my teeth and made my eyes wide. "I'm a monkey."

Officer Weston sucked in his cheeks. "I'm a fish."

We passed the time in this perfectly normal way until the bells jingled and my parents walked in.

"Mom. Dad!" I rushed to hug Dad like I'd just been rescued from kidnappers.

"An officer of the law?" I could feel Dad shaking Officer Weston's hand. "Here for the sentencing?"

While my head was still buried in Dad's middle, I heard Delton's mom come in. "I'm Sylvia Bean, Delton's mother. We met at the graduation ceremony."

"And I'm Cassidy's father." Dad turned me around and smoothed down my hair. "If it weren't for the family resemblance, I might try to deny it."

"Sylvia," Mom joined in. "We should apologize on behalf of our daughter."

"Oh, no, please don't. Delton's never been in trouble before."

"You say that like it's a bad thing."

"Well . . ." Mrs. Bean took a handkerchief out of her purse and dusted off the plastic seat before she sat down. "I've always believed that a child needs spirit to make his way in life. You know, a little backbone."

"I'm sure Cassie wouldn't mind giving Delton some of

hers," Mom said, not bothering to wipe off her seat. "She's got plenty of it."

"Please, everyone, be seated." I noticed Miss Melton-Mowry had a different tone of voice for the parents. "Your time is valuable and I don't want to waste it."

I knew better than to say anything about the value of my time. Adults and kids have never seen eye to eye on that subject.

"Miss Glennon here works for Private Reserve Academy, which, as you know, is an elite boarding school in Ravenna. I'm delighted to be one of the finalists for the position of headmistress of etiquette, and her grandmother, the founder, has asked her to observe my class."

All eyes went to Miss Glennon, who had the same look on her face that the rat had earlier. I'd seen that look before on Delton's face, right before he had to give his oral report on World War II Cessna aircraft.

"As a sort of final interview, we are invited to bring a few select students to the Egypt Valley Country Club, where many Academy families are members."

"Surely, you're not thinking of bringing Cassidy with you." Dad put his hand on the top of my head and turned it so that I was looking directly at Miss Melton-Mowry. "You must have other students who—"

"Grandmother was insistent that I choose the poorest-performing pupils," Miss Glennon said, folding her napkin and pinching the crease. "The hard-core cases. Those were her exact words."

"Hard-core, eh? Well, you might have found your girl, then."

"While Miss Corcoran has an excess of insouciance, Mr. Bean seems to suffer from . . . some social anxiety," said Miss Melton-Mowry. "They are excellent candidates to demonstrate the effectiveness of my teaching methods. I asked Officer Weston to stay because he has an event to prepare for and he needs the practice."

"I changed over to the graveyard shift to make it work," Officer Weston explained. "I haven't slept in nineteen hours."

"I feel your pain, Officer." Dad looked like he was about to say more, maybe about how grocery stores have to be open twenty-four hours a day, but he must have changed his mind. Turning to Miss Melton-Mowry, he asked, "So this will compensate for Cassidy putting your mannequin in the bin?"

"Delton was partly responsible for that," Mrs. Bean chimed in.

"He wanted to remove her arms so there were no identifying marks, but I said no."

I only said it to make Mrs. Bean feel good about Delton's backbone, but Dad squeezed my thigh, which in Corcoran-family sign language means "shut it."

Delton raised his hand to protest, but Miss Melton-Mowry ignored him.

"It will require a great deal of practice and extra lessons. I believe this is a fair trade-off."

"I was thinking some hard labor . . . maybe hours of leafleting cars in the parking lot during midday followed by picking up trash on the side of the highway."

"Brian." This time Dad got the squeeze. Mom knew I'd rather do anything than spend more time in etiquette class; she wanted me to suffer.

"Okay, sweetie." Dad put his hand over Mom's. "I'm beginning to warm to this idea, Miss Melton-Mowry. Cassidy as a little Eliza Doolittle."

"Excellent. Then it's all settled. I prepared a handout with the details. If you'll excuse me."

Miss Melton-Mowry stood up and Dad half stood before sitting back down.

Directing her gaze at Officer Weston, our teacher said, "When a lady excuses herself from the table, Officer Weston, it is customary to stand briefly in acknowledgment."

"Okay, sure. But why?"

"You won't get far asking the reasons for things," Dad said. "Originally, we were supposed to help them in and out of their chairs, but you could get decked for that nowadays. Think of it as the appendix of the etiquette world."

After Miss Melton-Mowry left the room, Dad leaned in my direction and said, "All things considered, you got off lightly, Miss Corcoran."

"Are you kidding me? She's worse than the Just Say No assembly." I glanced out the door, where something called the sun was shining to beat the band. "Well, now that's all settled, I think I'll just be moseying on home."

"*I* think we should start immediately." Miss Melton-Mowry had reappeared and was passing around a handout to the adults.

"But . . . what about lunch?" I sucked in my cheeks to make it look like I was starving.

"I'm sure Delton wouldn't mind sharing his lentil spread with sunflower shoots," Mrs. Bean offered, reaching into her bag and pulling out a package wrapped in wax paper. "We were going to the park after," she explained.

"That is very generous of you, Mrs. Bean, but I have some fruit salad in the refrigerator. In anticipation of this extra practice, I've already set the table in the back."

Mom leaned over to Dad and whispered, "Let's go to the Tortilla Factory."

It doesn't always help to have razor-sharp hearing. I would have pout-slouched, but I figured that was something that earned you the cattle prod in etiquette class. So, after we'd said our good-byes, I trooped to the back of the room and pulled out my chair with as much scraping as possible on a carpet.

There I was, sitting at a table with Miss Glennon, Delton, Officer Weston and Miss Melton-Mowry, so far away from where an aspiring hobo ought to be that I considered asking Delton to pinch me. Earlier in the week, Mom said we could go to Lake Michigan with a picnic after class; now she was at the Tortilla Factory and I was here!

Delton didn't seem disappointed to miss his picnic with his mom. He pointed to all the stuff on the table like it was the guts of a 1944 Cessna Bobcat, touching the tip of his finger with his thumb as he counted off each item: grapefruit spoon, salad fork, bread dish.

"Mr. Bean," I said, "you sure know how to make the best of a bad situation."

Miss Melton-Mowry stood watching us, waiting for silence, I guess, and the whole "all eyes on me" thing teachers are so crazy about. "Your waitstaff will serve from the left and clear from the right." Her hands hovered over the table like it was a Ouija board. "Now, since it is summertime, there may be a fruit cup."

"This?" I asked, pointing to what looked like a wineglass for Vikings. "Are we supposed to drink from it?"

"No. Look at the stem. Technically, it's a footed dish. I pulled it out of storage. I don't want anything to seem unfamiliar to you."

"Another clue," Miss Glennon added. "It's at twelve o'clock."

"Is it twelve o'clock already?" I strained to see the clock on the wall.

"They use that in the military," Delton said. "It indicates positioning. Everyone can picture where twelve o'clock is."

"Can you picture me cleaning your clock, I wonder."

"You don't have to get all worked up, Cassidy. I was just trying to help."

"There is far too much talking going on. Mr. Bean. Miss Corcoran. Posture."

Miss Glennon put her hand on my arm. "I like to think of myself as a dancer getting ready to go out onstage." She demonstrated, straightening her shoulders.

"I like that." I jerked myself up; my shoulders straight, I let my arms dangle. "I'll pretend I'm one of those puppets on a string."

"Miss Corcoran, you will stop talking this instant." Miss Melton-Mowry's eyebrows tried to link up, like two cable cars. "The truth of the matter is," she continued, smoothing the tablecloth, "we are going to sit at this table on this gorgeous sunny summer day until the lesson has been learned to my satisfaction. Do you think your parents will enjoy waiting outside—in their hot cars—for us to conclude?"

I shook my head. I did not.

"You may find your motivation there, Miss Corcoran."

"I'd like to get some sleep before I have to go on duty," Officer Weston said.

I wondered if arresting me for disturbing the peace would be considered going on duty. But I didn't say anything, because I *did* want to go home! Other than Magda's compost pile, this was the last place on earth I wanted to be. It was *so* unfair. Magda was probably sitting at the Bensons' kitchen table right now, eating sugar cookies and talking about her latest discoveries in putrefaction.

"Shall we continue?"

I straightened my shoulders—again—and reached across the table, my pinky as straight as if it was in a splint. "It's a perfect day for a cup of fruit." I took hold of the glass. "Should we pretend to eat now?"

And I swear I would have made a great show of pretending to eat in the politest way possible. Not because Miss Melton-Mowry wanted me to, but because it was the only way out of the situation. But! As I pulled the cup to my mouth, I saw what was in it—something squirmy and alive, with about a thousand legs. And, at the moment, it was panicked and imprisoned in my fruit cup!

"Ick!" I screamed, and threw the glass back to twelve o'clock.

"What on earth do you think you're doing?"

"There's a disgusting bug in there!"

"No there's not. It's right here." Officer Weston used his butter knife to bring the terrified little guy to eye level; but in a frantic attempt at escape, it flipped off the blade and—of course!—came scurrying toward me on its four thousand legs.

I jerked back from the table, my chair saved from toppling only by my kneecaps smacking the underside. "Arrrgh! Get it away from me or I'll do a runner."

"Oh, Cassidy," Miss Glennon said. "It's just a harmless millipede. It can't hurt you."

"Try telling that to my nervous system."

"Her flight response is on autopilot," Delton said. "She has an irrational fear of bugs."

"There." Officer Weston managed to slide his knife under the millipede again and flick it off the table. "Gone."

I smacked back down to the floor but kept my knees up, hugging them to protect my core. "It's not all bugs." I panted, waiting for my breath to stop running even though I was sitting still. "Just ones with a lot of legs."

"And worms," Delton added.

"Only if they're squirming. If they're dead, like in puddles, I'm fine."

"Is there something wrong, Miss Melton-Mowry?" Delton asked.

Rising from her chair, our teacher proceeded to speak: "To. Illuminate. Each. And. Every. Transgression. Here. Would be . . ." She reached over and set my cup upright. "For the record, Officer Weston, our cutlery is to be used for the purposes of eating and not . . . insect transportation. Miss Glennon, will you assist me in clearing the fruit cups so that we can fill them in the back?"

"So," Officer Weston said after they'd disappeared into the little kitchen. "Is this the part where we eat?"

CHAPTER 11

Fruit,
or Soup,
in Cups

"No." I took another slow breath. My heart rate was almost back to normal. "And in our experience, we're not going to."

"What is that noise?" Delton asked.

"My stomach. I get real hungry after I see a bug. My nervous system burns up energy like crazy."

Officer Weston rested his chin in his hand. "And I thought there were a lot of rules in the police academy."

"You'll be arrested by the etiquette police if they find you with your elbow on the table," I said, poking him. "We learned that day one."

"At least elbows don't leave a print." He straightened up. "Hey, Delton, you're not going to snitch on me, are you?"

Delton started in on how he'd been unfairly labeled, but he was interrupted by Miss Melton-Mackerel coming back into the room with her fancy glasses on a tray. I perked up. There looked to be some real food in them.

After she and Miss Glennon sat down, she said, "Well, then. Now that we're in a calm, quiet state, let's practice passing our fruit cups. We pass with the right hand and receive with the left. Place the glass at twelve o'clock, approximately eight inches from the edge of the table. No, Miss Corcoran, it's not a beer stein. Hold the stem between your thumb and forefinger, using your middle finger for ballast, if need be."

I didn't understand half the stuff she said, but I watched her and made it better by using my pinky as a rudder—straight as a board—like you see in all the Charlie Chaplin movies.

"Now, I would like you each in turn, beginning with Officer Weston, to take two bites of fruit."

Officer Weston stared into his glass. "I can't eat the pineapple," he said. "I'm allergic. It makes my throat close. Does that ever happen to you?" He looked at me as he speared a piece of pineapple with his fork. Holding it out, he asked, "Cassi— Miss Corcoran, would you like my pineapple?"

I stared at the little piece of pineapple, dripping with juice. Then I stole a look at Miss Melton-Mowry, who was pinching the skin on her forehead the way ladies on commercials do when they have a tension headache. "Sure."

After Officer Weston scraped off his pineapple bit using the edge of my glass, he cleared his throat. "Now, you said two bites, right? I want to get an A on this part."

"Two bites," Miss Glennon said.

Watermelon. Strawberry. Grape. It was impressive what Officer Weston could load onto his fork. He finished the whole dish in two bites.

I clapped. "Nice spearing technique. My turn?"

All eyes went to Miss Melton-Mowry, who was pressing her napkin to her mouth as if *she'd* just eaten a forkload of fruit. She gave a little flutter with her hand that I took to mean yes.

I was close to Officer Weston's performance except for needing fingers to steady the grape before I skewered it. I even remembered to chew with my mouth closed after skimming it off my fork.

Officer Weston gave me a thumbs-up.

Miss Melton-Mowry was fanning herself with a School of Poise and Purpose flyer. "Mr. Bean," she said.

Delton straightened his shoulders, picked up his spoon and skimmed it over the top of the dish, starting on the side closest to him and finishing on the side furthest away, where he tapped his spoon against the side of the glass before putting one measly piece of melon into his mouth.

Miss Melton-Mowry and Miss Glennon looked at each other, wide-eyed. Delton was going to need special tutoring.

"Mr. Bean?"

"I watched your YouTube video on eating soup and applied transfer of knowledge to the fruit cup." He patted his mouth with his napkin and set it on the table.

Elbowing Officer Weston, I whispered, "I told you he was a suck-up."

"That was brilliant. Soup and fruit cup in one fell swoop," he whispered back.

I raised my hand. "I need to see the grade sheet," I said. "I thought the point of this was to eat."

"To eat *politely.*"

"I chewed with my mouth closed. You chewed with your mouth closed, didn't you, Officer Weston?"

"You both drew attention to yourselves by trying to load an entire cup of fruit onto one forkful and making unpleasant noises as you ate. I think we should watch Mr. Bean demonstrate one more time. I'll have to go find another can of fruit."

Officer Weston was still stuck on the whole fruit/soup thing. "But you eat soup with a spoon and fruit with a fork."

"It depends on how the fruit is delivered to you. What Mr. Bean has mastered is the ability to discern what method is most appropriate for eating and then proceeding without drawing attention to himself. But that does bring up a good point. We're just as likely to be served gazpacho for our first course as we are—"

I sighed. Big-time. "How can I master gazpacho when I don't even know what it is?"

"It's a raw soup with a base of tomatoes and finely chopped vegetables," Delton informed us.

"That's not soup . . . that's salsa! Don't you eat that with tortilla chips?"

Officer Weston was still stuck on the spoon-for-the-fruit thing. "But he pushed the spoon away from him. That doesn't make any sense."

"Yes, it does. When one is eating soup, this gives it time to cool. And with a fruit cup, skimming the spoon over the far edge of the dish helps you catch any drips."

"It doesn't matter that it looks goofy?" I wanted to know. "It's like . . . rowing backward."

"I agree with Cassidy," Officer Weston said. "Even polite people must know that the way to get to your mouth is to go toward it."

"Miss Corcoran, you mean," Miss Glennon corrected.

It made me glad to have Officer Weston along. At least with two people pointing out how crazy the rules were, manners class was more of a fair fight.

Miss Melton–Marching Orders ignored us both. "You might also have noticed Mr. Bean's posture. He sat up straight and brought the spoon to his mouth rather than the other way around. And there was a peaceful silence as the food traveled to his mouth."

As our teacher congratulated Delton, I whispered to Officer Weston, "I thought you were supposed to eat the stuff, not take it on a trip."

"In fact, why don't you take another bite while Officer Weston and Miss Corcoran observe closely and then try to follow your example. Miss Glennon, shall we go find two more fruit cups? I need to confer with you in the kitchen."

After they left, Officer Weston poked at the tablecloth with his fork. "I guess it doesn't have to make sense if the future in-laws approve."

But I was still stuck on old Delton. He was supposed to be in trouble—like me!—and on day one of detention, here he was, the teacher's pet.

As soon as the door to the little kitchen had closed, I asked him, "What I want to know is who in their right mind would think of going on YouTube for etiquette lessons during summer vacation?"

"My mother." Delton set down his spoon and swallowed again, even though the fruit was history. "That's what she does. She searches out people on the Internet. Companies hire her to improve their online business. She did a whole inventory of Miss Melton-Mowry's Web presence."

"Well, then, why do you look so sour?" Officer Weston asked Delton. "You're at the head of the class."

"When Miss Melton-Mowry tells my mother how good I am, she won't be happy at all. She thinks I'm a congenital pleaser. Congenital pleasers don't make great men. She wants me to have more backbone."

Officer Weston took advantage of our teacher's absence to crack his knuckles. "Shouldn't she have sent you to rugby camp or something?"

"Oh, no. She doesn't believe in aggression. Besides, whenever she sets up playdates with boys who have original minds, they usually beat me up."

"But I want to beat you up!"

"Yes, but you don't."

"What's the point? It wouldn't be a fair fight. I don't like to see weaklings hurt. You know what you need, Delton? You need to watch our YouTube video on a good prank."

"Our . . . do you mean you and Jack? You make YouTube videos?"

"Of course we don't. But if we did . . ." I lowered my voice and gave old Delton the rules of the prank.

"So, the purpose of a prank is to annoy people—" Delton repeated, making notes on his phone.

"Right," I said; Officer Weston nodded.

"—but not hurt them."

"Sure. Gotta remember your karma."

"And cover up your tracks so no one suspects you," Officer Weston added.

Delton and I looked at him. For a member of the police force, Officer Weston seemed awfully familiar with the concepts.

110

"What? I was a boy once, too. There's a difference between a harmless prank and criminal activity."

"When they work right," I told Delton, "you can barely keep from laughing; you hold it in so hard, you get a stomach ache."

"So . . . Miss Information? That was a prank, right?" Delton could not let something alone until he understood it well enough to get an A on the test.

"It was supposed to be. If Miss Melton-Mopey had come out and seen a whole head of hair in the soup bowl . . . now *that* would have been the perfect etiquette 'don't.'"

"But how can you be sure your prank doesn't go wrong? I mean, look how miserable you are, Cassidy."

I sighed. "That's the trouble with pranks, Delton. They take on a life of their own."

Officer Weston nodded in agreement.

"Can you start small? Could I practice with a little prank?"

"I don't see why not," Officer Weston said. "When I was your age . . ."

But that was as far as he got because Miss Glennon and Miss Melton-Military were back with a basket of something covered in a napkin. I would say bread, but bread was something I liked. Surely, it could not be something I liked. *Or* she'd find a new way to torture us by instructing us to eat it crumb by crumb.

"Our second lesson today will be about bread," Miss Melton-Mowry announced as the two ladies took their seats. "Return to your dining posture, everyone."

We all sat up at attention, but somehow I knew we wouldn't just pass the basket around. Miss M&M would have to jaw about it first. I rubbed my grumbling stomach and waited.

"The basket is most likely to be in the center of the table. If you cannot reach it, you stand up, lean over with your left hand lightly pressed against your dress or jacket or tie so that it doesn't touch any of the items on the table and take hold of the basket with your right hand. Returning to your seat, you lift one corner of the napkin and take a roll between your thumb and forefinger, like so."

I wanted to say "Like a knuckleball?" because I knew it would make Officer Weston laugh. And in fact, come to think of it, a joke is a little bit like a small prank. But no matter how I "dithered," as old Mrs. Parsons called it, we still got to go to lunch at Stocking Elementary. Since eating here wasn't guaranteed, I chose to keep quiet.

"If there is an assortment—"

"Praise be," Officer Weston whispered.

Miss M&M raised her eyebrow, but she didn't stop talking. "At breakfast, for example, you might have a poppy-seed muffin, a scone, some banana bread. You must choose *with your eyes*. The first thing you touch is your choice."

I raised my hand. "But what if your favorite is at the bottom and you have to move something else around to get to it?"

"You mean like a cinnamon roll?" Officer Weston asked me. "Can you use a spoon, Miss Melton-Mowry?"

Miss Melton-Mowry set down the basket and replaced the cover. "We are not diving for buried treasure. You may have to forgo your first choice in favor of a more convenient option."

"You could say dibs on the cinnamon roll and pass it around until it's uncovered."

"You will say no such thing, Miss Corcoran. You will receive the basket with your left hand and you will pass it with your right. Fortunately, you will be spared the agony of such a choice today because all the rolls here are the same."

I put a lid on it. I was starting to salivate.

Miss Glennon took the basket and passed it to Officer Weston. "I'm gluten-sensitive," she explained.

"Of course, you may choose not to take any bread at all. Then just pass it along."

"If I'm feeling faint, can I take hers?"

"Never take more than one until everyone has been served. If, at some point during the meal, you feel you would like another roll, you must offer it first to everyone else. Like so. 'Would anyone else like another roll?'" Miss Melton-Monarchy held up the basket.

Officer Weston raised his hand.

"There's no need to raise your hand, Officer Weston."

"Well, what's the point of that?" I couldn't help asking the question. None of this made any sense at all. "If you let everyone go before you, the rolls will all be gone."

"The point, Miss Corcoran, is to be polite. The *point* is the reason you are sitting opposite me today. When we learn the rules of polite society, we open the doors of opportunity."

"Why don't we just open the doors of the kitchen?" I grumbled. "Are polite people *always* hungry?"

Miss Melton-Mowry decided to ignore me. It's a normal developmental stage for every one of my teachers. At some point, I'm just not there.

Of course, before we could get our one measly roll, we had to listen to another lecture about how you don't put the roll in your mouth and bite down like a normal person. What you do is leave it on your plate and pinch off a piece. Then there's a whole other slew of rules about how you butter it. And if you press too hard on that icy pat of butter and it lands on the floor, you can't rinse it off in your water glass like a sensible person. You have to leave it on the ground and eat your stupid old roll without it.

Polite people are sure to starve to death. A couple of bites of fruit and a roll the size of a golf ball took the whole hour!

As Miss M&M and Miss Glennon took the bread basket and the dishes back to the little kitchen, I whispered to Officer Weston, "Let's play a prank on Delton's mom."

"How so?"

"Well, she wanted Delton to take this class with me so he could get some backbone."

"Okay . . ." Officer Weston nodded.

"So, we tell her something she wants to hear. Will you play along?"

"As long as I don't have to break any laws or tell any lies."

"But you'll go along with mine?"

He looked up at the ceiling and whistled under his breath, which is sign language for "I know nothing."

finished

CHAPTER 12

Introducing Yourself

In the parking lot, Mrs. Bean ran up to us like the ducks at Riverside Park do when they see you have a bag of bread.

"Hey there, Mrs. Bean," I called out to her.

"Cassidy?" Mom was already in the car. She rolled down the window. "We need to get going." Mom has excellent radar for when I am about to tell a story.

"Be right there." I didn't break my stride. "You should have seen old Delton in class today, Mrs. Bean. We were learning how to eat rolls without sprinkling the crumbs all around and he got the whole roll into his mouth without losing a single crumb, didn't you, Delton?"

Mrs. Bean looked at her son. "That's wonderful! But . . . putting a whole roll into your mouth isn't considered polite, is it?"

It was the strangest thing. I'd never met a mother who seemed pleased when her kid was bad. Instead of staying in her car, *my* mom got out and joined us.

"Nope, but it is entertaining. We were cracking up, weren't we, Officer Weston?"

"Putting an entire roll into your mouth would satisfy the letter of the law," he told Mrs. Bean. "That is, if the goal is to keep the crumbs attached to the bread."

Mom eyed Officer Weston. He was getting on her radar, too.

"But how . . . how did you make polite conversation?" Mrs. Bean wondered.

"People who are unable to talk find . . . other ways to communicate. Silently," Officer Weston offered.

"Sure. Like sign language," I said.

Delton's head swiveled back and forth between me and Officer Weston.

I made a bunch of squiggly shapes with my hands. "Delton taught me this. It means 'Pass the salt.'"

As they walked to their car, Mrs. Bean asked Delton, "Did you learn sign language from YouTube as well?"

Delton glanced back at me and Officer Weston. We were cracking up, twisting our fingers all over the place like a couple of baseball coaches signaling the pitcher.

"Start small, Delton," Officer Weston called out to him. "You'll get the hang of it."

"Well, Mom, I think that's enough good deeds for one day."

I punched Officer Weston in the arm. "Time for me to get some normal-sized food and go fishing."

Freedom. Finally. As soon as lunch was over, I stuffed my retractable fishing pole into my backpack along with my binoculars for spying on people and called out to Mom to hang a GONE FISHING sign on my bedroom door.

"When will you be back?" she called after me.

"Tomorrow, latest." I slammed the screen door so I couldn't hear any more and pushed my bike over to Jack's. He was in the front yard, checking the oil in his lawn mower.

"Finish up," I said. "We're going fishing."

"Sorry, Cass. No can do." He looked sort of rumply, like he'd just got up, which was heartbreaking because it meant he'd stayed up late watching movies last night—without me.

"But you said you'd go with me today."

"I thought you'd be done sooner. I have to cut the Bensons' yard and then, after that, I have to cut the Sorensons' yard. I usually cut theirs on Friday afternoon, but I promised Sabrina I'd take her to Yoga for Teens."

"On a free summer afternoon, you're gonna be inside? Stretching?"

"That's a funny comment coming from someone who spends her days inside, drinking tea and learning to be polite."

"Funny thing is, I can't think of one polite word to say to a guy who breaks his promises."

"There'll be plenty of light when I get back. We can go after dinner."

"I got plans after dinner," I said.

"Like what. Moping?"

"Top-secret. Sorry."

"Well, who's gonna dig your worms, then?" Delton was telling the truth when he blabbed that squirmy live worms were on the official list of bugs that gave me the creeps.

"Me, that's who!" Fortunately, I was riding away, so Jack couldn't see my face. Like Mom, he always knew when I was lying.

I made a stop at the Westside Pharmacy and bought a bag of gummy worms. When I got to the park, I tried to see how long I could ride with my eyes closed, but I gave up pretty quick because even if I beat Jack's record of twenty-four seconds, how would I prove it?

As soon as I got to our favorite fishing spot, the one where nobody could see us from the path, I realized I hadn't done enough good deeds for the day, because a couple of sappy-looking teenagers were sitting there, holding hands and kissing.

Leaning my bike against a tree, I tore open the bag of gummy worms. Some little kids were riding up; their mom was far enough behind that I could stick a red gummy worm in each nostril and one in the corner of my mouth and start sleepwalking toward them like I was a zombie.

The little girl screamed, and the boy hit his brakes so hard he made a tire mark. Then they turned and hightailed it back to Mom. I thought about going to another path and lying in the middle of it with gummy worms all over me, like I was dead. Just thinking about that made me shiver. Gummy worms had never given me the creeps before—a definite sign I was getting worse. I would have pondered that, but I could see the little snitches' mom marching toward me. Time to disappear.

I headed for our second-best fishing spot, only to find that a couple of old geezers in waders had claimed it. *Geez!* The park was crawling with people! I ended up on the dock with a bunch of little kids. The fish seemed wise to my fake worms and I didn't catch a thing. When someone dropped a real worm on the hot wood, it wriggled like it was doing the tango.

I can't take it!

Grabbing my rod, I ran off.

What a sorry day. There was nothing to do but find our favorite oak tree and swing upside down on the branch we sanded last year for that very purpose. Sometimes all the blood sloshing around in my brain causes temporary amnesia.

I swung so long, I felt like my head was about to explode; instead, I had a brainstorm—if the world had to be full of people everywhere I went, then there must be *someone* interesting to spy on. I got back on my bike and pedaled home a different way, keeping a sharp lookout for crimes in progress or people doing the kind of embarrassing things you could sell to one of those funniest-home-video shows.

Nothing. Grand River has to be the most boring city ever! All I saw was a dog that had knocked over somebody's garbage can and was rooting around in it. I wasn't about to rat out a dog, even if he was making a huge mess.

But . . . something interesting *was* going on in that backyard. I screeched my brakes and let my bike fall near the mailbox. Over the back fence I saw a girl, her hair flying up and then falling in front of her face. She disappeared. It happened again. And she disappeared again. I moved closer to investigate. Could it be that someone had moved within a mile of our house and set up a trampoline? Jack would mow this lawn for free!

I crouched down and spied on her through a crack in the fence slats. She looked to be about my age. Boy, could she jump. And flip, too! This was an amazing discovery.

"I can see you, by the way," she called out as she flew ten feet up in the air. "Your bike, too. It's on my mom's nasturtiums."

"Sorry." I ran to get my bike and shoved a couple of the smashed flowers into my pocket.

"Well, don't run away. Come and jump with me. The latch is up high so the little monsters can't escape."

Stretching up on my tiptoes to undo the latch, I said, "You have to be new. There's no way we would have missed this last summer."

"Newish. We moved here in January. I go to Country Day."

"The private school? What do you live *here* for?" Most of the kids who went to Country Day lived on the posh side of town. Come to think of it, half my etiquette class probably went there.

"I'll live wherever I like, thank you very much. I'm Livvy. Who are you?"

I thought about saying "I'm Miss Corcoran. It's a pleasure to make your acquaintance." And "Those were the finest nasturtiums I've ever smashed with my bike." And all the other malarkey we learned in etiquette class.

Problem was, I liked her already. "I'm Cassidy."

"Well, don't just stand there drooling, Cassidy. Climb on. We've only got forty-five minutes." To emphasize her point, Livvy did a backflip!

Three steps led up to the trampoline; I had to step over the sign that hung across the stairs—NO BOYS ALLOWED!

"What have you got against boys?" I asked, landing with a bounce on my bum.

"I have no use for them whatsoever. Don't tell me you do."

"It's just that my best friend—"

"Much to my chagrin, I am forced to share my home with three younger brothers—eight, six and four. . . ." Livvy bounced around me, making it hard for me to stay in one place. "They're horrible nasty creatures. The only time I get a break is when Mom makes them rest in their rooms between one and two p.m. I put up this sign and bounce alone."

"You're good" was all I could think to say. I was getting a little seasick rolling around so much.

"I am. I'm practicing my flips so that when I'm sixteen I can go to the Youth Olympics as a freestyle skier."

"Are you . . . close?"

"I'm twelve and a half. It's my parents' rule that I have to be sixteen. They want me to be sure the risk is worth it if I crack my head open." Livvy dropped to her knees to stop bouncing and went to sit on the rim. "Go ahead," she said. "You bounce now."

"I've hardly ever bounced on a tramp," I confessed.

"Let's see where you are. I'm an excellent teacher; I can teach anyone to flip, even uncoordinated people."

While I bounced, Livvy grilled me. After fifteen minutes, she knew all about my geeky sister, my etiquette lessons, my epic pranks and how bad I wanted to ride the rails. The only thing I didn't mention was Jack, since she seemed dead set against boys.

Knowing how much Jack would want to practice his

death-defying stunts on this trampoline, I tried again. "Little kids are a pain," I said, "but now that you're almost a teenager, you must have some use for boys. My mom keeps telling my sister that, anyway."

"Name one thing a boy can do that a girl can't do better," Livvy responded. "Honestly, Cassidy. You're not one of those kind of girls, are you?"

"No!"

In just twenty minutes, Livvy had me bouncing six feet in the air. "First lesson, you have to get your air sense. That means you learn how it feels to bounce and get height. Next time, I'll teach you the tuck. But I need to practice now. I don't have much time left."

"That's okay. I better get home. Thanks, Livvy."

"And come back, Cassidy. I was beginning to think Grand River was the most boring place on the planet, until I met you."

"Me too," I said as I pedaled away.

Back at home, I made an Indian sweat lodge out of my covers and buried myself right in the middle. I wanted to think about my most recent discovery—Livvy. That couldn't be her real name, could it? It had to be short for something. I hoped it wasn't . . . Liver. It had been a long time since I had a secret all of my own—one I didn't share with Jack. Maybe I would never tell him about her. Whenever he hung out with Sabrina, I could disappear over to Livvy's house. I was just getting started imagining all the things we might do together when Magda came in.

"Have you seen my sports glasses?"

"What do you need them for?" Magda hadn't used her

sports glasses since Mom made her try out for volleyball in the sixth grade.

She didn't answer. Just sat on my bed and waited. Magda knows I can't stand an unanswered question. I pawed my way out of my sweat lodge. "What are you doing in that ridiculous outfit?"

"Does it look ridiculous? They're yoga tights. I borrowed them from Mom."

"You look like one of those walking-stick bugs."

"Thanks for the vote of confidence. At least I can console myself that everyone else is going to look the same way on Friday at Yoga for Teens, so it won't matter."

I threw the covers back over my head. "What can happen to your glasses in yoga? Don't you just moan and lie around like a corpse?"

"For your information, that's chanting the *om*. I'd rather not go at all, but Mom says if I don't get some exercise this summer, I have to work out with her at the gym."

When Mom works out, her face gets so beet-red people think she's having a heart attack. Even her eyebrows sweat! Plus, she sings out loud to the '80s songs on her MP3 player.

"You should go, too," Magda said. "Jack's going. And you are eleven-teen, according to Janae."

"Bree's going, too, I suppose."

"She's the one who really wants to go."

"Say, Magda." I untangled my legs and jumped off the bed. "Do you think my karma will get better if I go?"

"I don't know. What were you going to do instead?"

I couldn't think of a thing. Last summer, I usually hung out with Jack. Kicking around an empty house didn't seem all that appealing. "Watch TV, I guess. Play *Angry Birds*."

Magda shrugged. "You could give it a try."

I was beginning to think the whole world was swinging upside down from the oak tree and I was the only normal person left. Me? In Yoga for Teens?

"All right, all right. Uncle! Mag, you got any more of those tights?"

start

CHAPTER 13

If You Must Regret

"Cassidy, you're here, too! I didn't know you were coming." Bree squeezed me tight like I was the surprise guest at her birthday party. I couldn't make heads or tails out of the girl. Could anyone be so nice? Did she really like *everybody* or was that something they taught you in the South? It gave me the idea to bring Delton Bean over to her house and test the theory.

"Come over here, Magda, Cassidy; put your mats by me and Jack."

"We don't have mats."

"They're in the back. I'll show you."

As Bree pulled me into the back room, I tried to catch Jack's eye, but he was busy unrolling his mat.

"You'll need a mat, a strap, a set of blocks, a yoga blanket . . ." Bree kept piling stuff in my arms until I could barely see.

Staggering back into the main room, I almost ran into Jack, who grabbed my yoga blanket. "Here, I'll help you set up," he said.

He had on the same silly tights we did, but they looked better on him, like he was a circus acrobat or something. Since I had to borrow a pair from Mom, too, mine looked like Great-Grandma Reed's support hose.

"Magda, Cassidy, I'm so glad you could come." Janae gave us each a hug. "I see Bree is helping you get your props. Excellent. When everyone is seated, I will give my dharma talk and then we'll get started."

With all the mats lined up just so, I started sneaking looks at the other ten kids who should have been fishing, skateboarding, playing kick the can or any other normal summer activity, but were instead sitting cross-legged with their hands pressed together, breathing like they were about to blow out their birthday candles.

I sat there like everybody else, huffing my breath in and out so Janae could see I took things seriously.

"Stop it!" Magda turned around and poked me. She sat in front of me, Bree was behind me and Jack was behind her, which meant I was stuck in a teen-girl sandwich.

"Good afternoon, everyone. I want to welcome those of you who are new today. My son, Jack, and our friends Bree, Magda and Cassidy."

The other students welcomed us, pointing their folded hands and ducking their heads, smiling like they were in the best dream ever.

"Before we begin, I'd like to talk a little bit about *samskara,* so let's settle into our posture."

What is it with these teachers? They could never just do a thing. They had to natter on about it first. Did they do that in medical school? "As you can see, this man is bleeding to death, but before we sew him up, let me teach you a thing or two about blood."

I watched as Janae did this very strange thing to get her back end closer to the floor; it involved grabbing her cheeks—yes, those cheeks!—and tugging on them.

Then she put her hands together and said some gibberish in yoga language.

"Cassidy, once we've greeted each other, you can let your hands float down to your sides. There's no need to remain in prayer pose."

Is that what we've been doing? I looked around to see if any of these smart alecks were like Delton Bean and had watched the video on floating hands; since all their hands were on their thighs already, I just fluttered my fingers a little and got there, too.

"*Samskaras* are the general patterns of your life," Janae began. "Our karmic inheritance, you might say."

I perked up. Was this some secret about karma?

"They are the thoughts and actions we perform every day. Repeating *samskaras* strengthens them. We often speak of *samskaras* as making a groove in our mind, like the ruts that a tire makes when it goes over the same track again and again. It's hard to resist falling into the track when you travel that path.

"*Samskaras* can be good, like practicing your yoga postures at home; or they can be bad, like eating too many potato chips."

I let my hand float up into the air. I had an important question. "How many is too many, exactly?" I asked. "Potato chips, that is."

Janae smiled. "I'm sure others would like to know the answer to that question, too, Cassidy, but I'm afraid I don't know."

"It's just that my karma's been going south lately and it never occurred to me that it might be the potato chips."

"That is for you to decide. In fact, that's why we set an intention before we begin each class. It might be to pay more attention to what's going on with our body as we take a pose; or, it might be more general—to be kinder, for example. This is how we form new positive *samskaras*—by setting an intention.

"So, let's take a moment to set our intention before we chant *om*."

I closed my eyes like everybody else; well . . . except for one little slit. Was this like making a wish?

I intend to get Jack to let me wear the tool belt and also stop swanning around Sabrina Benson.

I intend to spend more time on Livvy's trampoline.

I intend to make time speed up so boring etiquette lessons and, while I'm at it, this stupid yoga class are over.

I had barely begun intending before Bree and Magda started to moan like they'd got a golf ball stuck in their throats. What was there to do but moan right along with them?

When you thought about it, I had a great deal to moan about.

"Cassidy, Cassidy! I appreciate your enthusiasm, but we only chant *om* three times."

"Oh. Sorry." I could see Magda's shoulders moving. She was giggling.

"Let's begin with a few standing poses." Janae told us all to stand in the middle of our mats and then gave us a bunch of instructions to activate our knees, descend our shoulders and float our heads?! After all that, we stood straight as boards.

"Now what?" I whispered to Bree.

"Nothing. You're in it."

"In what?"

"Mountain pose."

After another ten minutes of instruction, we stood there with our arms over our heads. "This might be more boring than etiquette class," I whispered to anyone who was in range.

Another ten minutes and we were leaning forward, touching the floor. I let my head float around a little bit and saw that Magda, like me, could barely get the tips of her fingers to the floor. Jack could touch with his knuckles, but Bree was folded up like a clam!

I'd had enough; it felt like someone was doing a tap dance on the back of my legs. But Janae had to walk around checking everybody first. Bree tilted her head, cheerful as ever, and waved.

"That's another sign of growing up," Janae said as she bent over me. "Your hamstrings get tight." She pressed on my back and the tap dancers turned into a road-construction crew with jackhammers. It was the kind of move that would get her a karate chop on the playground.

"Just play with the edge," she said. "It will get easier with practice."

"Sure," I said. "Like eating soup while rowing backward."

Of course, that was an inside joke. I blamed the dizziness I felt standing up for wishing Delton was here to appreciate it.

"Let's get a partner," Janae announced.

Before you could say "Jack be nimble," he was standing next to Bree with one of those yoga straps in his hand.

"It's much easier to demonstrate the proper technique of downward-facing dog with a partner to help us," Janae said.

I looked around. Magda and I were the only ones without partners. "Do we both need a leash?" I asked Janae, taking a small bow when the other kids laughed.

At least *they* weren't robots!

"A strap, you mean? No, just one will do."

"I ought to put this around your neck," I whispered to Magda, "for getting me into this."

"It's not as bad as jogging," she whispered back.

"We're in this stuffy room listening to a bunch of instructions for standing up! And it's summer vacation! I've beat up third graders for less."

"Oh, Cassidy. You don't beat up anybody. Besides, the purpose of yoga is to still your mind. Stop thinking so much."

"If my mind gets any stiller, I'll be the living dead." I started to do the zombie walk I'm so famous for at Riverside Park, but Magda grabbed my T-shirt.

"I'll go first," she said, and got down on all fours.

"In the downward-facing-dog posture," Janae said, "our goal is to feel the full extension of the thighs all the way down the hamstrings. Let me demonstrate with Bree."

From down on all fours like a dog, Bree straightened her arms and legs. Janae stood behind Bree and looped the strap around her thighs. Then she pulled back on both ends.

"The strap helps to relieve compression in the spine and allow for a full extension of the shoulders and arms as well."

In the world according to Cassidy, the logical question would be: "What would you want to do a thing like that for?"

"Do you understand the instructions, Cassidy?"

I nodded. Magda straightened her legs and I put the strap around them, up high, like Jack was doing to Bree. He was leaning back and pulling, so that's what I did.

"Don't pull so hard, Cassidy!"

"I'm not pulling. I'm leaning back like we're supposed to."

"Well, then, don't lean back so hard. I can't—"

"Do you two need help?" Janae appeared at my side.

"No thank you. We're done." Without communicating with her partner, Magda collapsed on the floor, taking me down with her.

"Get off me!" she said, bucking me like a bronco. As my knees hit the floor, I heard a crunch.

"Oh no!" Magda was groping around. "My glasses!"

"Don't blame me," I said, rubbing my knee. "You're the one who pulled me over."

"You're the one who was torturing me with the strap!"

"Magda, I'm so sorry." Bree was down on the floor with us. She tried to straighten Magda's glasses before setting them on her nose. "You love these glasses."

"They're fine." I pushed them further up the bridge of Magda's nose. "See. They're not even broken."

"Only, one lens is above my eye and one is below."

"Don't worry, Magda." Janae was smoothing Magda's hair. "We'll get this sorted. Has everyone switched partners?"

Magda grabbed a strap. "Not yet. Get down on all fours, Cassidy."

In retaliation for mangling her glasses, Magda tried to

stretch my thighs past their elastic limit. But since her glasses kept falling off and she's so pathetic without them—squinting and blinking like a mole hitting the sunshine for the first time—her technique was not very effective.

Finally, Janae had her sit over by the coats and shoes because we were using a prop that looked like a broom handle and Janae was worried Magda might be a danger to herself and others.

"I thought you weren't supposed to wear them when you exercised," I said as we waited for Mom to come pick us up.

"I couldn't find my sports glasses! You know that. Plus, you're the one who said yoga wasn't a contact sport."

I felt bad about Magda's glasses. Really I did. But they didn't look as bad as the pair I ran over with the vacuum cleaner *or* the pair I stuck in the microwave when she snitched on me for fast-talking the Zinderman kids out of a half-dozen Oreos at their lemonade stand.

The lemonade was way overpriced!

"Don't worry, sweetie," Dad said to Magda at dinner. "After the vacuum-cleaner incident, I took out insurance against loss or damage to your glasses. We'll get you a new pair."

"See," I said, "it's not that big of a deal."

"Actually, I don't see." To prove it, Magda stabbed the table with her fork.

"In the meantime," Dad continued, "I think that strap I use for my glasses when I play racquetball will help keep these aligned so you can avoid walking in front of a bus."

"At least it's summer," Magda said. "And no one will see what a freak I look like."

"We must have an old pair around somewhere." Mom intentionally passed the mashed potatoes to Dad instead of me so he could be the one to finish them off.

He dumped the rest of the bowl onto his plate. Obviously, he had never taken any etiquette lessons.

"Funny thing is, *all* my glasses look like these." Magda tried to give me the evil eye, but she just looked like a crazy old lady.

"You know what cats think?" I said, hoping to head off a trip down memory lane about all the unfortunate accidents that had happened to Magda's glasses. "Delton was telling me about it before class the other day. Cats think if they can't see you, you can't see them. That's why he puts his cat in a pillowcase to take it to the vet."

"Don't change the subject, Cassidy," Mom said. "Just because you'd rather not—"

"I'm not changing the subject. I was thinking if we were more like cats, then Magda would think no one could see her glasses."

Everyone stopped eating and stared at me.

"Don't you get it? It's like Magda's in the pillowcase. . . . Isn't anybody following me?"

As if on cue, the rest of the Corcoran clan shook their heads—no.

If only they gave grades for obfuscation.

ready for next plate

133

CHAPTER 14

The Unexpected Visitor

Fortunately, Jack knocked on the back door and saved me from having to explain further.

"Good evening, Corcorans. I stopped by on the off chance that Cassidy has any room in her lousy—I mean, busy—schedule to go fishing with me."

"See ya. Bye!" I said, aligning my shoulders for a straight pass through the exit.

"Hold on there, cowgirl. We're not finished," Dad said, his mouth full.

I could have pointed out—politely—that one of our family members wasn't finished because he'd hogged all the mashed potatoes.

"And you haven't been excused yet," Mom (the self-appointed stand-in for Miss Melton-Mowry) added.

I put my palms on the table; I wanted to be ready to push off as soon as I heard the magic words. Mom is a marathon chewer. She held up her finger, swallowed and said, "What is that rule about correct dining posture? Hand position?"

"C'mon, sweetie. She'll sleep better if she works off some of the energy she stores up from etiquette class all week." Dad wiped his mouth and dropped his napkin on the table.

Putting down her fork, Mom took a deep breath. "Promise to be home by eight-thirty."

I nodded, leaning even further forward. She straightened her place mat. "And your napkin goes where?"

"We haven't covered the end of the meal yet, Mom."

"Really? I thought . . ." She rubbed her temple, remembering.

Geez! She was killing me. A moan escaped from my throat.

"Ready, set, go!" Mom called out, like it was a real race, and Jack and I were out the door like a shot.

Fifteen minutes later, we were sitting back to back on our log over the water, feet tucked up, rod in one hand and one of Janae's granola cookies in the other.

I had just finished telling Jack about being starved in etiquette class when he got his first bite. I don't like watching the fish struggle on the line, so I concentrated on watching the evening sun glowing pink and purple, like it did in the summer.

Even though it's called the Grand River, it's not that deep—no motorboats allowed—and the current runs so slow that you can get twice the bang for your buck and see two sunsets—the real one and the one reflected in the water.

Jack unhooked the little guy and threw him back in. "How's Miss Information?"

"Not back yet."

"Where do you think she is? Visiting relatives?"

"I don't know. Let's not talk about her." With the smell of barbecue drifting through the air, I didn't want to talk anymore about etiquette class. We could hear kids shouting over a soccer game on the ball field. Somewhere, a radio was playing. The bumps of Jack's spine pressed into my back and a soft breeze kept the mosquitoes from settling. It was the perfect summer night.

"Maybe tomorrow afternoon we can play Frisbee golf," I said.

"Maybe. But only if I get my lawns done."

"What is it with you and the lawn-mowing?"

"I told you. I have goals. I'm saving up."

"Saving up for what?" I swatted away a mosquito that was trying to land on my nose.

"For things, that's what."

"Jack Taylor." Dropping my legs so I didn't fall in the river, I twisted around to look him in the eye. "I know pretty much every single thing about you. Why won't you tell me what you're saving up for?"

"Because it's none of your business."

"Because it has to do with Bree Benson, doesn't it? And your hairy legs. And how you have goals all of a sudden."

"What's that supposed to mean?"

"I heard Mom telling Magda. You get hair on your legs and you start getting all funny about girls. Older girls."

"What's the point of that?"

I twisted back around. "You tell me."

"Well, I'm not the only one who's acting funny. You think etiquette class is ruining your summer vacation, but you complain about it for twice the time you spend there!"

Ugh. I felt like smacking myself in the head with my fishing rod. Why did I have to ruin the perfect summer moment by bringing up Jack's hairy legs?

"For your information, an hour in etiquette class equals two hours of normal time. You should try it. You could use some manners."

"Cassidy?"

Just to remind me that my karma was still *Titanic,* the next perfect-summer-night sound I heard was Delton Bean calling my name.

"Delton! Are you stalking me?"

Coming as close to us as he could without stepping on the log, Delton said, "No. Not exactly."

"How did you know I was here, then?"

"Well, fishing is your go-to topic for polite conversation and we only have one river in town *and* this is the public park."

"Spare me the details."

"Hey there, Delton." Jack stepped over me and jumped from the log to the shore. The way he rocked it, I had to grab on tight to keep from falling in. "You didn't walk here, did you?"

"No. My mom drove me. She's reading on the park bench by the swings."

I shimmied along the log, scraping my thighs. "Let's skip how creepy that is to the part where you tell me *why* you're here."

"Do you eat the fish you catch?" Delton asked Jack.

"Nah. They're too little."

"Unless we're having sushi." Brushing bits of bark off my thighs, I added, "Then we roll them in a little seaweed and bite their heads off first."

"In his state-of-the-city speech last January, the mayor did say we've contained septic sewer overflow by almost one hundred percent and the river is rebounding."

"Delton . . ." Taking a step into Delton's personal space, I asked again, "Why are you here?"

"I . . ." Delton stepped backward. "I've been experimenting with a new way to cure my issues with public speaking, and Mom . . . Mom thought you'd want to know right away—you know, transfer of knowledge to help with your anxiety over . . ." He gestured toward Jack's cottage-cheese container filled with worms.

I took another step, moving in until my nose was almost touching Delton's. "You told your mom I was afraid of worms?"

"Technically, not just worms, Cassidy, but other invertebrates, too. You're also afraid of arthropods, as you demonstrated this morning with the millipedes; and I've seen you flinch at a struggling pill bug, which is also an arthropod, but . . ." Delton looked down at his hands, counting off the things I was afraid of on his fingers. "Though pill bugs do belong to a different subphylum. They are terrestrial crustaceans."

"Delton! Focus. You'd better tell me right now or I'll—"

"It's called EFT; that stands for Emotional Freedom Techniques. It draws from the field of energy psychology, which doesn't have rigorous backing from the scientific community, but there's a lot of anecdotal evidence to suggest—"

"For Pete's sake, Delton! What is it?"

"Well . . ." Delton tugged on the tails of his shirt. "You think about your phobia or look at a picture and you let yourself experience the fear vicariously, all while tapping on your meridian points."

"My what?"

"I know meridians," Jack said. "They're energy points in your body. You use them in acupuncture."

"That thing where they poke needles in you?"

Jack was kneeling by his bike, working a stick out of the spokes. "Yeah, you know my aunt Nalini. She's an acupuncturist."

I shook my head. Getting needles stuck into me didn't sound much better than hanging around a bunch of squirming worms.

"But there aren't any needles," Delton said in a rush. "You experience the fear while tapping on your meridian points with your fingertips; it helps you calm down."

I wasn't convinced. "So . . . where do the worms come in?"

"They don't. You're just thinking about them, and all the time, you're talking your way through it. First you experience the fear, then you overcome it—no worms necessary."

"It's that easy? You can do it without any bugs?"

"Well, you have to practice a little. Here, I wrote down a script for you." Delton patted his shirt pocket. When that didn't turn anything up, he jammed his hands into his pants pockets. "I'm sure I brought it with me. I'll be right back. I must have left it in the car."

"Don't come back, Delton."

"But . . . why? I thought finding a cure would make you—"

"I'm on summer vacation. I'm chilling. I don't want to do this right now."

"Should I . . . bring it to etiquette class Monday?"

"Yeah. Sure. That'd be great."

Delton turned to go. At least he knew when he wasn't wanted. "Oh, Cassidy," he called over his shoulder. "I pulled a prank."

"Great. You can tell me all about it at class."

"I don't think it's a topic for polite conversation." He stopped, waiting for me to ask him more, but I didn't.

"You gotta give old Delton some credit," Jack said after Delton was out of earshot. "He is trying hard to get in good with you."

"And that makes my life better . . . how?"

"I don't know. He's pretty smart." Spinning his tire to make sure it was all clear, Jack added, "And you *do* need to get over this fear thing. It's spreading. I've noticed."

"Noticed how?"

Jack stood up and dusted off his shorts. "Ever since you fell in the river last summer, you don't walk the log anymore."

"So?" I hate it when Jack is right. I fell off the log last summer and hit the bottom of the Grand River. It might be nice for frogs, but it's mucky and stinky and there's leeches; ever since, I've been shimmying in instead of walking it like a balance beam. It's not so easy on your thighs, let me tell you.

"Mom says we create our own reality. You believe you're going to fall in again . . . or at least you're so afraid of it you won't balance on the log anymore." Sticking his rod under the bungee cord on his bike rack, he added, "Now that I think of it, you believe your etiquette class is torture and it is."

140

"I don't think. I know. You don't."

"And you think mowing lawns all day is a walk in the park? It's hot and sweaty and—"

"But you don't have to!"

"Yes, I do. If I want—" Jack broke off. "Just forget it."

"Right. Forget it."

"Fishing's no good tonight, in case you hadn't noticed." Jack grabbed his handlebars. "I'm going home."

He didn't say good-bye or even wave, just took off on his bike.

I thought about hanging around. I had my Frisbees in my backpack, but what fun was that all by myself?

Ugh. Nothing was right.

In fact, it was the perfect nothing-is-right Friday night of my eleven-teenth summer.

Until I thought of riding my bike over to Livvy's. But . . . she probably had to help put the little monsters to bed.

Well, so what? I knew more wrestling holds than the average girl, and even a couple of bedtime stories—though they might not be fit for young children.

I got on my bike and pedaled in the direction of Livvy's house; it would be a refreshing change of pace to hang around with a girl who found boys as infuriating as I did.

There was plenty of squawking and splashing going on in the backyard when I got there.

"Hey," I called out to the kid whose head popped into view. It must have been the monsters' turn on the tramp.

"Hey, yourself. O-livia! Some girl wants in."

Next thing I knew, Livvy's head appeared over the top of the fence. "Cassidy! Permission granted."

The fence door swung open and I was greeted by the world's youngest pirate, complete with eye patch and plastic sword. "We're thwabbing the deck," he said.

Must be the four-year-old, I thought, following him around an inflated kiddie pool, where another pirate was diving for treasure with a snorkel and mask. The third and oldest pirate was bouncing on the tramp, a hose in his hand.

"If you spray her, I'll make you pay. Big-time." Olivia, in a polka-dot bathing suit, bounced on her butt and then off the trampoline entirely. "When you spray a warm trampoline, you can jump higher," she explained. "Care to try it? It's not for the faint of heart."

"Not yet." I stood there, taking in Livvy's crazy world, as she flopped down on a plastic lawn chair and opened a cooler. "Want a juice box?"

"Sure."

"I want one." The Fence Pirate ran over and pinched the material of Livvy's suit. "Pwease, Wivvy."

"You had yours already. Go back and guard the door. I saw three more girls out there trying to get in." Giving him a little push, Livvy used her other hand to reach into the cooler and toss me a juice box. "I'm babysitting. Could there be a less lucrative job than babysitting your own brothers?"

"I don't know." I tore the plastic off the juice-box straw with my teeth and tried to find a spot on the ground that wasn't soaking wet.

"Maybe you can stay until after I put them to bed. I want to tell you about the prank I played on my aunt Agnes. I followed your rules to a tee. Even she had to laugh after she got the Onesie off her schnauzer."

I started to tell her about the time Jack and I tied helium balloons to Miss Hennessy's attendance clipboard, but it wasn't easy with the random sprays of water, the shouts about alien girls approaching, and cutting Jack out of every scene.

"I meant what I said about that hose!" Livvy shouted at the Trampoline Pirate, whose bouncing practically created a rain shower in the yard. "I will take your battleship apart piece by piece."

Reaching under her chair, she pulled out an umbrella. "I'd introduce you," she said, "but none of my friends can remember their names. They're just one bratty snarl that doesn't listen worth a hoot."

Livvy flicked open the umbrella just in time to save me from a stream of water as the Tramp Pirate did a flip while keeping hold of the hose.

"Now do you understand why I feel the way I do about boys?"

I nodded. "I think so."

Poking the Water Pirate with the handle of her umbrella, Livvy said, "Turn over, Leonard! You'll look like a shriveled old man if you stay under any longer." She slurped the last of her juice box, crumpled it and threw it back in the cooler. "I can't wait to get out of here. Will you write to me?"

"Depends," I said. "Where are you going?"

"Camp."

"I guess. I went to Girl Scout camp last year, but due to an unfortunate experience with a canoe during nature exploration, I don't think I'll be—"

I was interrupted by a cold jet of water in my face. "Hey! Give a girl a fighting chance, why don't ya?"

"Louis! That's it. Battleship destruction begins now." Livvy jumped up and ran to the back-porch slider, her bathing suit streaming with water.

Louis let out a howl like something you'd hear on the nature channel and chased after his sister.

Leonard sat up and adjusted his goggles. "What did I miss?"

Wringing out my ponytail, I said, "Not much. A water fight, battleship destruction and possible injuries to your older brother."

"You don't say." Wiping the fog off his goggles, he held out a wrinkly hand. "I'm Jacques Cousteau, by the way, famous deep-sea explorer."

I shook it. "Calamity Cassidy. About to take to the open road. Tell your sister I said good-bye, okay?"

On the way home, I resolved to come back *only* during pirate rest time. As I pedaled up our driveway, I saw Dad standing in sprinkler territory, looking up at the flagpole.

"What is in my hand, Cassidy?" he asked me as I let my bike fall, also in sprinkler territory. Not that it mattered to me. I was already soaking wet, a fact Dad didn't seem to notice.

"Your flag."

"Then what is that?" He pointed up the flagpole to what looked like a big brown pillowcase.

"Search me."

"It was a rhetorical question. I know what that is. It is Mrs. Delaney's best nightgown."

Never mind that my day so far would measure on the seismic Richter scale of rottenness. I had to know more. "Really? How do you know?"

Because she rang my doorbell a few minutes ago and handed

me my University of Michigan flag, that's why. It was pinned to her clothesline."

I had to look down at the ground so Dad couldn't see my smile. When I'd wiped it off my face, I looked back up. "You don't say."

"I do. She then wondered if I might know the whereabouts of her missing nightgown. We followed the logical path."

I know my dad. He likes a good prank and he liked this one. He was trying not to smile, too.

"Could she ID it?"

"Yes. After she found her driving glasses."

"So . . . why didn't you pull it down?"

"There's a problem with the pulley. It seems to be stuck."

I covered my mouth—and coughed. "Would you call that a mechanical failure?"

"You could say that . . . yes. Cassidy, did you and Jack do this before you went fishing? Or was it swimming? I thought bathing suits were required at Briggs Pool." Dad handed me the ends of the flag so we could fold it together, military-style.

Before I took hold, I raised my right hand. "Scout's honor. We did not do this."

"You're not a Scout, Cassidy."

"No, but I respect the institution. Seriously, Dad, this is a sweet prank. I would own up to it if it was mine."

"And the dunking you got? That occurred . . ."

"On my way home, I was ambushed by a water fight. Kids these days . . ."

We finished folding and I handed the flag to Dad.

After he'd returned my salute, he said, "Any ideas for how to bring her down?"

My first thought was to volunteer Jack to shinny up there and get it. "Not really."

"Well, then, I guess Mrs. Delaney will have to wear her second-best nightgown to bed this evening. That doesn't seem like too big a tragedy."

"I guess not."

He put his arm around my shoulder as we walked into the house. "According to Mom, you have successfully completed week two of your etiquette class. No further misdemeanors, I trust?"

"Dad!"

"As your parole officer, I need to check in on your doings from time to time. Why don't you grab one of the clean towels in the laundry room? According to my sprinkling plan, we don't need to water the carpet until next week."

On my way up the stairs to bed, I took a closer look out the window at our new flag. A laundry pin had been knotted in the rope to keep it from sliding through the pulley.

I watched the nightgown flap in the breeze. Nothing broken. And yes, I totally cracked up watching Dad explain to Mrs. Delaney that we couldn't get it down . . . yet.

If only I could learn etiquette as well as Delton Bean learned pranks.

CHAPTER 15

Using Tact

As I finished up etiquette class number one for the week, I chose Donna Parker for polite conversation.

"Miss Parker, didn't you tell us that you went to Country Day?"

"Why, yes, Miss Corcoran, I did." Donna always straightened up when someone asked her a question, like she was the teacher.

"Do you by any chance know a girl named Livvy?"

She thought about it. "Livvy. Can't say I do. Does she go to Country Day? What is her last name?"

"Um . . . not a hundred percent sure. She has a trampoline and three younger brothers."

"You mean Olivia? Olivia Dunn? We're on the gymnastics team together."

"You're a . . . gymnast?"

"That is so strange, Miss Corcoran. You know, on the first day I thought you reminded me of someone. And that's who it is! Olivia! Miss Dunn, I mean."

"How, exactly?"

Donna paused; I knew that pause. She was wondering how to put it politely. "Well . . . uh . . ." She leaned in. "What's the polite-conversation word for 'smart aleck'?"

"High energy . . . original mind . . . future politician?" I replied, quoting my report cards from memory.

"Yes! Something like that. Do you know her?"

"I met her last week. I plan to spend more time on her trampoline in the near future. As long as the monsters are resting, that is."

"Oh . . ." Donna bit her lip. "You don't know, then."

"Know what?"

"She spends most of the summer at gymnastics camp in Wisconsin. She wants to go to the Olympics, you know."

"She said she was going, but she hasn't left yet. I saw her last night. I didn't know it was all summer."

"Well, I know she's packing. Her mom called my mom and asked if she could borrow my brother Spencer's sleeping bag. It's got mosquito netting built right in and he's studying abroad this summer, so he doesn't need it."

I went back to my seat without excusing myself from the conversation. It figured. Just when I thought I'd found someone as interesting as Bree was to Jack, I learn she's going away all summer. Class ended and all I wanted to do was go some-where to think this over. Delton and I were supposed to get a five-minute break between regular class and etiquette suspen-sion, but what's a break if your only choice is sit at the table and stare at your reflection in the dinner plate? There wasn't even any room to pace!

It made me all of a sudden mad as a hornet at Miss Melton-Mowry. Kids *need* to work off their excess energy! I'd get my fill of Delton for the next hour, so I refused to start making polite conversation before then.

Hmph. If we didn't get any personal time, then neither should our teacher.

I knocked on Miss Melton-Mowry's office door before I opened it. Even though I did things in the correct order, I don't think she heard me, because her eyes were closed and she was leaning back in her chair—I could see her knees!—listening to something on the radio. I'd never seen this look on her face before—it might have been a smile.

I cleared my throat.

"I was listening to Debussy," she said, quick sitting up and pushing her skirt over her bony knees.

"I thought you weren't supposed to lean back in your chair."

"There is such a thing as a private moment, Miss Corcoran. You don't think I sleep with correct dining posture, do you?"

"Well . . ." I never thought about Miss Melton-Mowry sleeping. Or putting her feet up.

"Debussy is my favorite classical composer. This is one of his arabesques. For me, it is like a four-minute mini-vacation where I am transported . . ." She stopped talking until she'd got her shoulders back in coat-hanger order and tugged her blouse straight. "But surely you didn't knock on my door to talk about the music."

"No, I . . ." I was, in fact, going to ask her if we could cover the polite way to eat a melting candy bar. I wanted to make it so she didn't get a break, either.

But instead of saying what I'd planned to say, I listened to the music with her. It was all right, a bunch of fancy piano stuff my mom might have chosen when it was her turn to pick the radio station in the car. It seemed to fit with the way I felt—having Livvy snatched away when I'd only just met her.

"So . . . where do you go? When you're transported."

"A riverbank. This music reminds me of water; there was a time when I was younger . . . I used to pack a picnic lunch and we'd sit near a bridge by a mill and dip our feet in. Do you hear that? At the end? The way the piano fades out, like little drips of water?"

I nodded. I did. "Have you ever . . . do you ever go to River-side Park?"

"The public park? No, I don't."

It was probably better that she said no, because if she'd said yes, we might have something in common; *that* would not be good for my reputation.

"Maybe I should. Why don't you tell me more about it during polite conversation?"

"Okay." I pulled the door closed, turning the handle like she taught us, so you could barely hear it.

Turns out, Miss Melton-Mowry was right about the music. It didn't change anything, but it did make me feel a little better. By the time I was sitting across from Delton, I remembered what I wanted to talk to him about. "Good morning, Mr. Bean," I said, diving right in. "How was your dinner Friday night? After we saw you at the park?"

"Very pleasant, Miss Corcoran. We had tuna-noodle casserole."

"Tuna-noodle casserole? Really? I thought you said you were going to have pranks and beans."

"Pardon me?" Officer Weston leaned closer to hear.

"I said, I thought Mrs. Bean was serving *pranks* and beans." At the risk of having Delton follow me around like a puppy, I shook his hand—and no funny business. "A fine job, Mr. Bean. Your execution was flawless."

Delton pinched his earlobe. "Thank you, Miss Corcoran," he said. "I do take pride in my work."

"I need to think up a new prank for one of the lifeguards at Briggs Pool. You're not afraid of water, are you? We'd have to do it during open swim."

"Mrs. Dennon says my fear of water is healthy," Delton replied, but before I could ask what that meant or even who Mrs. Dennon was, Miss Melton-Mowry joined us at the table; another round of torture was about to begin.

"I'll fill you in about Delton's prank later," I whispered to Officer Weston. "Hey, look. Miss Information's back."

"She looks well," Delton said. "Wouldn't you agree, Miss Corcoran?"

"Looks to me like she's got a crick in her neck."

Miss Melton-Mowry tapped her wineglass with her fork. "Today, we're going to take a break from our table manners to discuss in more detail what makes a lasting impression. As we have seen, formal social situations are a bit like a dance, where we learn how to move through space, how to keep the correct distance between ourselves and our speaking partner and how to introduce ourselves.

"Now I want to show you a little technique that will keep the conversation going smoothly. When the conversation flows easily, dining guests are more relaxed and they will associate you with a feeling of ease. So . . ." Miss Melton-Mowry turned in her seat to face Delton. "Let's say I have just met Mr. Bean and asked him how long he has lived in Grand River. He might say something like 'eight years,' at which point the conversation would come to an end. *But,* if he gives his partner a little information about himself and follows that up with an inquiry, he can keep the conversation going."

"I thought we weren't supposed to talk about private stuff," I said.

"Nothing too racy, Miss Corcoran." There was that smile again! "I will demonstrate. Mr. Bean, please ask me how long I've lived in Grand River."

Delton sat up in his chair and gestured to our teacher. "Tell me, Miss Melton-Mowry, how long have you lived in Grand River?"

"Most of my life, Mr. Bean. I think one of my favorite things about Grand River is our art museum. And how long have you lived here?"

"I was born in Grand River and have lived here all my life." Delton paused, his giant brain recalculating like a GPS to figure out how to turn the conversation around. "I think my favorite spot in our city is Rosa Parks Circle. My mother and I often walk there after visiting the museum. Do you enjoy Rosa Parks Circle, too?"

Officer Weston pinched me and whispered, "This is like watching golf on TV. Or cricket."

"What's cricket?"

Officer Weston mouthed his answer. "Bo-ring."

"You must be discussing your favorite place, Miss Corcoran. Would you care to share it with us?"

"The oak tree in Riverside Park, of course. The one by the sign that says DON'T FEED THE DUCKS, with a view of the first tee in Frisbee golf. It got struck by lightning so there's a big burn mark— What?"

By the way everyone was looking at me, I'd clearly messed up. "There's a lot of oak trees. I want to make sure you get the right one."

More blank stares. "Oh, right. I forgot. It's like we're playing talking hot-potato." Standing up, I hopped from one foot to the other, juggling my imaginary potato between my hands. "Riverside Park where the ducks live," I said, underhanding my invisible spud to Officer Weston. "And you?"

"What if mine is Riverside Park, too?" Officer Weston asked Miss Melton-Mowry. "Is that like wanting the same roll in the bread basket?"

We all waited for Miss Melton-Mowry to answer. She was looking at me, probably trying to decide if she needed to remind me that hopping from one foot to another was *not* the sort of thing polite society ladies did.

"No, of course not," she said after a minute. "You have now found a mutual point of reference, which makes the conversation even easier. That very thing happened to Miss Corcoran and me before class."

"Really?" Delton was so surprised he talked out of turn.

"But I already knew it was her favorite," Officer Weston persisted. "We covered Riverside Park day one."

Miss Melton-Mowry flipped forward a page in her instruction book. "Well, then. As long as we all remember the rule of three. One, answer the question; two, tell a little—emphasis on the *little*, Miss Corcoran—about yourself; and three, turn it back to your companion with a question. Shall we practice?"

Of course, I got Delton.

"So, how long have you been imprisoned in etiquette class, Mr. Bean?" I said, sticking out my lower jaw like a gorilla to make him laugh and earn himself a demerit.

"What a delightful choice of verb, Miss Corcoran. I've only had the pleasure of this class for a little over two weeks, but I've already learned the proper setting of a table as well as how to politely introduce myself. And what have you learned?"

"I've learned that it would be mighty easy to assassinate a queen with some of this tableware . . . but my favorite part has been helping you grow your backbone."

"What a coincidence. I have something here to grow yours." Delton slipped a folded piece of paper out of his pocket. "Here's the script I was telling you about. I recommend thirty minutes of practice a day for optimal results."

I took the paper and shoved it in my back pocket. "On top of this nonsense? You gotta be kidding me."

"Please excuse the interruption," Miss Melton-Mowry said.

We froze—but not before I made my face look like I'd just seen a corpse rise out of the grave.

Miss Melton-Mowry waited for my face to return to normal-boring.

"I've just demonstrated the next part of our lesson. Inevitably, you will need to break into a conversation. You do that by saying 'excuse me,' and then waiting for the intended party to finish and give you his or her attention."

"What if they never give you their attention?" I asked. "I've known my sister Magda to talk through about a hundred 'excuse me's.'" I turned to Officer Weston. "Especially if she's talking about something geeky like how mold blooms."

"On the Senate floor, they call that filibustering," he said. "It's like a talking marathon."

"Excuse me, Officer Weston." Miss Melton-Mowry stood as still as Miss Information, waiting for our attention.

When we gave it to her, she continued, "You see, in polite society, people do yield the floor. In fact, 'excuse me' is a very useful term. It also signals when you must leave the table. *Or* when you need to ask someone's pardon if you must step into their personal space, *or* to beg their pardon for coughing, sneezing—"

"Burping, farting . . . ," I added. "What? I was just trying to be helpful."

"Even polite people fart," Officer Weston said when he saw Miss Melton-Mowry shaking her head no. Miss Melton-Mowry put her fist over her mouth and coughed, the sort of move you made when you were trying to cover up . . . a laugh.

"Thank you for that insightful bit of information, Officer Weston. To continue, 'excuse me' is a useful phrase, but it should not be confused with 'I'm sorry.' With the exception of sneezing and coughing and . . . other things, 'excuse me' comes before the action. 'I'm sorry' comes after it. Let's say you would like to move past someone and this requires stepping into their personal space. You would say, 'Excuse me,' or even 'Pardon me,' before you move. However, if you inadvertently bump into someone, spill something on them or step on their foot, then a sincere apology is what is called for. Sincerity is most important when apologizing. Let's practice, shall we, Miss Corcoran?"

"By all means, Miss Melton-Mowry. I have a great deal of experience in this area. You want me to demonstrate how to say you're sorry like you really mean it, right?"

She nodded, but narrowed her eyes a little, wondering if I was up to something. I stood up and shook out my arms and legs.

"We learned in drama class how to get into character," I explained. "I'll pretend that you're my art teacher and my paintbrush just dripped on your new white shoes."

Once I'd wrung myself out, I stood completely still until I was an art student who'd just made a terrible mistake. Dropping to my knees, I pressed my cheek to her shoe and cried out, "Forgive me, master. I'm so sorry."

"Miss Corcoran, what do you think you're doing?"

After I'd hugged her shoe, I threw myself down flat on the floor. "Prostrating myself. I saw it on a BBC mystery series once. It's as sorry as you get."

"Good heavens. Get off the floor and straighten your blouse."

Now it was Delton and Officer Weston's turn to "cough."

I've still got the touch.

Standing up, I pushed the hair out of my face. As it turns out, a sincere apology, according to Miss Melton-Mowry, is looking someone in the eye and saying you're sorry—and meaning it. After Delton and Officer Weston and I practiced bumping into each other a few times and saying we were sorry, we passed the test and were ready to move on.

"Now we come to one of the least talked-about and yet most critical aspects of making a good impression. Body odor."

I pushed past Delton to get closer to Miss Melton-Mowry. Finally, something I wanted to hear. As a future hobo, I have more than a passing interest in body odor. When I'm on the road, I'll go days without so much as seeing a bar of soap; it makes sense to practice. Last summer, I managed four days without a bath by running the water in the tub, sitting on the toilet seat and singing at the top of my lungs. I guess a kid can't generate all that much stink, because I got away with it until Mom found the twigs in my hair.

As I stood next to Delton, I thought back to my last bath. I knew there were at least two trips to the park with Jack, four rides on my bike, some ground rolling and a sprinkle of Grand River water.

I'd slide by.

Miss Melton-Mowry asked Officer Weston to stand up. She walked all the way around him. If I was the teacher, I would have given her a personal-space violation. But in case you haven't gone to school for a very long time, teachers get to play by a different set of rules. She stopped when her shoulder was almost touching his shoulder and sniffed.

"Smoke," she said. "French fries. Fried eggs."

"*You* smoke?" I asked Officer Weston.

"No, he does not. If he did, the odor would be much stronger. But his collar"—she sniffed again, detecting—"bears the scent of others' smoking."

"I had a few with the guys down at Wet Your Whistle the

other night. We shot some pool. Jerry smokes in his car. It makes us all stink. Elizabeth won't come near me after I've been out with Jerry."

Even *I* thought smoking was disgusting, but what possibilities this opened up for driving my parents crazy! I pondered how to get Officer Weston to take one of my shirts along the next time he went to the Wet Your Whistle.

"And they're home fries, by the way," he added. "I had breakfast at Lennie's before class."

"Grease does not discriminate between home fries and French fries, Officer Weston, and there's a fleck of yolk on the corner of your mouth. Let's just say that Elizabeth's relatives will form opinions about who you are based on how you smell."

"But how is that a bad thing, Miss Melton-Mowry?" I wanted to know. "There's always a line out the door at the Wet Your Whistle. Doesn't that mean he's popular?"

"Yes, Miss Corcoran, to some people—and I think we can include you in that group—Officer Weston is a wonderful man who likes to shoot pool and spend time in diners. But Elizabeth's relatives might not be so inclined to see those as positive attributes."

"But what do *you* think, Miss Melton-Mowry?" I said, knowing I was putting our teacher on the spot.

"You're asking for my personal opinion?"

"Sure."

"I like Officer Weston very much. He's genuine, and . . . that's a rare quality these days. However, he is not paying me to accept him the way he is, Miss Corcoran. Just as your great-grandmother did not pay for these lessons so that you could remain . . . in your present condition. My job is to help you navigate any fine-dining or polite-society situation. Needless to say, we're not there yet."

Officer Weston didn't take it personally. "I like you, too, Miss Melton-Mowry. At least I don't have *that* kind of BO," he added. "I showered this morning."

I kept my arms straight down by my sides, military-style, just in case I had a little of *that* kind of BO.

"The point is to not draw attention to yourself by the way you smell. Cooking odors and smoke can be very distracting. It's best to smell . . . clean . . . refreshing. Maybe a slight scent . . ." By this time, Miss Melton-Mowry was standing in front of me and Delton. "No strong odors from the shampoo, no cloying aftershave. I have no idea what you had for breakfast, Mr. Bean. Well done."

"I always brush my teeth after I eat."

Officer Weston and I exchanged our "what a suck-up Delton is" look.

"But I was at Lennie's," Officer Weston said in his own defense.

"I have a travel toothbrush for when I eat out. It folds in half. My mother keeps it in the glove compartment."

I would have responded to that, but Miss Melton-Mowry was headed my way. I didn't know how much odor a banana slathered in peanut butter and a half a bag of gummy worms would give off, but I wasn't taking any chances. I held my breath.

Miss Melton-Mowry didn't come into my personal space, just looked back and forth between me and Delton. "Your issues are somewhat different from Officer Weston's since you're not old enough to frequent bars and drive around with friends who smoke. Still . . ."

She paused.

What happened next was very *un*-Miss-Melton-Mowry-like. She looked like she didn't know what to say.

Clearing her throat, she began, "You are getting older and . . . I can't stress enough the importance of personal hygiene."

Officer Weston leaned in my direction and took a sniff. "Not sure Elizabeth would sit next to you, either, Cassidy. Er . . . Miss Corcoran." He got even closer and whispered in my ear, "You kinda stink."

I quick-sniffed under my armpit. The fact that I did—not just kinda—stink came as a real surprise to me.

"Can you smell the peanut butter and bananas?" I whispered back.

"Not over that."

pause

CHAPTER 16

Cake Is Eaten with a Fork

As soon as I jumped out of the car after manners class, I heard Jack's whistle signaling me to come over. He'd been waiting to show me the harness he'd built with his dad—the one that allowed him to scale walls without killing himself.

I'd hoped to at least swipe a washcloth under my armpits before anyone else got in my personal space, but he didn't give me the chance! As we headed into his dad's workshop, I pressed my arms to my sides and told him about Delton's prank.

"Mrs. Delaney's nightgown? Off her clothesline? That is sweet. But so is this . . . take a look." Jack held up a rope that looked like a lot of his other ropes . . . maybe a little thinner.

"Wow." I tried to match his excitement.

Holding it out for me to touch, he said, "Feel how soft it is . . . really going to cut down on the sliding burns. Plus, it's thin enough for me to clamp it with my toes."

"Impressive." I handed the rope back and, very nonchalant, asked, "Say, Jack, do you ever notice . . . my BO?"

"Sure. It smells like chicken soup."

"That's not so bad."

Jack tossed his new rope up and over the beam that crossed the length of the workshop. "Unless you've been riding your bike or fishing . . . or wrestling. Then it smells more like . . . let me see . . . the duck pond."

"Ugh. That stinks."

"I didn't used to notice it. My sniffer must be getting more sensitive." He tacked one end of the rope to the cleat on the wall and got the harness off his dad's workbench. "See, it's got padding here and here." He pointed to the chest part of the harness, followed by the leg holes. "And the outer part is nylon so it doesn't cause friction. You want to put it on?"

"Nah."

Of course I want to put it on! But that would mean Jack had to hook me in, which involved him getting close to me while I smelled like the duck pond. When the pond started to dry up in the summer, all you could smell was the green scum and the duck doo-doo left behind. For the first time in recorded history, I almost left off hanging out with Jack to go home and take a shower.

What is the world coming to?

Now he was giving me a funny look because he *knew* I'd want to try it on and swing from the beam in the ceiling. "Suit yourself."

162

Pretending not to care, I watched as he stepped into the leg holes and buckled the chest. Then he jumped up and fastened himself to the swinging rope with one of those clips that mountain climbers use.

Soon he was swinging around the workshop like Peter Pan while I pretended it was no big deal.

"Delton's prank is impressive, Cassidy. He might give us some competition next year."

"I don't think so."

"Name one of our pranks that beats Mrs. Delaney's nightgown," he said, passing overhead.

I shrugged. Jack had a point.

"C'mon. You'll have to remember for the history books."

"Maybe the time we tied Miss Hennessy's helium birthday balloons to her attendance clipboard?"

"That was pretty good." Jack made a grab for me on his next pass. "Stick your foot up in the air. I want to see if I can grab one of your socks."

I did what I was told. *What difference does it make if I lie on the floor and get sawdust in my hair? I already have BO to beat the band.*

"Maybe the time we put cat kibble in Mr. Fenster's trail mix? Hey! You're tickling me!"

"Hold still! The kibble was amateur. I say it was the time we gave Mr. Janescko a new title."

"*That* was epic."

What we did to our principal's door didn't just make us legends at Stocking Elementary; it resulted in the name of our global organization. It was the summer between third and fourth grade when Jack and I realized the funny thing that happens when you put our names together. You can bet we were going to use that. So on the very first day, during the all-school assembly, we found a "Jack" in the first grade and a "Cassidy" in third and we snitched their name tags. A little clever cutting later, we marched past the office to our fourth-grade classroom and stuck the stolen name tags on the office door, right below MR. JANESCKO, PRINCIPAL.

In class, Jack kept looking over his shoulder at me so I could practice my "I'm sorry, can you explain that one more time?" look. The look that says, in one expression, "So you think that I—and Jack—put those name tags *together* under Principal Janescko's name? But why would we do that? And look, my name tag is right here."

Dense as iridium.

You can't take a photo of your fourth-grade teacher being called down to the office and returning to give *you* a look. A look that said "Could she? Could they?" And then uncorking a brand-new bottle of extra-strength Excedrin.

"So what's our next one? We haven't done a prank in ages."

Thinking about Delton made me remember the piece of paper in my pocket. I pulled it out and unfolded it. "I know what I'm going to do. I'm going to make my fear of bugs disappear."

"Really?"

Next thing I knew, Jack had swiped the paper. He's the only boy I know who can swing around like Superman and read at the same time.

"So . . . how does this work again?" he asked. "You say this stuff while tapping on your energy points?"

"I guess."

As the piece of paper fluttered back down to me, I thought, for some reason, of that music Miss Melton-Mowry had been playing in her office. Paper drifting through the air *was* sort of like water dripping off your toes.

Weird.

I looked over the sheet. "It's a script. And I'm supposed to say this stuff while tapping on my meri—what did you call 'em?—my energy points."

"Meridians. So . . . go ahead." Jack struggled to get himself out of the harness while he was still swinging. In the end, he had to go upside down and wrap his legs around the rope so he could reach the clips to undo himself.

Why couldn't I have challenges like that? Why was I the one with the rotten karma and the weird fear of bugs? Jack must have been some rich banker in his former life—one who rescued people from losing their farms.

I sat cross-legged, trying to read the script while tapping all the places on the diagram.

"This fear I have of bugs . . ." Tap the top of my head. "It overtakes me. . . ." Tap my eyebrow. "It feels like I'm threatened . . ." Tap beside my eye. "Like they're going to bite me." Tap under my nose.

"Yuck!" I threw the paper down. "This is ridiculous. It's like trying to pat your head and rub your belly at the same time. Besides, I'm not afraid they'll bite me."

"What is it, then?"

"It's more like . . . they're . . . I don't know if it's me or them that's . . . so scared. Like I'm *their* scared."

"Like *you* are the bug?"

"I don't know! And how am I supposed to feel the fear when

I can't stop thinking about where I'm supposed to poke myself next?"

"Here." Jack kneeled down beside me. "Put the paper on the floor and I'll tap while you say it. Maybe picture a squirming worm on the dock. That oughta get you in the mood."

My stomach started to feel squeezy again. I don't know if it was the vision of a struggling worm or the fact that Jack was in BO range.

"Go." Jack started rapping the top of my head with his knuckles. "Be the worm."

"This fear I have of squirmy worms . . . Ouch, Jack!"

"Do the next one."

"It overtakes me. You're not supposed to poke me in the eye." I swatted his hand away.

"Well, you're feeling better, aren't you? I mean, I can tell you're not feeling afraid. In fact, I'm guessing you want to punch me right now." Jack kept going, this time tapping under my chin—which wasn't even on the picture.

"Stop it." Pushing him away, I scooted back a few feet.

Jack looked at me, surprised. He was dangerously close to moping—which was my specialty, not his. "Just trying to help, Cassidy. You can't keep quitting everything."

"Jack?" Bree pushed open the workshop door. "Oooh, you got the harness. Can I try?"

"Sure." Jack jumped up and ran over to unhook the rope and bring the harness down.

"Not now," Bree said. "I came to find Cassidy. Mama and I have a surprise for you."

I did a quick inventory of what a Benson surprise might look like. On the upside, it could be more of those sugar cookies with the electric-blue frosting. On the downside, it could be something to make me more like them—a manicure? Sweetness lessons?

I got up and dusted off my clothes. I didn't feel like hanging around Jack with duck-pond BO, but it might come in handy to drive the Bensons crazy. They were always scrubbed. Plus, as long as I was with Bree, Jack couldn't be. "Lead on," I said in my best robot voice.

I figured we were headed to the Bensons', but Bree walked up our back-porch steps. "It's in here," she said, yanking open the back door and bounding up the stairs to my bedroom.

"Ta-da!" Bree had to stop to catch her breath. "A perfect re-creation of an elegant luncheon, complete with your own Miss Information."

I looked at the card table set up in my room and crammed with so much china that you couldn't put your elbows down on it even if you wanted to. Mom had obviously loaned the Bensons her Bunco table, complete with folding chairs. Mrs. Benson sat in one and Pat the Bunny sat in another, his fat tummy squeezed into *my* favorite shirt.

"Where did you get all this stuff?" I asked. Then added, "He's going to pop the buttons!"

"Don't you like it?" Mrs. Benson unfolded her napkin. "This is my grandmother's china. I thought before we put it in the china cabinet, we'd set it up so you could practice."

"You realize that Jack and I wrestle in here," I said. "The china is not safe."

Mrs. Benson studied her napkin for a minute before she answered. "Well, we can certainly practice. I was . . . thinkin' about keepin' it out to have a tea, anyway. You know, invite the neighbor ladies. Except for your mama and Jack's mama, I haven't . . . well, I don't seem to be . . ."

"The neighbors aren't comin' over," Bree said. "They always do that down South when someone moves in."

Talk about recalculating. I was about to be trapped into another etiquette lesson—in my private refuge, no less. As soon as I caught wind of what they were up to, I reviewed my drive-'em-crazy escape routines—zombie, blind tightrope walker, one-legged ballet dancer—but something was wrong with Mrs. Benson. She looked . . . sad.

"If you really want to get to know the neighbor ladies," I told her, "you need to serve wine and cheesy snacks and play Bunco. They're crazy for it."

I wasn't sure why the neighbor ladies loved Bunco so much. It was a toss-up between "No kids allowed—ever!" and the wine; there was always lots of shouting and, if you spied on them, red cheeks and slapping each other on the shoulder.

"I don't know how to play Bunco." Mrs. Benson looked at Bree, who was sitting across from her with her napkin unfolded on her lap. "Is that a Yankee thing?"

"Probably." I flopped onto the empty folding chair. Very unladylike. "Look, let's get through this tea game and I'll show you how to do it. This is an etiquette lesson, right? I'm assuming there's no real food involved since Mom *never* lets us have food in our rooms."

I unfolded my napkin, wondering if sucking on it would make my hunger pangs go away. Pat has no lap, so I had to tie his napkin around his neck.

"Well, your mama said, and I quote: 'I guess there could be

special dispensation for practicing etiquette.' So . . . I brought a cake." Mrs. Benson leaned over and pulled up a dome-covered cake plate hidden beneath a kitchen towel. "I'm known for this cake back in Decatur."

Bree whipped off the towel. "It's *always* the first picked at the December Decatur Cake Walk given by the Junior League."

There in front of me, in all its towering glory, was the biggest cake I'd ever seen. "It's got three layers," Bree continued. "Chocolate, vanilla and red velvet—and the frosting is whipped cream and sugar and toasted coconut."

One look at that cake could make a girl forget that cookie butter had ever been invented. This was serious business.

"Ladies," I said. "Teach me how to eat this cake like they do down South; then we'll get out the dice and master Bunco."

It was the least I could do.

"That's the spirit." Mrs. Benson patted my knee. "And while I'm dishing it out, we can practice our polite conversation."

"Can the bunny have a big piece?" I asked, wondering if I could get an extra piece of cake for my new friend, Livvy. If she really was the same as me—like Donna said—this cake would definitely help me rise in the ranks. "Can you send cake by mail? Just theoretically."

"Cassidy," Bree said. "You're jumping ahead."

"The first thing to remember," Mrs. Benson began, "is to ask if each guest would like cake. Some people pass on the cake because they're watching their figure or for health—"

"You don't have to worry about that here," I said. "I'd like a big slice, please."

"It's not considered polite to request a size," Bree informed me.

"What if I open my eyes really wide? Do you think the cutter will get the idea?" Stretching my eyebrows up to my hairline, I managed to get a laugh out of Mrs. Benson.

"You're a true original, Miss Corcoran," Mrs. Benson said. "Would you like a piece of cake?"

I thought we'd just covered that, but since this was etiquette practice, I knew it didn't have to make sense. Nothing else had made sense today, come to think of it. Miss Melton-Mowry *smiled*, I said no to the harness and now here I was—in my bedroom!—having polite conversation with ladies who wore so much stuff on their face we could be in a play.

"Yes, Mrs. Benson, I would love a piece of your special cake."

Patting my other knee, Bree whispered, "Nice compliment."

Mrs. Benson made a couple of deep slices with her knife, slid one of those wedgy things underneath the piece of cake and balanced it over my plate.

I knew I was supposed to wait before digging in, and that licking the frosting that trailed on the plate was considered something close to a jailing offense, so I set my plate in front of me and folded my hands in my lap.

"Actually . . . ," Bree said, handing me her empty plate, "it's most polite to continue passing the cake until everyone has been served."

"But what if the next piece is smaller than mine?"

"It could be bigger." Mrs. Benson cut another hefty slice.

"Okay." I put the new piece in front of me. "I guess that makes sense."

"Knock, knock!"

"Dad!" My dad never gets home early on Mondays. I almost jumped out of my chair, but since we were practicing our manners, I said, "If you ladies will excuse me, I'll get the door."

Charging into the hall, I gave him a bear hug.

"Word has reached me that there is an etiquette practice going on up here involving a cake that, well, I might have some special interest in."

Since there weren't words in Corcoran language to describe what was being passed around the Bunco table, I pulled Dad into the room and pointed.

"Olive Ann, Sabrina, what a nice surprise," Dad said, though he couldn't take his eyes off the cake. "I came to inform Mr. Bunny there is an urgent need for his services downstairs—the clover in the lawn has gotten out of control." Dad picked up Pat by the ears and deposited him outside the door. "I will, however, be happy to assist in any way that I can."

It was so much more fun to play manners with a cake like this in front of me. Could it be a trick, I wondered. I waited for more instructions, but after Mrs. Benson had served us each a piece, we all picked up our forks and took a bite.

Dad patted his lips with his napkin. "Olive Ann . . . truly. I have never tasted a cake so divine in all my life."

"Thank you, Brian. That is high praise coming from a man in the food business."

I could have told her that my dad thinks of graham crackers as dessert, given how one hundred percent against sugar my mom is; but honestly, even I knew this was the kind of cake you only get once in a hundred years. The frosting was creamy, the cake was moist and every layer melted in your mouth.

"There's nothing in all the world like Mama's pound cake

and biscuits . . . oooh, and her cheesecake brownies," Bree said. "She even made special-order cakes for all the weddings they held at the Landis Valley Country Club."

"Trouble is, with everyone watching their weight and eating fat-free this and that, my cakes aren't as popular as they used to be."

"These are special-occasion cakes, Olive Ann. They have a place in our diets. In fact, I'd like to feature this cake in our bakery department—special order only. You'd have to bake them in our kitchen, of course. Do you think you could do that?"

"Well . . . I don't know. It's a lot to think about so soon after the move."

"It's not really work, Mama, when you love to do it."

"I do have time on my hands these days."

I wished Mrs. Benson could spend some of her time subbing for Miss Melton-Mowry at etiquette class. We might not all be so half-starved by the end of class.

Dad stopped talking then and concentrated on his cake. Since I knew more about etiquette, I decided to help him along with some polite conversation.

"I was just telling Mrs. Benson that if she wants to meet the neighbor ladies, she should learn to play Bunco."

"Mama doesn't drink alcohol," Bree said. "Or swear *or* take the Lord's name in vain."

I swallowed and looked at Dad. Was there a way to play Bunco without the wine and the colorful words?

If he knew, he wasn't telling, which brought that topic of conversation to a screeching halt.

❊

Neither Dad or I or Magda had much appetite for dinner; of course, my sister managed to score a piece of cake *without* the china or polite conversation.

"I think Olive Ann is having trouble adjusting to Michigan," Dad told Mom as she tucked into her lentil loaf.

"She might be the nicest person I've ever met," Mom said. "I'm going to invite her to Bunco. She'll meet a bunch of women there."

"As long as you don't force her to drink wine," I said.

"Or swear," Dad said.

"Or take the Lord's name in vain, whatever that means," I added, pushing my peas and carrots into square-dance formation.

"Does saying the Rosary before you throw the dice count?" Mom asked. "Maura Delaney's been doing that since day one."

"You know what Olive Ann is . . . ?" Dad stopped talking and contemplated his forkful of lentils. "With her sweetness and her encouraging manner? She's a natural teacher. Maybe she could teach a cake class. That'd be one way to find her tribe."

"What a wonderful idea, Brian. She's perfect for your new demonstration kitchen. Let's try that first . . . and wait a bit on the Bunco." Mom looked around at our plates. "Why isn't anyone eating my lentil loaf?"

excellent

173

CHAPTER 17

Notes of Apology

"Today we will focus on the little inconveniences, such as spills, and how to handle them in a fine-dining situation."

I straightened my shoulders into coat-hanger order. I swore I was in that movie where you wake up and it's the same day over and over again. It was our second class of the third week—but who was counting? Since the Fourth of July holiday fell on a Monday, we were having three classes this week to make up for missing next Monday! That meant, this week it was the same day over and over *and over* again on Friday, too.

Miss Melton-Mowry didn't seem to mind at all. "Let me demonstrate what I mean," she said as we watched her haul Miss Information out of her seat and drag her over to the space between me and Delton. There was some trouble with getting her to stand. Even after our teacher finished setting her up, Miss I swayed a little, the same way my mom does after she's had a classic margarita at the Tortilla Factory.

We always went to the Tortilla Factory on the summer solstice. Now it was the last week in June—the sweetest time in summer. The days went on forever; you could lie on your back and watch the fireflies and the bats come out at dusk; the dirt smelled like perfume and playing kick the can could last until your parents dragged you in to go to bed.

Or . . . you could learn how to get a waiter's attention.

"All right, then. Let's say you have spilled a bit of water. Simply drop your napkin over it like so and, when the waitstaff appears, indicate in a low, modulated voice that you would appreciate another napkin. Let's begin with you, Miss Corcoran. Miss Corcoran?"

I tried to pull myself out of my etiquette coma and focus on what Miss Melton-Mowry was saying.

"Um, can you define 'modulated'?"

"Quiet and controlled. Like so." Miss Melton-Mowry dropped her napkin on the table and looked up at Miss Information. She gestured at the napkin and pressed her lips together like the napkin was covering up something rotten. " 'When you have a moment, could you bring me another napkin?' " She waited a few seconds—we all did, as if Miss Information would finally open her mouth and say something. " 'Thank you,' " Miss Melton-Mowry said at last. " 'I would be most obliged.' "

"But what if you need your napkin before she gets back?" I wanted to know. "What if she takes a powder in the kitchen?"

"In polite society, Miss Corcoran, spills are rare. When we control our movements, we reduce the risk of an accident. The risk of having two accidents in a short space of time is very low."

I hated to disagree . . . but . . . Miss Melton-Mowry had obviously never read *The Nine Lives of Magda's Glasses*. Putting a slipknot into the corner of my napkin, I stuck my butter knife in it.

"What are you doing now? You need to stop playing with your napkin and return it to your lap."

"It's not a napkin. It's a white flag." I waved it for demonstration purposes. "I'm surrendering. Geez, Miss Melton-Mowry, we're not robots; we're kids. And in case you haven't heard, with kids—accidents most definitely do happen." I glanced over at Officer Weston, who was clearly *not* a kid, and at Delton, who was sitting as stiff as, well, a zombie robot. "Present company excepted."

"Miss Corcoran, *kids* are baby goats. And yes, children have accidents, but *you* are not a child any longer. You are a young lady who will replace her cutlery and return to the subject at hand."

"Yes, ma'am." I dropped my knife back on the table and unknotted my napkin, but not before gesturing in a twenty-one-gun military sort of way.

"There is no need to salute. Now, Mr. Bean . . ." Miss Melton-Mowry turned to Delton. "How would you get the waiter's attention? Remember, as we discussed last week, speaking in a loud voice is distracting. If the waiter is not nearby, you'll need to use your body language."

"Well . . ." Delton sat up and cleared his throat like he was going to recite the Pledge of Allegiance. "In your video on fine dining, I seem to recall that you can get the waiter's attention by looking at him, and . . ." He paused, searching his massive data bank for fine-dining details. "Hmmm . . . sometimes you can do it by directing your energy; but if that fails, you can . . . you could . . ."

"Poke him?" Officer Weston prompted.

"Clock him in the shins?" A favorite of mine.

"I remember!" Delton forgot himself and snapped his fingers. "Arch your eyebrow."

"You can't be serious," Officer Weston said. "How's he going to see *that* across a crowded restaurant?"

"Let's practice, shall we? Now, Officer Weston. Please direct the intensity of your gaze at Miss Information and draw her to your assistance."

Officer Weston screwed up his face like a rock had just landed on his foot.

"All right, and if that doesn't work, then you can raise your hand slightly. Try that, Miss Corcoran."

I let my hands float up from the table like I did in yoga class, only they floated a little too far and knocked Miss Information off balance; she fell forward like a chopped tree, smacking her head on the table—where it stayed—while the rest of her fell to the floor.

"Miss Corcoran! You do try my patience. The purpose of these lessons is to demonstrate the correct way to behave in a fine-dining situation. Your aim is to be polite, gentle, seemly. You are *not* to draw attention to yourself. Does it exist—in the realm of your imagination—to conduct yourself in a manner appropriate to the young lady you *seem* to be, at least on the outside? Need I remind you that there is more at stake here than your . . . entertainment!"

There were more words, but I was focused on using the intensity of my gaze to tell Miss Melton-Mowry that her spit was landing on our tablecloth and my napkin wasn't big enough to cover the spray!

"Excuse me, Miss Melton-Mowry?" Officer Weston had returned Miss Information's body to a standing position. "If you hand me the head, I think I might be able to fix it."

"This!"—Miss Melton-Mowry picked up the head and thrust it at Officer Weston—"was made by the gentleman who repairs all the antique clocks for the royal family in Dubai. It is extremely unlikely that you can *fix it*! But by all means, Officer, give it a try."

Miss Melton-Mowry was having what my dad calls a Michelin-three-star tirade, tugging first on her sleeves and then on the bottom of her blazer before closing her eyes and pressing her hands to her very red cheeks. "Do you believe in miracles, Mr. Bean?"

"I'm going to be an aeronautical engineer, Miss Melton-Mowry. Miracles are not a mechanically valid—"

"Well, start believing. Now! And that's an order." When her eyes finally opened, Miss Melton-Mowry stared at us as if she wasn't sure why we were there. "I need to excuse myself for a moment. Just . . . practice polite conversation."

Officer Weston blew into the hole in Miss Information's neck and tried again to insert the screw into it. "You should go apologize, Cassidy."

"Me? What did I do?"

Officer Weston and Delton stayed silent, letting me figure it out for myself. "I didn't mean to make her so mad—" I broke off, trying to think of something to say to defend myself. But I couldn't. I'd really done it this time. I beheaded her best doll— twice!

Bending Miss Information's body so that she sat in his lap, Officer Weston tried to screw her head back into place, but her hair kept getting caught in his shirt buttons. Delton helped out by pulling the hair into a ponytail and holding it above her head.

"You're so natural at being a pain, you can't even see it," Delton said, smoothing Miss I's hair back down and tucking it behind her ear. "I think her collar's stuck in the neck seam," he told Officer Weston.

"She's only trying to do her job and make us civilized, Cassidy." Officer Weston managed to unpinch Miss I's collar, but now her head tilted again. She looked at us with her head cocked like that—like she wished she could figure us out.

Figure *me* out, I should say.

"We need an even bigger screw," Delton said. "Maybe a plaster screw with an anchor bolt."

"We better leave her headless until we get one. I'm afraid if she loses her head again, there will be permanent damage." Officer Weston carried Miss Information back to her chair and set her head in her lap.

"But *why*?" I persisted. "Why do we have to be civilized?"

"It's called growing up, Cassidy," Delton said. "And it's going to happen whether you want it to or not."

"It already has happened to me. How'd you like to be doing this when you're twenty-seven, Cass?" Officer Weston asked me.

That was definitely nightmare material. "All right, all right. I'll go apologize."

I pressed my ear to the door of Miss Melton-Mowry's office and heard music again. It wasn't the same as before. I closed my eyes and tried to picture the river and the drops of water, but I couldn't do it. This wasn't river music.

I knocked.

"I'd like a few moments to myself, please."

"I know," I said, opening the door anyway. "But I was thinking . . . well, maybe if you put on the water music you'd feel better. This sounds more like . . . a bunch of birds in a tree, screeching at one another."

Miss Melton-Mowry was looking at a photograph, but when I opened the door, she slipped it into the top drawer of her desk.

Even I knew it was rude to ask her about the picture. "My sister Magda found a photograph of my great-grandma," I told her. "She was hunting poachers in Africa."

Miss Melton-Mowry took a tissue from the box on her desk and pressed it to her cheek.

"Miss Corcoran, when someone tells you they need a private moment, you should respect their wishes."

"I know." I stood there wondering if apologizing trumped respecting Miss Melton-Mowry's wishes. "I . . . just wanted to say I'm sorry. I know I'm obnoxious. My great-grandma used to say I got on her last nerve."

"You do . . . have a knack."

"I am sorry," I said again, and was surprised to find that I really meant it. "I pushed you to the brink. When I do that to my dad, he calls it the full moon of madness."

"Maybe . . . you were right about the music." She pressed

a button on her radio and found something better . . . not the water music, but . . . calmer. "What makes me feel sorry is that I haven't been able to demonstrate the importance of these lessons. To you, they are just an endless series of pointless rules designed to keep you indoors and bored half to death."

I nodded, but stayed quiet, since the only honest thing to say was that I couldn't have agreed with her more.

"But they're not, really. Manners are useful; they are the means by which . . . people can enter another world, you might say. They can bridge a gap that exists between their stations in life—" Miss Melton-Mowry broke off, possibly because she could see I didn't have the foggiest—as my dad would say— what she was talking about. "Well, there's no point in repeating myself."

"We could chant *om,* maybe. That's where you take a deep breath and moan. If you do it three times, you pretty much forget what you were sore about."

"Thank you, but I think I'd rather try to find some Debussy."

I had almost closed the door when she said, "And that was a nice apology, Miss Corcoran. It felt . . . sincere."

The best part of a bath is pretending your toes are shark teeth bobbing just above the surface of the water, coming closer and closer to your head until—they devour you!

"Don't blame me." Magda sat on the edge of the tub while I mopped up the floor with an old bath towel. "I didn't force you to play *Jaws* in a bathtub that was dangerously overfull."

"It wouldn't be so disgusting if you'd actually cleaned under

181

here when you drew our bathroom from the chore list." I had made it to beneath the sink, where a bunch of Magda hairs climbed up the porcelain. "Next time, I'll make my toes an iceberg and re-create the story of my life as the *Titanic* crashes into it."

"For a girl who wishes she were a boy, you'd make a darn good drama queen."

I didn't have a snappy comeback to that. I was beginning to understand what my dad meant when he said, "Whatever happened to my happy carefree Hopalong Cassidy?" I really was turning into a world-class whiner.

"Mom wanted me to give you this." Magda held out a razor.

"You want me to . . . hurt myself? I'm not that depressed, Mags."

"No, she wanted me to inform you that shaving your armpits will help with your, um . . . body issues."

"You mean my BO? Is everybody talking about it? Geez." For the first time in my life, I was happy to have a reason to keep my head down and scrub. It's creepy to think of people talking about what's happening under your arms.

"Well, it makes sense, in theory. We have about three to four million sweat glands, and your forearm, for example, doesn't smell when you're sweating there. At least mine doesn't."

Head down, I kept swabbing the deck, but I was listening.

"The smell people associate with sweat isn't actually sweat. It's what results when the bacteria that live on our skin break down sweat into acids. Therefore—and I wasn't able to definitively solve this with an Internet search—it seems like common sense that the more sweat is trapped on the hairs that grow under your arm, the more bacterial action, thus the stronger the odor will be."

I was about to protest that I didn't have any hair under my arms, but the truth was I did. Not a lot . . . but some. "I bet Great-Grandma Reed didn't shave under *her* arms while she was chasing poachers and whatnot."

"Probably not." As usual, Magda had that look she gets when she's contemplating chemical reactions. "The distinctive smell we give off doesn't have to be perceived as bad. That's a cultural notion. Our body odor is a result of genetics, our diet, our lifestyle, the medications and supplements we take. Our ancestors loved the smell of their family members. And just think of the way dogs want to get into your—"

"Magda! It is possible that you are the most disgusting sister on the planet. Just give me that and make yourself disappear!"

Reaching out, I swiped the razor before putting my hand back down on a pile of fifteen-year-old-sized toenail clippings.

do not like ✗

CHAPTER 18

Food Stuck
in Teeth

The Friday before Fourth of July weekend, I set my intention to do no harm to the already headless Miss Information. In fact, as she sat next to me with her hand resting on her genuine-human-hair head, I realized she was proof that this was not the same day. At the beginning of our last class, her head was on her shoulders.

"So much of our etiquette training has stood the test of time," Miss Melton-Mowry began. "However, fears over the spread of disease have changed how we *politely* deal with basic body functions, and today we will focus on those changes. I know that schools teach children the most sanitary way to cough or sneeze . . ."

This seemed like basic stuff, making it safe to play a round of Frisbee golf in my mind.

"Is that right, Mr. Bean? Miss Corcoran? . . . Miss Corcoran?"

"I see what you're saying, Miss Melton-Mowry." I'd been caught daydreaming—a hole in one that sailed right over the duck pond, to be exact. "But I wonder . . . ," I continued, hoping Officer Weston and Delton would help me out. "Does everyone feel that way?"

Delton covered for me by giving Miss Melton-Mowry the rundown on how we'd learned to cough and sneeze into our elbow in preschool, more or less bringing me up to speed.

"The trouble is, coughing into one's elbow has a way of drawing attention to oneself," Miss M&M said after Delton's impressive demonstration. "There are subtler ways, especially if you're not infectious. The back of the wrist is an excellent alternative. Let's practice that for a minute, shall we?"

Officer Weston raised his hand. "Excuse me, Miss Melton-Mowry, but I have an etiquette emergency. Can we cover things that get stuck in your mouth? Last night, Elizabeth had a piece of spinach in her teeth . . ." He opened his mouth and pointed to his front two chompers. "Right here."

"And you alerted her to this how?"

"Like I'm doing right now. I pointed."

"Yes, well. We can add that to our list." Miss Melton-Mowry looked up at the ceiling and then back at us.

"I'd appreciate it. The word 'clod' came up again right before she stomped to the ladies' room, but I have no idea what I did wrong. I mean, it was as plain as the nose on her face. How was I supposed to have polite conversation when a blob of spinach was playing peekaboo with me?"

A noise escaped from Delton's mouth that sounded suspiciously like a giggle. To cover it, he raised his hand. "Miss Melton-Mowry, if this is the time for special requests, I'd like to know if there's any special etiquette for picnics. Our neighborhood Fourth of July picnic is this Monday and both Miss Corcoran and I will be in attendance. I remember, last year, Cassidy—"

"Seems to me that Mr. Bean and Miss Elizabeth could use a good dose of etiquette class," I said. "You for changing topics, Mr. Bean, and Miss Elizabeth for stomping. Even *I* know that stomping isn't polite."

"Miss Corcoran is correct. We need to stay on task, and I'm afraid picnics are not in our purview at this time. You'll have to . . . do your best with transfer of knowledge, Mr. Bean. Officer Weston, I'm sure we'll breeze through this lesson and have time for . . . blobs of spinach at the end of class. Now, to practice."

Miss Melton-Mowry demonstrated a fake cough, holding the back of her wrist up to her mouth. We all copied her.

"There is no need to make contact with your wrist, Miss Corcoran. Simply hold it up to shield others from your cough. Remember the point is *not* to draw attention to yourself."

"That's a big challenge for Cassidy," Delton said. "Uh, sorry. Miss Corcoran."

To show Delton how very wrong he was, I stopped goofing around and coughed politely, using the back of my wrist. "How about sneezing?" I asked. "Same drill?"

"Thank you, Miss Corcoran. Yes. Same drill. The only tip

I have for you here is to remember to keep your nose down slightly."

"I get it. To control the force of the blast?" Officer Weston asked.

Miss Melton-Mowry coughed into the back of her hand again, but it was pretty obvious she was laughing this time. "Officer Weston, your language is so . . . colorful."

"Yes it is," I agreed. "When you get hitched to Elizabeth, you'll have to talk in black-and-white."

"I know." Officer Weston shoved his hands in his pockets and studied the floor.

Getting married to a girl who thought etiquette was the bee's knees made me wonder about Officer Weston's mental state. Did this start with his hairy legs, too? Did all men and boys lose their marbles over a pretty girl? He once let it slip during polite conversation that he called her Honeybun, since her real name is Miss Honeycutt. Seems to me, a honeybun should be covered in cinnamon glaze, not red lipstick. Why would a perfectly good guy like Officer Weston give himself a life sentence of talking about the fine weather and never getting the last of the mashed potatoes?

I'd seen this honeybun after class. She wore big sunglasses and she made him kiss her on the cheek so he didn't smear her lipstick.

"Now, don't be discouraged, Officer Weston," Miss Melton-Mowry was saying. "Let's practice yawning politely and then we'll move on to spinach."

I didn't need practice yawning since I'd got plenty of that during previous etiquette sessions. We learned from Miss Melton-Mowry that you could cover up little yawns by pressing your lips together. If it was a whopper and pressing your lips together meant that your eyes bugged out, you used your handy-dandy wrist back to shield your companions from knowing that you were bored out of your mind!

"Now, to Officer Weston's emergency. It's equally likely that we'll encounter this issue at our luncheon. Alerting someone to an unpleasant situation such as food stuck in her teeth can be accomplished in the same way you summon a waiter—using the intensity of your gaze."

I raised my hand. "But didn't you say staring at people is rude?"

"Staring, especially staring cross-eyed, Miss Corcoran, *is* rude. But, as we've seen, the intensity of your gaze can be very useful. Observe. Without Miss Information's head, I'll have to use Officer Weston as my example. Let's say that he has something stuck in his teeth. Now watch my face closely."

We all watched as Miss Melton-Mowry straightened her shoulders, picked up her knife and fork and pretended to be cutting up food. She put an imaginary piece of food in her mouth and started to chew it. Smiling, she looked around the table, still pretending to chew and swallow.

Finally, after another two bites of invisible food, she stopped and looked at Officer Weston. Her eyes opened wider as she tucked her chin. Even though her head was down, she kept looking at him. After about thirty seconds of this, she set down her fork and knife, picked up her napkin and patted her mouth with it.

"Now, if you didn't know what all this was about, Officer Weston, how would you feel when I looked at you this way?"

"Um, like you were trying to hypnotize me?"

"That's not entirely off base. I am using my body language to help direct your thoughts."

"Couldn't you just slip me a toothpick? All that staring gave me the heebie-jeebies."

"If we were in a diner, possibly. But we'll be at the Egypt Valley Country Club, where they don't provide each table with a toothpick dispenser."

"Oh, that's not a problem. I always have some right here." Patting his front pocket, Officer Weston continued, "I have a gap between my two front teeth. More like a crevice, really. It's a magnet for popcorn." He demonstrated the effectiveness of the toothpick.

"I am well aware of what a toothpick can do, Officer Weston. What I am trying to teach you—and the result Elizabeth hopes to achieve by having you take this class—is that we have evolved from ancient times when men stuck twigs in their mouths to dislodge bits of food. What we want to do is accomplish the task with a minimum of distraction."

What better way to accomplish the task than with a toothpick?

"Putting foreign objects into your mouth is not considered polite," Miss Melton-Mowry said. I was beginning to think she could read my mind!

"But it's not foreign," Officer Weston protested, reaching into his pocket for the box. "These Diamond toothpicks are made in the USA."

Miss Melton-Mowry tweaked the creases of her blouse collar. "Let's try Delton, shall we? Delton, if I'd looked at you that way and you suspected I was alerting you to something in your teeth, what would you do?"

"I'd excuse myself and go to the bathroom to check."

"Exactly. There are two reasons for these subtle maneuvers, Officer Weston and Miss Corcoran. One, it is not conducive to the appetites of other diners to see someone mining their mouth for bits of food at the table. Two, it is a courtesy to the dining companion who may have food lodged in her teeth to draw as little attention to it as possible."

"But what if you're wrong and your food gets cold?" I wanted to know. "Cold food is not conducive to my appetite."

Miss Melton-Mowry directed the intensity of her gaze at me. There was something to this staring stuff.

"In polite society, Officer Weston, couples often develop subtle cues that they give each other in situations such as these."

"You mean like how Jim Leyland used sign language to tell Verlander to throw a slider?" Officer Weston proceeded to do a good imitation of the former Detroit Tigers' manager calling pitches from the dugout.

"More subtle, Officer Weston. Remember subtlety."

He moved from hand gestures to wiggling fingers.

"More like . . . a touch on the shoulder or a meaningful look."

"Like this?" I put my hand on Miss Information's shoulder, ducked my head and batted my eyelashes.

"Yes, more like that."

"What were you conveying, Cass—Miss Corcoran?" Officer Weston wanted to know.

"I was suggesting she might like to excuse herself to the ladies' room to see if she could find her missing head."

❋

That afternoon, I got on my bike and retraced my route all the way to Livvy's house, timing my arrival to be the same as when I'd first seen her jumping head; I was hoping to get another sighting. Nothing. Quiet. No dog. No bouncing. There was a car in the driveway and a tricycle on the front walk, so I leaned my bike up against the mailbox, careful not to let the wheels smash any more flowers, went up to the front door and rang the bell.

A mom answered, drying her hands on a dish towel. "Hello," she said.

"Hello there. I'm Cassidy Corcoran." I held out my hand and shook hers, never mind it was still wet. "I'm so pleased to make your acquaintance." It doesn't hurt to make a good first impression on moms—especially moms whose houses smelled like they'd been baking with cinnamon. "I was wondering if Miss Olivia was at home."

"Livvy? My Olivia? Are you sure you have the right address, dear? Livvy doesn't . . . well, she doesn't usually have friends with manners like yours."

Was that a compliment? Or no? I waited for her to answer my question.

"Where are *my* manners? I'm Mrs. Dunn, Livvy's mom." Mrs. Dunn set down her dish towel and picked up an envelope and a piece of paper from the table in the hall. "Did you say Cassidy?"

I nodded.

"Livvy's gone to summer camp already, Cassidy."

"Oh. Do you know when she'll be back?"

"At least eight weeks. That is, if all goes well." Mrs. Dunn put her hand on my shoulder. "I'm sorry you missed her. But . . . she left something for you."

"For me? Are you sure?" I held out my hand for the envelope.

"I'm afraid you have to swear an oath first. Would you be willing to do that?"

"Pinky-swear? Spit-swear? If there's blood involved, I might have to request a Band-Aid."

"I'm sure raising your right hand would be sufficient."

I raised my right hand while Mrs. Dunn squinted at the paper. "Her handwriting . . ." She turned again and picked up a pair of glasses from the hall table and read: "Do you, Cassidy sorry-I-forgot-your-last-name, promise to commit the Chipmunk Code to memory, to destroy the original, and to never divulge this key or any message created with it to anyone under the age of twenty-one, most specifically and especially any living boy? PS All animals and birds except talking parrots are okay."

Mrs. Dunn looked up at me.

"I do."

"Well, then. There you are." At the exact moment she handed me the envelope, we heard a loud thudding noise on the stairway behind her. I stretched until I could see the three monster pirates sliding down the staircase on what looked like an upside-down bath mat.

"Man the controls, Captain! We're going down!"

Mrs. Dunn threw her body in front of the door so they wouldn't slide right outside. "Lovely to meet you, dear," she said, and slammed the door.

There was no point in going right home. Nosy Magda was sure to smell a mystery, and since she was a living person, I couldn't let her see the code. No. This was mine. I kept on riding to Riverside Park and found an empty swing set. Tearing open the envelope, I pumped my legs a few times and looked over what Livvy sent.

Cassidy, here's my address. After you memorize the Chipmunk Code, which was created by me and my last best friend, Judy Hansen, you should write me a letter in code. It is deadly boring here when we're not doing flips, so make it interesting and that's an order!

Chipmunk Code

For every letter of the alphabet, the Chipmunk Code had a picture. *A* was a heart. *B* was a kite. *C* was a candy cane. So now I had to memorize this and write Livvy a letter? We never got to the point where I told her I don't like memorizing *or* writing. Couldn't I just steal Magda's phone and text her? Pumping higher, I stuck the code in my back pocket, wondering if Livvy wanted *me* to be her new best friend. I liked the idea of being best friends with a girl who had a trampoline, but if I couldn't use it all summer, what use was that?

I needed to think more about this, but swinging cross-legged and cross-armed is a life-threatening activity. Would falling out of a swing and breaking my neck be interesting enough for Livvy Dunn, I wondered. For someone I'd just met, she had a lot of requirements.

"Cassidy, may I borrow your hands after dinner?" Dad asked me as we were finishing our exciting dessert of yogurt and pineapple bits.

"Do they have to be connected to my body?"

"As a matter of fact, they do."

"Borrow your hands" usually meant Dad had a "fix-it" project, and *that* meant he needed my help. He's not good with tools, like Jack or his dad, and I can tell it really bothers him when Mom suggests we ask one of them for help, like she did last week when there was a leak under the kitchen sink.

The good news is, during Tigers season that meant Dad and I would go down to the basement and listen to the game on Granddad's old transistor radio. I would have Dad all to myself—no Magda dissertations on mold!—for at least half an hour, and sometimes things even got fixed.

Tonight we carried the silverware drawer down to the basement. "Lucky you," Dad said as he emptied the forks and spoons onto the counter. "You can practice setting the table while I work."

"Maybe." I pushed the pile away. "If we have time. Let's fix something first."

"Mom tells me these drawers aren't gliding, but the wheels work okay. . . ." Dad turned the drawer over and held it up to his eye, looking down the drawer glide like it was a telescope.

He handed the drawer to me so he could tune in the ball game. It was the third inning.

"Tigers are down, two to one." The crackling of the radio and the familiar voice of the announcer, Dan Dickerson, made the back of my neck prickle. Listening to the Tigers in the basement with my dad was like . . . I don't know, like playing an epic game of freeze tag. It just felt right.

"I'll take it back now." Dad held out his hand for the drawer.

My fingers were covered in grease after running them along the glides. "Uck, what is this? Engine oil?"

"It's not the first time Mom's complained. I applied some WD-40 to them a few months ago."

"I think that makes them stick worse, Dad."

"Oil doesn't make things sticky, Miss Cassidy. It makes things slippery."

I patted Dad's shoulder, trying to come up with a nice way to say it. "I can see how you would think that, but when you put oil on something exposed like these glides, it attracts dust and dirt and *that's* what makes it stick worse."

"Really?" Dad swiped along the glide and got a black stripe on his finger. He sniffed it—just like Magda always did!

"Turn up the volume, Dad. I think Avila just got on—"

"So you're saying I made things worse?"

"What I'm saying is we can fix this. Hand me that bottle of Oil Eater, will you?"

Dad handed me the bottle and a clean rag. Then he sat in one of our lawn chairs so his ear was closer to the radio. "Two on and two out. Kinsler's up."

I started rubbing. "Dad, if I was sworn not to tell something to a boy, would that include you?"

"Though I am male, I am not technically a boy. So, depending on how much you needed to talk about it"—Dad stopped talking and looked at me—"I would say since I'm no longer a boy, it does not include me."

So I told him about Livvy. How she was all of a sudden there . . . and then not there. How she seemed to want to be my new best friend . . . and how her code reminded me of hobo signs, but it wasn't so easy to memorize, especially on top of all the stuff I had to learn about manners.

"Very interesting." He handed me a new cloth in trade for the blackened one I gave him. "This young lady seems . . . mercurial."

"What's that mean?"

"It means that . . . her mood changes a lot. But then, she also sounds . . . adventurous. I can see why you're drawn to her."

"Donna Parker says I remind her of Livvy."

"She does, does she?"

"I guess I'll memorize the code. At least it makes more sense to me than etiquette class."

"Only if you want to, Cass. This assignment is voluntary."

"What I really want is for me and Jack to hang out like we used to . . . and to take him over to jump on the Dunns' trampoline between one and two while the little monsters take their rest."

"Come here." Dad pulled me onto his lap. "Let's listen to the game."

If I worked my way to the side of the chair and put my head on Dad's chest, I could still fit, with one ear listening to his heart and one listening to the game. Brian Corcoran didn't have to prove he was a fan; his heartbeat took off for the races whenever

Dickerson announced a hit: "It's a fly ball right over Sizemore's head . . . but no! Caught at the bleachers. Tough luck, Tigers!"

"How's it going down there, you two?" Mom called down at the top of the fifth.

"Fine." I jumped off Dad's lap and he picked up the drawer.

"We're cleaning the glides," he called up.

"You must be doing a thorough job." She waited for an answer, but when we didn't give her one, she closed the door.

"Are we done, Cass?" Dad asked.

"Are you kidding? The game's tied."

Running his finger over the clean glides, Dad asked what more we could do that would last four innings.

"What we need is something to make them slippery . . . something that doesn't attract dirt."

"Uh . . ." We heard the crack of the bat. I'd lost Dad to the game again. "Darn. Caught in foul territory. Slippery, slippery . . . soap?"

"I said that *doesn't* attract dirt, Dad. Try to focus, will you?"

"I've never been good at multitasking."

"That's okay. I have another idea. Keep your ear glued. . . ." I went upstairs and asked Mom for some wax paper.

"I suppose this is a full nine-inning project," she said, handing over the box. "You can tell your dad I enjoyed my quality time with the dinner dishes."

"Sure." Slamming the basement door, I ran back downstairs.

Mom opened it behind me. "I hope he's at least quizzing you on place settings. You have to set the table in your next class."

"Roger that."

"Nothing's changed," Dad told me. "Still no outs."

I tore off a sheet of wax paper and rubbed it along the clean glide.

"And what will this accomplish?"

"Just an idea I have." I didn't mention that it came from watching Mr. Taylor run a piece of wax paper over the teeth of his jacket zipper to get it unstuck.

We polished the glides for a while, then gave up and listened to the end of the game. Tigers eked out a three-to-two win.

But even sweeter was when we were back upstairs and Dad said, "Cassidy, you are a genius!" as I reinserted the drawer and it slid smoothly along the track. "Thank you, sweetie!"

After a big bear hug, he added, "Now to that other little chore . . . memorizing the place setting."

"Ugh." I stuck out my tongue and crossed my eyes. "What difference does it make where everything goes as long as you can reach what you need?"

"But you wouldn't know whose is whose, would you? It makes it easier with rules."

"That's what all grown-ups say."

"Think about baseball. Imagine if the players decided to run to home whenever they felt like it. It would be a free-for-all and no fun to watch. But when the batter runs to first base while the third baseman is stealing home . . . that creates a tension. Then we're on the edge of our seats."

"Etiquette creates tension, too . . . it gives me a tension headache."

"In etiquette there are rules for different reasons. Let's say you had a delicious meal set in front of you and you went to take a drink of water and the person on your right was drinking from your glass and the person on the left was drinking from his glass. How are you supposed to get any water?"

"Excuse yourself and go to the water fountain?"

"All right, then, say it was Cherry Coke."

Dad was upping the ante. Mom doesn't keep Cherry Coke in the house and we are only allowed to drink it when we go out to eat—which is about twice a year!

"Then I'd have to wrestle somebody."

"And your fries would get cold."

Dad had a point. I hate it when he has one of those.

"Okay, so teach me how to do this."

"You need to make a mental diagram. When we reorganize the store and I have to memorize where we've put everything in the new layout, I try to match it with something I already know. Like . . . our backyard. I'll tell myself, 'Okay, produce is now along the Fensters'—excuse me, the Bensons'—hedge; dairy is by the back steps; sundries are in the fire pit . . .'"

"What are sundries?"

"Bottle openers, disposable lighters, that sort of thing. Let's have a look at that place-setting diagram." Dad grabbed the diagram off the fridge and stared at it. He put his hand on my head and massaged it, which is how my dad does some of his best thinking.

"It's as plain as the nose on your face, Miss Cassidy. Or should I say a plate. Home plate, to be exact. If I were imprisoned—pardon me, attending—etiquette school, I'd memorize the place setting on a baseball field. And I'd make this"—he grabbed a dish from the drainer—"home plate."

CHAPTER 19

Picnics Can Be Perfectly Awful when Bungled!

"Jack! Wait up. There's something I want to show you." With all the etiquette classes I had to take and all the lawns he had to mow, I'd barely seen Jack all week. With our volunteer time at the Humane Society (Mom's pathetic substitute for letting us get our own pet) and geocaching in Aman Park with Dad (who always has to practice Cache In Trash Out), here it was, Sunday night, and we hadn't even talked about possible pranks for tomorrow's picnic.

Now he was crossing our backyard with what looked like a big sausage in his arms. It's not easy to hide a big sausage, especially one with a bow tied around it, but that's what he tried to do as I ran to catch up with him.

"What's that?"

Jack squished the package to make it smaller. "Nothing."

"So . . . that's air inside that paper?"

"You mean this?" He looked at the bundle in his arms like he'd never seen it before, like it was no big deal. "Oh . . . just some—"

I made a grab for it, but he was too quick for me. Still, I tore an edge and *something* flew out. We were losing light fast. I dropped to the ground to see.

"It's not like I want to keep it," I told him. "I just want to see what . . . flowers? You got flowers in there?" I held up a sad droopy flower.

"Since you *have* to know, I accidentally Weedwacked a bunch of Mrs. Delaney's hydrangeas and she told me to get them out of her sight."

"So you tied them up in butcher paper and were taking them to Bree?"

Jack grabbed the flower and tried to push it back inside with the others. It was hard work. Hydrangeas are big and floppy. "Mom did that for me. She said that's how they come from the florist. What's wrong with that?"

"Nothing. You're really . . . gone on her, aren't you? Bree, I mean."

Ignoring my question, Jack set the flowers on the ground and held out his hand. "Well, what have you got? You were going to show me something."

"Nothing. Nope."

We both stared up at the glowing orange ball through the trees . . . silent.

"Suddenly there's a whole lot of nothing in this backyard,"

Jack said, right before faking left and grabbing the photo I was holding.

Blasted Jack Taylor! He was faster than . . . green grass through a goose.

"So, who's this? Great-Grandma Reed again?" Sitting down on the back step, Jack studied the picture in the porch light.

"Magda found it on findyourancestors.net." I sat down next to him. You couldn't really tell who was who in the photo since all the people were bundled up in big jackets with hoods. The caption on the back of the photo read: "Saving baby seals in Gdansk."

"Which one is she?"

"The lady who sent it to Magda said she was second from the right."

"You're sure this is Great-Grandma Reed?"

"Pretty sure, yep. Those people on findyourancestors.net spend a lot of time figuring out who's who. The lady who helped Magda is the granddaughter of this guy." I pointed to the man standing next to my great-grandma. "She says he was her boyfriend."

"She was really something, wasn't she?"

"What I can't figure is why she sent me off to etiquette school and not, I don't know, wilderness training. How much etiquette do you need to save a baby seal?"

"None, would be my guess." We sat there a minute, watching the fireflies. The light went off in the Bensons' kitchen.

"Oops." Jack jumped up and picked up his flowers. "Gotta go. See you at the picnic tomorrow, right?"

"If you're lucky. You should have cleaned the grass clippings off," I told him. "She's gonna know you didn't buy 'em."

"I tried, but they stick worse than cat hair."

"I'll have to start charging you to cross my backyard, you know," I called after him. "You're wearing a path in the grass."

"I can go by the road if you want."

"Jack!" Maybe Livvy was right. Maybe boys weren't worth the trouble.

"Later, Cass."

I wasn't about to stand there and watch—well, not from the back porch, anyway. I sat down near the bushes and listened as Bree got all emotional, saying things like "These flowers smell like summer" and "Every girl likes to be surprised," and Jack saying he was sorry about the grass clippings and Bree saying she knew just the thing to do to perk them up—immerse the buds in cold water for just a minute—and did Jack want to come in and have a glass of Arnold Palmer while she did it.

Which is just about the time I felt something really big crawl over my hand; I flung it off as I jumped to my feet, screaming like I was being hit with a billy club. Bree made a little yelping noise and asked Jack what was happening. Jack said it was nothing, just Cassidy, who always does that when she sees a bug.

And then the Bensons' back door closed.

The only way to properly mark time during summer is with the holidays—Memorial Day, Fourth of July, Magda's birthday and Labor Day. Memorial Day is one of my favorite holidays of all time. Celebrating it means you get a day off school and you're kissing distance from the last day. I try to feel sad on Memorial Day for all the soldiers who died for my freedom, but I don't think they'd mind me celebrating it—my almost freedom from school, that is.

Labor Day's a different story. You're about to head into a whole year of . . . labor. Who needs to be reminded? Magda's birthday is at the end of August. I do get a piece of real cake, but the summer's almost over and Magda gets the most boring presents imaginable.

Which brings me to Independence Day. On the downside, ever since the city decided to close the pools a week early to save money but keep the Fourth of July fireworks display, Mom has made us boycott the celebration downtown. I feel this is a violation of my rights as an American citizen, but no one in the Corcoran clan seems to care much about those. On the upside, it is now legal to buy fireworks in Michigan, making our neighborhood Fourth of July party a lot . . . longer. The explosions start around the third week in June and finish up about July 10.

Usually by now, we'd have gone to Lake Michigan, camped out at Michigan Pioneer Experience Park and even tubed down the Pine River. But who has time for dull stuff like that when you're learning to be a young lady and cough into your wrist?

Maybe that's why I vowed to soak up as much fun as I possibly could at the Fox Hills Fourth of July neighborhood picnic. I planned to eat more bratwurst and potato salad and drink more root beer on tap than your average young lady—*plus*, I would light more crackling balls and ground bloom flowers, and twirl more giant sparklers. Plus, *plus*, I would convince Mom to let me sit on the roof to watch the Deanders' teenage sons shoot off bottle rockets. (I have found if you want to be near the action on the Fourth of July, find some teenage boys and a dad who drives a pickup truck.)

But by now, you probably have a sense of how things trend for Cassidy Corcoran. There's karma that goes south and there's karma that treks to the South Pole—yours truly's. Yes, I was first in line for a brat—I even had two paper plates nestled together so I could keep my baked beans and my potato salad separate. But there came Mr. and Mrs. Fenster with wretched Percy, and Mom and Dad called me out of line to make polite conversation with them!

"It's so nice to see you, Mr. and Mrs. Fenster," I said, keeping my knees bent in the neutral position for a quick getaway. "How are you enjoying the Sunny Pointe Senior Center? I'm surprised, with all the concern over allergies and fleas and whatnot, they let you keep Percy." As soon as he heard his name cross my lips, Percy snarled at me.

"Percy's a senior, too, dear," Mrs. Fenster said. "And we do have our own condominium."

"Fine weather we're having . . ." I watched the neighborhood kids jumping in line for brats. Now I'd have to wait for the next round! A pair of redheaded twins, who looked to be about seven, cut in at a bend in the line. If I could get away with it, I might—

"Can you hear me, Miss Corcoran? I asked how your manners class is going." It seemed Mr. Fenster was determined to keep me from my brat. He leaned in. "Those are Mrs. Delaney's grandkids, by the way—visiting from Washington State. Mrs. Fenster and I call them Thing One and Thing Two. You know, after the two whirling dervishes in the Dr. Seuss book."

Though I had no interest in talking literature with Mr. Fenster, I did see what he meant—I counted at least six personal-space violations on those two while I was having my polite conversation.

"Young people today have an appalling lack of manners," I responded. "If you'll excuse me . . ."

I was about to sweet-talk my way into the food line when I heard Mrs. Benson calling my name. "Cassidy . . . can you . . . ?"

She looked positively lost in all the hustle and bustle of the Fox Hills Fourth of July celebration. "Honey," she said. "I brought that cake you liked so much, but there doesn't seem to be a cake table. In Decatur, we had a whole separate tent for desserts so the frosting could stay perky out of the sun."

I tried to imagine Mrs. Benson's cake on our dessert picnic table, which looked more like Hobby Lobby on the day after Christmas, with all the red-striped Rice Krispies Treats and boxes of neon Popsicles shoved into buckets of ice. There wasn't room for a flour and butter and sugar sculpture like hers.

Unless I *made* room for it. Taking the cake stand from Mrs. Benson, I said, "I'll make sure it doesn't melt." I figured holding that cake would gain me entrance to the back of the table, where the moms stood swatting away kids who tried to fill their plates with only desserts.

"Excuse me, ladies. You probably haven't met Mrs. Benson, but you will want to after you taste this cake."

Mrs. Cramer and Mrs. Lowe looked at me funny; I couldn't tell if it was because I was speaking in fine-manners language or because I'd just parked the Cadillac of desserts on their gingham tablecloth.

"Sounds like someone's been to a manners class," Mrs. Lowe said.

"Bingo." I gestured toward Mrs. Benson. "I'd like you to meet Mrs. Benson, the cake baker."

"Call me Olive Ann," Mrs. Benson said, reaching over me to shake hands. "Goodness, it's warm. Not like Decatur—we just moved here from Georgia—but certainly a hot one. I confess I'm worried about this cake."

According to Miss Melton-Mowry, Mrs. Benson had just fed these two ladies a couple of key pieces of information about herself; in fact, she'd given them a big serving of polite conversation. But the only thing they passed back to her was silence.

"Not sure where to put this," Mrs. Cramer said, finally, setting it down near the edge of the table.

"I want some of that." I looked up to see Thing One (or was it Thing Two?) bypass the salads and other sides and zero in on Mrs. Benson's cake. As soon as he got close enough, he put his hand on the glass cover, leaving a barbecue-sauce print.

"I call the first piece!" The other one pushed his brother's arm, smearing frosting against the glass.

Using the intensity of my gaze wasn't about to cut it with these two. I threw my arms around the cake cover in a variation of the cross-armed surfboard, ready to do what it took to protect Mrs. Benson's masterpiece. Unfortunately, she was moving in to defend at the same time.

"It's all right, Cassidy, I'll just take that—"

I was doing hold-the-fort and she was doing duck-and-cover. If we were in a WWE wrestling match and the cake was our opponent, we'd win the round for . . . crushing it.

"What is the matter with kids nowadays?" I asked Mrs. Benson as I scraped a third of the crumpled cake onto a paper plate.

"Would you ladies like to try a bite?" Still game to make friends, Mrs. Benson looked as crushed as the cake when Mrs. Cramer shook her head. "No thanks. I don't do gluten."

"No processed flour or sugar for me," added Mrs. Lowe, frowning.

By the time I cleaned up the mess and delivered Mrs. Benson to my dad, who offered her a virgin strawberry margarita with frozen blueberries—in honor of our great flag—all that was left were wrinkly, overcooked brats; Mrs. Pearce's quinoa salad with toasted sunflower seeds; and some half-melted Rocket pops.

And when it was dark enough for the neighborhood fireworks to begin, I'd only managed to convince Mom to let me watch out my bedroom window. Instead of getting a clear view of the Deanders' backyard or a fighting chance of seeing a starburst from downtown, I saw Jack demonstrating for Bree his ability to swing upside down in the oak tree while twirling two extra-long sparklers.

There was nothing left to do but construct the world's largest sweat lodge—which would probably require stealing all of Magda's and my parents' bedding. I was considering how to make this dream a reality when someone knocked on my door. Given the *Titanic* direction of my karma, I thought maybe it was Miss Melton-Mowry with some homework I'd forgotten to complete.

But no. It was Delton Bean.

"This is your room?" Delton asked as his eyes did a full one-eighty. "I would ask to come in, but—"

"Yes, it's booby-trapped. Plus, we have WWE wrestling tournaments in here; *plus,* I didn't invite you."

"No." Delton looked positively cheerful. "But *I* want to invite you over to Riverside Park. Your mom told me I'd probably find you moping up here."

"Riverside Park? Now?"

"Yes. My mother says that if you agree to wear the life vest, I can take you out in my uncle Roger's canoe and show you how to set off a sky lantern. I make them myself."

"Delton, you have to be the weirdest kid I have ever met."

"'Young man' is a more accurate term for an eleven-year-old, Miss Corcoran. And 'weird' is not a fit word for polite conversation. 'Quirky,' maybe? 'Eccentric'? 'Unconventional'?"

"Okay," I said. "Uncle. I'll wear the life vest."

And faster than a hot knife through butter—as Jack would say Bree would say—I was clipping it on at Riverside Park.

Mrs. Bean was not about to let us out of her sight; she did agree to sit on the park bench at the end of the dock, though, so she could follow our progress via the kerosene lamp we secured to the middle seat in the canoe. After we'd paddled for a minute, she disappeared into the darkness.

"Cassidy, I think . . . I might . . . I may have found another way to address your . . . anxiety."

"You mean with the bugs? Is that why you brought me out here, Delton?"

I squinted, trying to get a look at his face in the darkness. Was there any way he could know what happened last night with Jack?

"No, I brought you out here to help me launch my sky lanterns. But my dad says you should have business before pleasure."

Thinking of what Jack said to Bree sent a shiver down my

spine: *That's just Cassidy. She always does that when she sees a bug.*

Well, I didn't feel like being "just Cassidy" anymore. "I hope this doesn't involve smacking myself in the forehead, because that did not work."

"Tapping, not smacking, but I agree. EFT tends to draw unwanted attention, especially when you do it during Joys and Concerns in Sunday school. This one's a little different. It's called desensitization. You learn relaxation techniques and then look at pictures of what psychologists call a graduated list of the things you fear, from lowest to highest. Looking at or thinking about your fears while in a relaxed state breaks down the fear response. You can't feel anxiety when you are in a relaxed state."

"You're going to put me in a trance, aren't you."

"No. Deep relaxation isn't a trance. But it does work, Cassidy. After a week of practicing, I got everyone's attention at dinner at my grandparents'—I stood up, raised my glass of grape juice and said 'Cheers'—but I didn't break out in a sweat or anything. Next, Mom says she'll have me order at the counter when we go to Mr. Burger. You really have to shout at that place."

"All right. Deep relaxation is okay, but no hocus-pocus. Promise?"

"Promise."

Now that we'd taken care of business, I grabbed the sides of the canoe; I was about to threaten Delton with the move I got famous for during my one and only stint at Girl Scout camp when I realized I'd forgotten something. "Thank you, Mr. Bean," I said. Sincerely. Re-creating the Battle of Tippecanoe could wait.

"You're welcome. Now, let's row over to that dead log. I need to get set up." While I held on to the log to keep us still, Delton lifted the kerosene lamp and hooked it on a snag. Then he opened the box and pulled out big stiff triangles of tissue paper. I shone his flashlight on them so he could see.

"They're polyhedrons . . . ," he began to explain. "Three-dimensional objects with flat sides and straight edges. A bi-pyramid is the most common—" He was interrupted by the sound of a cell phone buzzing.

Delton pulled his phone out of his pocket. "Hi, Mom. I know visibility is low. We talked about the mist on the way over to Cassidy's, remember? Can you see the kerosene lamp? Uh-huh. That's where we're moored. You'll see the lanterns in a minute."

After several more assurances about the buckles on our life vests being fastened in accordance with the manufacturer's instructions, Delton ended the call. "Just remember, when I said it, it was true."

"So, you're going to make these things float?" I held up the paper ships. "Doesn't seem likely."

"Float *up*. They're like mini hot-air balloons. Problem is, there's not much visibility. We'll have to paddle after them to keep them in sight."

"I think I've seen these on TV. They lit up hundreds at the same time. I didn't know you could make them."

"I use the South American method as opposed to the Chinese. The Chinese used sky lanterns during wartime. They favor a large globe with a stiff paper collar—"

"Delton, can this please *not* be like manners class, where you talk something to death before you actually do it?"

"Sorry. Will you light this tea candle for me?"

I did what I was told and Delton placed the lighted candle in a little holder that hung down under his poly . . . whatever. He held it in his hand for maybe ten seconds before the hot air filled the lantern and it hovered above the canoe all by itself. Then, slowly, it started to rise. The light from the candle made the colored tissue paper glow, like a giant firefly bobbing in the air.

"Wow, I can barely see it anymore. Do another one."

"First we'll follow it. Turn your flashlight off for a minute." Delton pushed away from the log.

"Don't you want your lamp?"

"We'll come back for it . . . it's where we're moored, remember?"

"Delton! Are you pulling one over on your mom?"

"I prefer . . . ignorance is bliss."

Once we were further out, we could see the lantern again. We paddled downstream, following the bobbing light until it burst into flames and fell into the water.

"My dad and I design them to do that," he said as we pulled alongside the burned bits and he hauled the wire skeleton out with his oar. "We do it over water so they're not a fire hazard; plus, this way I can reuse the armature."

I lit another candle. Delton placed it in the wire basket of an airship that was pink and purple; it looked like its own setting sun as it rose into the sky.

After three more lanterns, we were almost to the Sixth Street Bridge; Delton's phone was blowing up with texts.

"Better head back," he said. We paddled in silence. Even though the current wasn't that strong, it was much harder

212

going upstream. But the clouds had lifted and here we were canoeing at night under about a million sky lanterns. It was the kind of place a hobo might find herself—minus the bright-orange life vest.

Suddenly, from behind, I heard a sonic boom that almost brought back Tippecanoe. "What was that?"

Delton looked at his phone. "Right on time. Downtown fireworks, Miss Corcoran."

"You mean . . . *city* fireworks?"

"Yep. I heard you complaining to Officer Weston about not being able to see the fireworks anymore." Delton dropped a metal claw over the side of the canoe and it sank in the mud.

"But . . . we're not even close to downtown."

"True, but the river is straight from here to downtown. Usually there are lots of boats out . . . I see a few . . . but the weatherman said the visibility was so poor tonight, it wouldn't be worth watching from the river."

The familiar whiz of an amazing firework about to explode made me look up; above my head, a thousand dancing sparklers lit up the sky.

"My dad has all kinds of gauges in the backyard; he's a bit of an expert on barometric pressure. He said the fog would lift just in time."

"I think your dad should get nominated for the Dad Hall of Fame, Delton. You can tell him I said that."

"I promise to relay your message."

"And now . . . let's shut it and watch the fireworks."

"Agreed."

It is hard to lie back and get comfortable in a canoe; but when your boat is bobbing gently in the water and the world's best kaleidoscope is exploding over your head, you don't really mind how hard the seat is.

"Delton Maximilian Bean!" Mrs. Bean shouted from the dock as we paddled in. "You were not supposed to stay out for the fireworks. You don't have your noise-canceling earbuds."

"Sorry, Mom. Can't hear you over the ringing in my ears."

Mrs. Bean investigated Delton's head like he'd just come back from the war, turning his face this way and that to make sure all the parts were in place.

"That was the best fireworks show ever, Mrs. Bean!" I said, laying on the enthusiasm. "I think your plan worked. Your son is now full of do-daring!"

Mrs. Bean held Delton at arm's length, regarding him like maybe she wasn't sure about this do-daring idea of hers. "Well," she said, finally. "I'm glad you enjoyed it, dear."

We drove home and, before I could make my getaway, Delton whispered, "Take this, Cassidy. You have to practice your breathing techniques before you look at even the smallest bug."

"Roger," I said, shoving the folded piece of paper into my back pocket. "Over and out. Oh . . ." I reached into the front seat and punched him in the arm . . . not too hard. "You're all right, Delton. Thanks. And thank you, Mrs. Bean. Happy Independence Day."

start

214

CHAPTER 20

Attire for the Summer Luncheon

"With our big luncheon only a week away . . ." Miss Melton-Mowry flipped through her notebook with so much energy she tore a page.

"Tick, tick, tick."

"That's not helpful, Officer Weston. As I was saying last week, we'll need to discuss what to wear. For men, business casual would normally be fine. That would be an open-collared shirt with a blazer; but, since we're trying to impress, I'd like you to dress in business attire—that would be jacket and tie. For the ladies . . ."

I stopped scratching my mosquito bites. I hoped, on top of everything else, I wasn't going to hear the five-letter word that always comes up around weddings, funerals and fifth-grade graduations.

"Cassidy will have to wear a dress, won't she?" Delton said.

"No I won't."

"A dress is the correct attire for a summer luncheon, Miss Corcoran. I'm sure your mother will find something appropriate."

"We can leave my mother out of this, Miss Melton-Mowry. I don't wear dresses. I . . . I'm allergic."

"Allergic?"

Officer Weston leaned closer and whispered in my ear, "Make this fly and I'll buy you an ice cream sandwich."

"It's just that I get all itchy and twitchy when I put one on." I stood up to demonstrate, doing a pose I learned in yoga that looks like you're trying to scratch an itch between your shoulder blades. Since Miss Melton-Mowry didn't seem impressed, I threw in a few zombie moves for good measure.

"Be that as it may, you'll have to find a fabric that doesn't irritate your skin. Need I remind you, Miss Corcoran, that you are participating in this event as restitution for damaging my property?"

I glanced over at Miss Information, whose head was still in her lap. I'm pretty sure Miss Melton-Mowry left it there to remind me even when *she* wasn't reminding me.

"No. But how come they invented dresses, anyway? You wear one and you can't climb on the monkey bars or swing on the swings unless you want everyone and their uncle to get a free show."

"Jersey's a good choice," Delton said, risking a massive demerit to consult his phone under the table. "It's a soft knit fabric and it moves with you, so it would be appropriate for your active lifestyle."

"Give me that." I tried to swipe Delton's phone. "I want to look up 'straitjacket.'"

"Mr. Bean! Put your phone away this instant. Miss Corcoran knows how important it is to live up to her agreement. I am sure—"

"If I don't wear a dress, will I go to jail? Even though I'm a kid?"

"We lock kids up, too." Officer Weston yawned and put his elbow on the table so he could prop up his head. He probably had to work a double shift to make up for all the time he spent in etiquette class. "C'mon, Cassidy. Let's learn the rules of polite society. I've only got a couple of weeks to get reformed myself."

"I will be very pleased to wear a dress to the country-club luncheon, Miss Melton-Mowry," I said in my best robot zombie voice (though I did not stick my arms out).

"Thank you, Miss Corcoran. Let's review the cutlery now, shall we?"

"I don't know how a person is supposed to enjoy lunch when she's all wrapped up like a Christmas present in bows and ribbons," I said to Delton as we stood at the window waiting for our moms.

"From my observation, most girls seem to enjoy wearing dresses."

"Well, you must be observing some very strange girls."

"Cassidy, I was thinking . . . do you want to come over tonight? I've compiled an impressive list of insects that you—" Delton was interrupted by his mother coming through the front door and throwing her arms around him.

"Hello, Cassidy," she said, after she'd kissed Delton's head maybe four times. "How are you on this beautiful day?"

"Well, to be honest, I've been better, Mrs. Bean. I tried creating my own reality during etiquette class and making a power outage, but I couldn't even get the lights to flicker."

"Delton is enjoying class with you. What did you say about Cassidy the other night after the fireworks, Delton? Oh, I remember. You're a real live wire."

"A live wire would have worked, too. Usually they evacuate the entire area when there's a downed power line. Or maybe a sewer backup."

Mrs. Bean looked at her son. I could tell she was wondering what the polite-conversation response to a sewer backup was.

Despite all the etiquette mind-washing, I still had the touch.

"Say, Mrs. Bean, would you mind if I came over tonight so Delton and I could practice our, um, cutlery skills?"

"Of course not. In fact, if you like, you could come over *for* dinner and practice. We've been setting the table just like Miss Melton-Mowry does so Delton will be ready for your big luncheon."

"Oh, that's okay. We're doing that at my house, too. Miss Information was supposed to have dinner with us tonight but she's under the table."

"Don't you mean 'under the weather'?"

"Right. Under the weather."

Honestly. *How did I get here?* I mean, making polite conversation with Delton Bean's mom? Asking to go over to his house? I told myself if Delton could teach me not to flip out when something squirmed or crawled in front of me, then I could run off on my own—no Jack required.

"It's a deal, then," I said, looking around for my own mom. Enough chitchat.

Time to go to the park.

"If my stomach wasn't rumbling like Saturday afternoon at the River City Raceway," I told Mom once we were in the car, "I would have you drop me off at the park."

"I'm afraid we have another errand after lunch, Miss Cassidy. I just spoke with Miss Melton-Mowry about the luncheon. It seems we'll be needing a dress for you."

"Ugh." I curled up in the backseat. *"Help me, I'm melting."* I was doing my best Wicked Witch of the West impression, but Mom didn't even glance in the rearview mirror. I stayed a puddle for thirty seconds before I said, "Seriously, Mom?"

"Seriously."

"The torture just goes on and on."

"Let's not worry about that now. What did you learn in etiquette class today?"

"I learned there really is such a thing as being bored to death."

"But you're not dead."

"Not yet. Etiquette class is like arsenic poisoning. It takes time. I promise you, by the end of the summer, I'll be pushing up daisies."

❋

"Look at that face." Magda passed me a paper napkin, which I was required to fold and place next to my fork, now that we officially set the table at the Corcoran Estate. "You look like you ate a whole package of Warheads."

"You'd wear this expression, too, dear sister, if Mom was making *you* shop for a dress." I set down the butter knife, business side toward the plate, and the spoon next to that.

Mom smacked a peanut butter and jelly sandwich down on the table in front of me. "You wouldn't have to shop for a new dress if you hadn't wrecked your graduation dress."

"How was I supposed to know all that lace wasn't flame-retardant? FYI, serve from the left, Mom."

Mom sat down and put her elbows on the table and her chin on her fists. "FYI, this isn't exactly how I hoped to spend my summer afternoon, either."

Instead of pointing out her many etiquette don'ts, I said, "I know. I'm sorry, Mom. Maybe we could cut off the parts I burned?"

"You'd look like Cinderella in the part of the story where she was being abused," Magda chimed in. "Bad idea."

Swiping my finger across my plate, I stuck a jelly-covered digit in my mouth. "I've got a better idea. Let's take a break from being miserable. Want to eat lunch on the roof with me, Mom?"

"Your finger is not a utensil, Miss Corcoran. And the roof isn't . . . I know! We could all eat together outside on a picnic blanket. Remember when you girls were little and we used to lie under the oak tree while I read *Anne of Green*—"

"Sorry, Mom." Magda pushed back from the table. "I'm conducting an experiment that needs constant surveillance. I say we let Cassidy commune with nature by herself." Grabbing a handful of potato chips, she stuck one in her mouth before adding, "She needs time alone to set an intention to be civil while you're shopping."

"I can eat in the oak tree," I offered.

"Fine, but no higher than the second floor. Oh, and I almost forgot. This arrived in the mail for you today." Mom handed me an envelope covered in skulls and crossbones, except for the part with my name and address written on it.

Grabbing it out of my hand, Magda said, "This looks like hate mail. Maybe it needs to spend some time in my laboratory to ensure it doesn't contain any suspicious substances."

"It's top-secret," I said, trying to grab it back.

But Magda held it out of my reach. "Top-secret from the Door County Academy of Gymnastics?"

"It's the kind of letter that should only be read in a tree." Mom took the letter from Magda and handed it back to me. Then she put my sandwich in my lunch box and threw in a couple of extra cookies, maybe to show there were no hard feelings about her picnic idea.

With my lunch-box handle in my mouth and the letter in my back pocket, I climbed up our oak tree to the piece of plywood Jack and I had wedged into a spot where three big branches split off from the trunk. I was glad Magda and Mom had seen my supersecret letter from Livvy filled with the code no one but me could read because I'd spent *hours* memorizing it over the weekend. Well, it felt like hours. Maybe Magda would mention it to Bree, who would mention it to Jack, who would discover he wasn't the only one in the world with secrets.

But first things first. I was starving.

Balancing the lunch box on the plank, I opened it, broke off half of a half of sandwich and crammed it into my mouth.

"Tree etiquette," I said with my mouth more than full. "One, always eat with your mouth open and spray as many crumbs as possible. While mumbling. Two, if you wipe your mouth, do it with the back of your hand and then, if the food is good, three, lick it off. If not, swipe it on your shorts. Four, never, *ever* use a napkin. It will either blow away or you'll drop it. Save a tree and use the tails of your shirt if you have to."

Impressed with my new set of rules, I searched the ground for someone who might be eavesdropping. How do you know if you're funny if there's nobody to hear you? Even Bree wasn't around.

I leaned back against a gnarly branch and slipped the letter out of my pocket. I also pulled out the piece of paper Delton had given me in class; that one could wait.

Careful not to tear any of the great pirate art, I used my fingernail under the flap and worked to get the letter open— mostly—without tearing. This was going to be great—for once, I'd done my homework. Only three people in the world— me, Livvy and Judy Hansen, whoever she was—could read it.

Only, I couldn't read it. I stared at the letter for a full minute. It was written in code all right, but it wasn't the code I'd memorized! Instead of moons and lightbulbs and candy canes, there were angles and squares and dots. It was a different code! I crumpled up the letter and stuffed it into my lunch box. Did she have so many friends and codes that Livvy Dunn couldn't keep them straight?

Of course, I couldn't cross my arms and legs in the tree, so I just sat there fuming. What was the matter with that girl?

To calm down I tried chanting *om;* I even looked cross-eyed at a cardinal that had the great misfortune to land near me in case that would help. Instead, I ended up throwing one of my cookies at it.

If I climbed down now, I risked taking my anger out on another human being, which meant I'd be grounded for life for assault—probably on my older sister.

There was nothing to do but read the note of instructions Delton had given me—written in plain English.

"Cassidy, I copied this off the Internet. Read it through at least a few times before you try imagining an invertebrate."

Full-Diaphragm Breathing and Progressive
Relaxation for Panic Disorder
by Dr. C. T. Mills (anxietydoc.com)

Panic disorder? Was that what Delton thought I had? *Was* that what I had? Maybe some full-diaphragm breathing would help me forget the *hours* I had wasted this weekend learning the Chipmunk Code!

When people experience a phobia, they often report being short of breath. Some feel they can't breathe at all. However, if you can say "I can't breathe," you can, in fact, breathe, because we speak by making air vibrate.

The trouble is, you are only breathing with your upper body or your chest. You need to learn to breathe with your belly.

Geez. You'd think a doctor would know that your stomach was in your belly, not your lungs.

I stuck the paper under my lunch box and ripped the straw off my juice box. Slurping—loud—I balanced a cookie on my nose. Then I tried to touch it with my tongue before reading more.

What you want to do is activate your diaphragm, the muscle that inflates your lungs. To do this, place one hand on your belly and one on your chest and practice breathing with only the belly hand moving.

I followed the instructions. Though this was difficult to do in a tree, I think I figured out what all those pale-faced teenagers were doing in yoga class—breathing from the bottom of their stomachs. The next thing I was supposed to do was close my eyes and check in with different parts of my body. Starting at my feet, I tensed them up and then relaxed them. Then I went to my calves. Then my knees. How were you supposed to tense your knees, I wondered.

The cool part was, all this distracting was making it easier to forget how much I wanted to punch a certain someone.

"Cassidy, it's time to go," I heard Mom shout from the base of the tree.

"I'm meditating," I shouted back.

"Well, you'll have to finish in the car."

"Who meditates in the car?" I asked after my face had been scrubbed with a washcloth and a comb yanked through my hair. Like a four-year-old.

"People with schedules. My book club is tonight and I still have to make my spaghetti pie."

"Are you going to cook one for us?"

"No, I'm going to let you starve. Of course I am, though I do have conditions."

"You're not going to make us eat like we're polite society at dinner again, are you?"

"Yes, I am, in fact. And if you're lucky, I'll let you demonstrate for Norma Pearce when she comes by to pick me up."

"Seriously?"

"Not really, but I do have some conditions for this store visit, young lady. I want you to promise there will be no zombie act, no cross-eyed looks, no stuttering, no sneezing fits, no diabetic comas, no fainting spells, no sudden blindness. In other words, behave yourself. There's a spaghetti pie on the line."

Mom pulled into the parking lot, parked crooked and slammed the door after she got out—Corcoran sign language for "not in the mood." I had to give it a try anyway.

"C'mon, Cassidy."

"I can't . . . I can't feel my legs."

"Did I forget to say 'no paraplegic stunts'?" Mom yanked on my arm and half dragged me into the store.

"Good afternoon, ladies. Can I help you find something?"

"Are you sure you're up to the challenge, Ms. . . ." Mom squinted to read her name tag. "Evans?"

"I just celebrated my ten-year anniversary at Stetler's." She pointed to a star next to her name. We started the long walk to the juniors' department.

"Good . . . a veteran. Cassidy here needs a dress for a summer luncheon at the country club."

"Oh. I see. You might find this section more . . . appropriate." Ms. Evans did a half-turn and started to walk in the opposite direction.

"It's not our country club. She'll be a . . . guest."

"Gotcha." We did another about-face and headed back in the direction we'd come from.

"What do you think Great-Grandma Reed would have worn?" I asked Mom.

"Battle fatigues, I imagine, from the photos you and Magda have been finding."

I started to ask where the camouflage section was, but I resisted. I was hoping to see sunlight again at some point today.

"What's your favorite color, Cassidy?" Ms. Evans asked me.

"Don't say—"

"Black. What? Mom, you know I'm always in mourning when I have to wear a dress."

"She likes blue," my mom said. "It brings out her eyes."

"Mmm." Ms. Evans flicked through dresses on the racks, holding one out every now and then to consider it. You'd think *she* was going to the lunch at the country club.

I pretended to be looking, too, but really, I was backing away. Before they imprisoned me in a dressing room, I was hoping for a few turns on the escalator.

"It's a hard age to buy for," Ms. Evans was saying to Mom. "Not a little girl, but not yet a young lady, either."

"You can say that again."

I left juniors and got lost in misses. Who knew there were so many ways to look like a flower? Over the top of a rack of dresses, I saw Bree. Or I *thought,* just for a minute, that I saw

Bree. It was only a mannequin; still, from the back it looked a lot like her. Same hair, same headband! And a dress she'd probably wear on her first day of high school. I went closer. The skirt felt like tissue paper—only stiff—and there were flowers on the sleeves. I got a vision of two floats colliding at the May Day parade. Disgusting.

I ran to my mom and pulled her back to the dummy. "I want this one," I said.

"You can't be serious."

"It is beautiful," Ms. Evans clucked. "So feminine. Funny, I hadn't pegged you for a girly-girl."

"Oh, I'm as girly as they get, Ms. Evans." To cement the deal, I winked at her.

"Cassidy?" Mom was squeezing my arm.

"Have you and Ms. Evans discussed this fine weather we're having?" I asked Mom. "Because if not, I'd like to get in on that. Personally, I favor clouds . . . just one or two, for variety."

"What are you playing at, young lady?" Mom whispered as Ms. Evans dove deep into the rack to find a dress my size.

Drawing my shoulders back for dining posture, I raised my nose up an inch and sniffed. "Mrs. Corcoran. I don't want to play at being a young lady. I want to be one." I unlatched Mom's fingers from my arm and took the dress. "Thank you, Ms. Evans."

In the dressing room, I wondered, *Do you need a map to get into this thing?* First there were buttons, then a zipper, then these little thingies that looked like baby fishhooks.

"It'd be easier to crack a safe," I mumbled, yanking it over my head with my eyes closed. Once I had it over my head, I groped my way to the mirror, eyes still squeezed shut. When I finally opened them, I threw my hands up to protect me from the girl staring back at me.

"Disaster" was too kind a word. I sat down on the little bench they put in every dressing room to give myself a pep talk.

You can do this, Cassidy. Create your own reality!

I stood in front of the mirror again. Maybe if I pulled my hair out of the collar and mussed it up like I've seen girls do on TV.

Funny, that's how my hair usually looked, especially if I managed to escape Mom and her long-toothed comb of doom. There was no doubt about it. I looked like one of those missing kids whose photos they put on the back of milk cartons.

What would Livvy think if she saw me now?

Then I remembered I didn't care what Livvy thought. Livvy only got an opinion when I received a letter filled with candy canes and kites and balloons. It's what Jack thought that mattered. Even though he'd lost his marbles, I still wanted him to be my best friend.

Plastering a smile on my face, I left the dressing room. "Perfect," I said, twirling around like a runway model.

"This is the dress you *choose* to wear to the luncheon?"

I nodded, keeping my smile in place.

"I'm going to make you sign an agreement to that effect before we cut off the tags."

"That would be lovely, Mrs. Corcoran." I scooted back into the dressing room to remove the monstrosity.

At the cash register, I pretended to look over the scarves while Mom and Ms. Evans had more polite conversation.

"How old is Cassidy?" Ms. Evans asked.

"Eleven."

"Girls change at this age . . . their interests change. I see it all the time."

"Trust me. She's up to something."

Moving over to the sunglasses, I tried on a pair. The best thing about sunglasses is that when you're wearing them, no one can tell if you're fibbing.

"One summer they're being dragged in here in dungarees; the next year they're asking to try on the perfume."

"Can I try on the perfume?" I asked Ms. Evans. "What are dungarees?"

"Blue jeans," Mom said. "And no you may not."

"Tell me you didn't cut the tags off," Magda said when Mom showed her the dress. She and Bree were up in Magda's room working on some DIY project for Bree that involved loads of pink fabric and a staple gun.

"Of course I didn't. She's up to something. I thought I'd give you first crack at breaking her."

Bree took the safety pins out of her mouth. "Never judge a dress until it's on."

"You want me to put it on *again*? Isn't it enough that I put it on in the store?"

"I thought you loved it," Mom said. "You told the saleslady that it made you feel like a pretty pink flower."

Magda pressed her hand to my forehead. "She's young to be exhibiting signs of delusional disorder."

"That was just polite conversation," I said, in my defense.

"Well, go try it on, then." Magda handed her wad of fabric

to Bree. "Maybe on your body it will undergo some alchemical transformation."

"It's so feminine," Mom said, shoving the dress at me. "Take it to the bathroom, Cassidy. And when you have it on, picture yourself at Cousin Laurel's wedding in August, too. Maybe even the first day of middle school."

I went into the bathroom, but instead of trying on the dress, I pressed my ear to the door.

"Mom, she is not wearing that dress. If you think Cassidy—"

"Maybe she's trying to catch the eye of a certain someone, Magda? A certain someone who is trying to catch the eye of a certain someone who loves . . . pink?"

I almost came charging back out, but then Bree said, "Well, bravo for Cassidy for fighting for what she wants. I say, let's help her."

I couldn't hear any more because I proceeded to try to commit suicide by suffocating myself in a wad of gauzy fabric. The smile was a little harder to make stick than it had been in the store. Looking in the mirror, all I could think about was the time I dropped a perfectly good billow of rainbow cotton candy on the ground at the Michigan State Fair.

"I'm not sure I can handle the sight of this twice in one day," I heard Mom say. "I'll leave you girls to it."

"Oh, Cassidy." Magda adjusted her glasses like she was trying to focus me. "You look like a wedding cake."

"Your instincts were correct, Magda." Bree reached out and touched the sleeve of the dress. "Don't cut the tags off."

"Bree! Are you up there? I got the curtain rod you wanted from Ace Hardware." Jack came bounding up the stairs. "It wasn't so easy riding up Fulton Street with it bungeed to the back of my bike, but that's where years of walking the top of the fence—"

I put my hands in front of my face again, shielding me from Jack's expression.

"Cassidy? Is that you? Why are you dressed like a fairy?"

"Excuse me?" Getting huffy is a proven defense when you are caught doing something extremely stupid. "Are you saying you don't like this dress, Jack?"

"Why would I like it? It's . . . pink . . . and flowers. If you tried to climb out the window in that, you'd probably get strangled on the way down. Not to mention if you jumped onto a speeding train—"

"Fine. I get it."

Bree took hold of my shoulders. "It's not the dress, Cassidy—"

"It's definitely the dress," Magda said.

For the first time ever, I saw an unhappy look cross Bree's face. "It's *not* the dress. It's *you* in the dress. What I mean is, the dress is not you."

"It's like me wearing a bow tie," Jack said, handing the rod to Magda. "It doesn't work."

"Well, what *should* I wear?" I tried to sit on the edge of the bed, but all the layers of the dress made it so I just kinda leaned on it. "I can't go naked to the luncheon. I can't wear dungarees."

"What are dungarees?" Jack sat next to me. Like *he'd* been invited to this conversation.

Bree put her arms around me, which I didn't mind so much

because it blocked the view of my hideous dress from Jack Taylor. "Believe it or not, Cassidy, there are dresses for girls like you. Let me go next door and get my fashion magazine."

"Delton said I should wear jersey," I mumbled.

"I thought jersey was a cow," Jack said.

"Thanks, Jack!" I ran into the bathroom and slammed the door, hard enough to make my teeth rattle.

"No, wait." Bree stayed on the other side, talking to me. "I don't know who Delton is, but that's brilliant. Jersey is a fabric that was first used by Coco Chanel. Do you know who Coco Chanel is, Cassidy?"

"No, and with a name like that, I don't want to."

"She was a fashion designer in the olden days. She got women out of corsets—you know those tight things around their waists—and into dresses where they could move freely. And she used jersey to do it. Before that, jersey was only used for men's underwear."

"So I'd be wearing men's underwear to the luncheon?" At least this sounded more interesting.

"You better take this seriously." Magda had joined Bree at the door. "I can tell you right now, Cassidy. That dress goes above and beyond calamity into catastrophe territory."

"Magda, hand me your iPad. Come out, Cassidy, and I'll show you."

I stuffed the dress in the dirty laundry and put my shorts and T-shirt back on.

"She's not so bad," Jack said, looking at the screen Bree was holding up. "I like the cigarette holder."

"So I get to wear men's underwear *and* wave a cigarette holder?" I leaned over. It was still an old-fashioned dress, but it wasn't as bad as the one I'd just stuffed down the laundry chute.

"It says here on Wiki that Coco Chanel's qualities included ". . . genius . . . lethal wit, sarcasm and [a] maniacal destructiveness, which intrigued and appalled everyone.'"

"Let me see that." I took the iPad from Bree. "Do they have a store for her?"

"No, but she's still influencing dressmakers. We'll help you find something, Cass. Mama and I love to shop."

ready for next plate

CHAPTER 21

Business Meetings in the Home

"Hi, Mrs. Bean."

"Come in, Cassidy. We've been expecting you." Mrs. Bean stood back and gestured for me to walk through the door. She moved her arm exactly the same way Miss Melton-Mowry did when she taught us how to greet people.

"Will I meet the third Bean tonight?" I asked, trying to erase from my brain the image of Delton teaching his mom everything we learned in etiquette class.

"Oh, you must mean Dr. Bean. Yes, I'm sure he'll pop in to say hello." Standing in the Beans' hallway, all I could see was a lot of windows, some houseplants with very good posture, and white carpeting in the hall and the living room. White carpeting would never fly in the Corcoran household; according to my dad, the way I tore through the house, and with the chemicals Magda spilled, we should buy stock in OxiClean.

"I'm not sure it's proper that you go see Delton in his room, but if you're comfortable with that . . ." Mrs. Bean looked up the stairs, as if she wished *she* was the one being invited into Delton's room.

"I'm okay with it. I'm guessing . . . ?" I pointed at the stairs. She nodded.

"Well, it's been really enjoyable chatting with you; let's do this again soon, Mrs. Bean. Maybe a spot o' tea." I thought about showing off my Irish brogue, but decided I'd better get down to business.

Mrs. Bean covered her mouth to hide a mom-giggle. "Oh, Cassidy."

I bounded up the stairs, taking two at a time (my politeness muscle only lasts for so long and then I have to change locations). Stopping in front of a door with the name plaque DELTON BEAN on it, I noticed another sign hanging from the doorknob. It was like one you'd see on the door of a shop with the word OPEN on one side. Before I knocked, I flipped it over, and yes, it said CLOSED.

"Cassidy? Is that you?" Delton opened his door.

"What—could you hear me breathing?"

"I heard you stomping." Delton straightened the sign that read CLOSED. "Good. You flipped it over." He pulled me inside.

"So how come you're 'closed' now?"

"I had to work that out with my mother; 'closed' means that she is not to interrupt me. My therapist said a sign would help me articulate my boundaries."

"Your therapist?"

"Yes, I see Mrs. Dennon on a regular basis to work through my social anxiety and to help with my individuation."

I pinched myself. Was I really standing in Delton Bean's bedroom? It looked like I imagined a mental ward would—one of those places where they take everything out so you can't commit suicide. The walls were painted white, the carpet was—surprise!—white and the bedspread was white.

"You're noticing the minimalist appearance of my room, aren't you?" he asked me.

I quick-checked Delton's feet to see if he was wearing shoelaces—far and away the top choice for stringing yourself up in solitary confinement.

He was in slippers!

"My mom thinks a blank canvas inspires creativity. But . . . it's not as bad as it first appears." Delton walked over to some folding doors and pushed them open. There was a desk with a computer, some model airplanes on shelves and Delton's clothes folded neatly in stacks.

"Look," he said, pointing to a pile of shoes on the floor. "It's today's act of rebellion."

"You rebel with shoes?" I landed with a bounce on Delton's bed, creating at least a hundred wrinkles.

"They belong here." Delton got on his tiptoes to point out the spot on the shelf where his shoes belonged. "I piled them on top of each other for added effect."

"Well, Delton . . ." Rolling onto my stomach, I let my head hang over the side. "You are something. I'm not sure what, but . . . can we get down to business now?"

236

"Just one question . . . about the shoes. If you were my mom, would this make you angry?"

"That's the only square foot in this room that looks normal, Delton. You're a kid! I'd see it as a sign of hope. Now, where are you hiding all those bugs? Bring 'em on. I've mastered the deep-breathing stuff."

To demonstrate my mastery, I puffed out my belly and blew.

Delton sat down at his computer and typed in his password. "Go slower . . . more controlled. When I use the biofeedback machine in Mrs. Dennon's office, I get the best reading when I breathe slowly."

"Slow. Got it." I huffed slower. "My knees are great right now. Very relaxed." Half closing my eyes, I checked in with a few other places. "There's some tension in my fishing arm, but that's because I ought to be on the dock at Riverside Park instead of lying with my head over the side of your bed."

"The PowerPoint's ready." Delton swiveled around in his chair to face me. "But just to clarify about the shoes—"

"Delton, if you want me to teach you how to annoy your parents, I can do that. I practically have an advanced degree in Annoyance and Obfuscation. But earlier today *you* promised to cure *me*. I. Go. First."

My brain was pulsing with blood. I flopped on the floor to redistribute.

"Delton? Is everything okay?" Delton's mom was knocking on the door.

"Tell her you're giving yourself a tattoo," I whispered. Then, to be polite, I gestured. "Down there."

"I . . . I'm giving myself a tattoo. Just in erasable ink, but it's . . . down there."

"Down where? Delton? You have a lady present."

I drew my finger across my throat. Silence would be the best way to send Mrs. Bean to the moon without a spaceship. But of course Delton wouldn't cooperate.

"Cassidy's not looking . . . she's . . . meditating."

"I knew your room was an inappropriate place for the two of you to study. I told Arthur that and he didn't believe me. Arthur? Arthur?"

"I assume Arthur's your dad," I said after her voice disappeared down the hall.

Delton nodded. "Wow. You are . . . really good at that."

Polishing my knuckles on my shirt, I responded, "Yes, I am, Mr. Bean. I might be a little better at that than you are at sucking up to Miss Melton-Mowry. If only we got graded for driving parents crazy. Sigh. Okay, I'm ready to work."

"Here." Delton rolled a stool out of his closet and had me sit on it. "We'll start with pleasant associations."

The first picture that came up was of a big field and, at the top of a hill, a Frisbee-golf basket. "Is that a Mach Ten?"

"Not sure, but check in with your body. Is your heart beating a little faster?"

I leaned in closer. "Sure it is. I would love to play that course."

"It's important to understand that adrenaline works both ways. It can be generated because you are afraid and you want to run away *or* because you are excited. Let's bring you back to home base. Breathe."

"Home base. Cool. I like the sports metaphors." I took a deep breath and looked at the screen one more time. "Sorry. This just makes me wanna cut class and go play Frisbee, Delton."

The next slide was a picture of a pill bug, all curled up. I took a few loud breaths to show Delton I was still mellow. Without all those waving legs, it wasn't hard to look at. So of course the next picture was a pill bug on its back with *all those waving legs*. Latching onto Delton's shoulder, I squeezed hard.

"Ouch! Cassidy! Sit down and breathe. Mrs. Dennon says, 'Return to your body.'"

"I'd rather return to home base." I let go of Delton's shoulder and started checking in with my body parts—anything to stop the image of that bug on its back, struggling.

The screen went blank. "I thought we might need a break after this one," Delton said. "Do you want some water?"

Delton handed me a water bottle and I took a couple of swigs.

"Do you mind if I ask why, Cassidy? *Why* does that scare you? Pill bugs don't bite."

"I don't know." Wiping my mouth with the back of my hand, I set the bottle down. "Why do audiences scare you? They don't bite, either."

"I don't know, either. I . . . I think they upset me because I feel . . . vulnerable . . . exposed."

"Yeah, well, maybe that's why I don't like watching bugs squirm. It feels like it's me who can't turn over."

"Really? Then you're not so much afraid *of* them as you are afraid *for* them."

"I don't know! Does it make a difference why they give me the creeps?"

"It does, actually. With me, for example, Mrs. Dennon tells

239

me that it's okay not to be perfect. When I'm standing in front of the class, I feel like if I'm not perfect, something bad will happen."

"Like what?"

"Like I'll get a bad grade."

"I'm living proof you can survive that, Delton."

"So what bad thing will happen if you see a squirming bug?"

I thought about it. "It's like one of those movies where a man is standing on the sidewalk, minding his own business, and you see . . . the shadow of something—like an air conditioner—falling. You just . . . you want to run in and give him a good push so he doesn't get squashed . . . but it's all happening so fast you can't stop it."

I rubbed my eyes to get rid of the image. "Do you always keep your house so cold?" I asked, hugging myself.

"Your blood rushed from your extremities to your heart when you hit the panic button," Delton said. "I have a sweater if you want it."

"No thanks."

Delton sat back, making his office chair squeak. "All this time I thought you were afraid."

Honestly, I couldn't see why it made any difference, but Delton seemed happy about it. "Okay," I said. "I'm ready. Let's try again."

The next slide was of a girl fishing off a dock. She'd caught something. Her line was tight. I knew the next minute there'd be a fish struggling on the line. Slow breathing is tougher than it sounds. I tried counting one-potato, two-potato.

"Ugh!" I screamed as Delton switched to a slide of a worm squirming on a hook. "Delton Bean!" Running over to the bed, I jumped on it and covered my eyes. I counted through a whole bag of potatoes before I opened them again, only to see a tall man in a vest standing in front of me.

"Are you all right, young lady? Sorry to interrupt, Delton; the screams drew me in."

"That's all right, Dad. We're looking at an escalating slide show of Cassidy's irrational fears."

Dr. Bean pulled up the stool I'd just left empty and sat down on it. The smell of pipe tobacco filled the room. "Is this some new fad I have yet to read about?"

"No. I'm just showing her what Mrs. Dennon taught me so that she can apply transfer of knowledge to her reaction when she sees bugs."

"Hmmm . . . when I was a kid, we spent summer evenings trading baseball cards and playing hide-and-seek."

"Let's go back to the good old days." I jumped up and stuck out my hand—anything to get that vision out of my head. "Nice to meet you, Dr. Bean."

"And you, Cassidy. Your reputation precedes you."

"That's usually how it works."

"So you're the one who's been charged with infusing some spirit into Delton."

"I guess."

Dr. Bean pulled a toothpick out of his pocket and stuck it in the corner of his mouth. "But first, bugs."

Pipe smoke. Toothpicks. Maybe there was hope for Delton.

"Well, I don't want to interrupt. It's been very nice to meet you, Miss Cassidy. I wish you luck—with both challenges."

Dr. Bean closed the door on his way out.

"Delton, there's something I need to show you." Before I'd

decided to bring Livvy's letter to Delton's house, I thought over the oath I'd taken. *She* might not keep her promises, but I did. I decided since I was not revealing the Chipmunk Code or anything written in the Chipmunk Code, it didn't matter that Delton was a boy.

"I met this girl and then she went to camp and now she wants to write letters . . . in code."

"That sounds intriguing."

"Crazy-making is more like it. She gave me a code to memorize and then she sent me this." I pulled the letter out of my pocket and smoothed the paper on his desk. "This is *not* the code she had me memorize. Why would she do something like that, Delton?"

Delton put his face close to the paper, studying it. "There are several possible explanations for this, Cassidy, but first a question. How well does she know you?"

I thought for a minute. "She knows I have a sister who's addicted to mold; she knows I like hobos; she knows—"

"Does she know you like pranks? Because that's the most likely explanation. She's pulling a prank on you."

"On *me*? Nobody pulls pranks on me!"

"Well, you could call it by some other name, but I'm betting she's sitting on her bunk bed at camp right now busting a gut—as you say—thinking about you trying to read this letter."

"Are you serious? Because if it's true, that stinks! In fact, it stinks so bad . . ."

What was it Bree said when Magda let her smell the bottle of sulfur?

242

"That stinks bad enough to knock a dog off a meat wagon! I spent time on my free Saturday memorizing that stupid code."

The whole idea of being pranked made me so annoyed I had to get some air time on Delton's bed just to release the tension.

"Cassidy, it's not a good—"

"I'm just helping you rebel, Delton, by . . . making wrinkles." After a full sixty seconds of bouncing the way Livvy taught me, I landed in a sitting position to catch my breath.

"You know what, Delton?" I said, still huffing. "What Livvy doesn't realize is that *I* have a secret weapon."

"A secret weapon?"

"Yes, right here in this room. My secret weapon is your giant head."

"Me? My . . ." Delton started to get that look he gets when we're putting on our choir robes for the Christmas concert.

"Yes! I need your brains, Einstein. Is this gibberish? Or is it a code?" I jumped up from the bed, took his head in my hands and turned it back to the page. "Study."

"It does seem to conform to a certain pattern . . . clearly some sort of mono-alphabetic substitution . . ." Delton scanned the letter, talking to himself like he does when solving ninth-grade algebra problems while the rest of us work on graphing and tables.

Finally, he looked up at me. "It will take me a while to crack it."

"That Livvy has a lot of nerve. Do you know Donna Parker said I reminded her of Livvy?"

"I can't think why . . ."

"It's probably because we're both mercurial," I told him.

"I'm not familiar with that. Mercurial?"

"Really? I use it all the time. It means we change our mind."

"Mercurial . . ." Delton typed the word into his computer. "According to the Internet, 'mercurial' means 'volatile, temperamental, unpredictable, erratic, moody, impulsive, excitable . . .' With all that volatility, I'm not sure you and your new friend should be in the same room, Cassidy."

"Those aren't good words, Delton. Are you saying . . . ?" I wondered. "Was my dad saying . . . ? Do I annoy people as much as Livvy is annoying me right now?"

"Well, I haven't met Livvy yet, but from the evidence you've presented . . . and what I know about you after five years in elementary school, it is a workable hypothesis."

pause

CHAPTER 22

Signaling That You Are Finished

"It seems appropriate that we conclude our last class before our luncheon by covering how we signal to the waiter that we are finished with our meal. Now . . ." Miss Melton-Mowry paused, waiting for our attention.

"It's important to note that different countries have different approaches; so that you don't get confused, we'll confine ourselves to the American way. When you have finished eating, you simply put the handles of your fork and knife at the four o'clock position. The utensils lie across your plate with their tops near the ten o'clock position. Oh, and the knife blade should be pointing in. Let's all try that, shall we?"

It didn't take long to master putting our knife and fork across our plate—geez! Some of this stuff was so dumb. After about a million more reminders about what to wear, how to greet Mrs. Glennon and everything else we'd already covered in *exhausting* detail, our last etiquette-suspension class was over.

Of course, I was itching to get outside. Where was my mother? Can you call Child Protective Services if your mother is *continually* late to pick you up?

As I stood there with my nose pressed to the door, Miss Melton-Mowry leaned over my shoulder and said in a quiet voice, "I asked your mother if she would delay her arrival so that you and I could talk."

"You mean, more than normal?" What new form of torture could she have possibly dreamed up?

"I just want to go over a few things with you regarding the luncheon, Cassidy. In private."

I froze. *Did Miss Melton-Mowry just call me by my first name?*

"Class is over. We don't have to use formal address."

I double-froze. It would have been an Oscar-winning performance in freeze tag.

Miss Melton-Mowry sighed. "Let's take a little walk, shall we? Get some fresh air and sunshine?"

If you'd asked me, I would have said our teacher was allergic to fresh air; I was curious to see what she looked like in the sunshine. Could her skin get any whiter?

As we stepped out the door, the wind blew a coupon for the juice bar right up into Miss Melton-Mowry's face. She swiped it away, rearranged her shoulders into dining posture and tugged at the bottom of her blazer to make it all straight. We walked past the tailor, the dry cleaner and the dollar store. I would have peeked in to see what the candy selection was, but Miss Melton-Mowry seemed like she was on a mission.

"Watch out for gum at twelve o'clock," I said, pointing to a pink blob in the middle of the sidewalk.

"Thank you."

The wind blew harder. I had to grab my ponytail to keep it from whipping my face. Miss Melton-Mowry's hair didn't seem to be affected; when it moved at all, it went in one big piece. I would swear it was a wig, but I'd seen her part, with the strip of gray hair ladies get when they wait as long as they can before coloring it.

"Tell me, Cassidy, do you think you'll live in Grand River forever?"

First we were outside. Now she was asking me a personal question, the kind we never touched in polite conversation.

I decided to roll with it. "Me? Nah. I'm going out . . . on the open road. You know, sleep rough, gaze up at the stars . . ."

"There's not much use for etiquette around the campfire, is there?"

"Not that I know of, but if there is, I'll have a heap of it."

We came to the edge of the parking lot. The sidewalk kept going, and I could see that it connected to an apartment complex behind the strip mall. Between the two sat a deserted playground with just a swing set and a slide.

There's something sad about empty playgrounds.

"We can sit here." Miss Melton-Mowry pointed to a bench across from the swing set.

As we sat there in the hot sun, I wondered what was wrong with her plumbing that she wasn't sweating buckets.

"Well." She began by folding her hands in her lap. "It's not just campfires where people have no use for etiquette, Cassidy. It seems the polite rules of society are no longer required in the days of . . . reality TV and Internet chat rooms. I . . . I have a favor to ask of you. The truth of the matter is, my enrollment is down. Parents think if their children watch my etiquette videos, they're covered. But practice is so important. And the nuances . . ."

She stopped talking and looked at me. In the bright light, I could see where her lipstick line went just a hair south of her lips.

"I need this job, Cassidy. I am too old to be doing so much traveling. It's not the open road, exactly, but the climate of the Middle East and the change in time zones . . . Working at the Private Reserve Academy would be a way for me to—" She broke off and examined her polished nails. "Well, in addition to being easier for us, it would be an honor, of course."

"*Us?*" I knew I was in personal-question territory, but if there was a Mr. Melton-Mowry confined to a wheelchair due to war injuries who relied on his wife working just to get his pain medication, I wanted to know about it.

"Me and my cat, Mr. Jeeves. And Miss Information, of course."

"Oh. Can I ask—may I ask you another question, Miss Melton-Mowry?"

She nodded. "Very nice, Cassidy. Yes, you may."

"Who's in that photograph in your office? The one you keep in your desk drawer?"

Miss Melton-Mowry shaded her eyes, then smiled, remembering. "He was my . . . beau . . . the one who had picnics with me. By the water."

"Were you all stars and hearts for him? Like in the cartoons?"

"Stars *and* hearts and . . . maybe even smiley faces."

"Then why . . . why isn't he with you now?"

"It's . . . complicated."

There was that word again! The one grown-ups used when even *they* hadn't figured out the answer.

"We were in different stations in life. My parents didn't approve . . . it seems so silly now, but back then . . . I do wonder sometimes what would have happened if I hadn't been, well, such a dutiful child. More like you, perhaps, Cassidy. But my mother owned an etiquette school. We had visiting dignitaries all the time. I was her star pupil."

I nodded. Things were beginning to make more sense around here.

"She loved to tell the story of the time we had lunch at the Polo Club. We were out on the terrace. They had just cleared the palate cleanser—I think it was a melon sorbet—when a spooked horse stampeded onto the patio, foaming at the mouth.

"Ladies screamed, men tripped over their chairs. I didn't know what to do, so I kept my eyes on my mother."

"You didn't . . . run?"

"Of course not. I hadn't been dismissed. It's important to stay calm in an emergency. Some of the diners were cut by the glassware, but I"—Miss Melton-Mowry stared into the distance, remembering—"I . . . wasn't harmed."

"So is that what you wanted to have this little chat about? If there's a stampeding horse, then all eyes on you?"

Miss Melton-Mowry looked as if she was about to say something else, but instead, she reached over and patted my knee. "Not in so many words, but I think . . . yes, that is the import."

The following night—*the* night before the big luncheon—I did everything right. I turned off my e-reader an hour before bedtime; I dimmed the lights. I put on my cricket noises. I tried to read a very dull story about nucleo-pepper-something in one of Magda's *Scientific American* magazines. Nothing made me sleepy—I couldn't even scare up a yawn.

So when I heard Dad in the hallway around eleven, I called out to him.

"Cass, have I ever told you the human species is diurnal, *not* nocturnal?" he asked, sticking his head into my room.

I tossed the magazine on the floor. "About a million times . . ."

"Flip over," he said, sitting on my bed and rubbing my back. "Are you thinking about your big day?"

I nodded, my face in the pillow.

"Well, I can't see the future, but I do know one thing, Miss Cassidy. You're going to try your best."

"'Course I will," I said, lifting my head so Dad could hear. "You don't think I *like* going to extra-quette class, do you? Because if you do, Dad, I know some scientists who'd want to examine your head."

"No, I don't think you do."

"It's just . . . well, I set a good intention, but then I . . . I don't know. Something always goes wrong."

"Does something go wrong or does something get stirred up? By someone who is, hmmm . . . unengaged?"

"Well, now that you mention it, it is deadly boring in there. And there's no AC. Can you die of hot boredom?"

"I don't think so. My wish for you, Miss Cassidy, is that you learn how to be yourself *and* help others be themselves, too. You're not the only one trying to get through the day. Today, for example, someone broke a jar of molasses in the baking aisle and six carts rolled through it before my team was alerted. Do you know about the Great Molasses Flood of 1919 in Boston?"

No, I had to admit I didn't.

"Well, picture a scaled-down grocery-store version of a sticky federal-disaster site. In the break room, they were calling it the Grand River Molassacre."

"That's rough. Sorry, Dad. Want me to rub your back?"

"No, honey. It's all in a day's work. I calmed down by reminding myself that *you* would mostly likely have been one of the cart drivers. Be honest. Would you have been able to resist it?"

Why deny it? We both knew I'd be there, front and center. And sticky.

"Dad? I think I know how you feel." To cheer him up, I told him about Livvy's letter and how frustrated it made me when I tried to read it.

"I wondered when this day would come," Dad said. "I'm not trying to rub it in, sweetie, but it's called a dose of your own medicine."

"Well, it stinks, especially since I memorized the other one."

"I know. I'm sorry. You do know exactly how I feel. Grrrrrr . . ."

Growling like a bear meant . . . bear hug!

"I think I'm ready to go to bed now, Dad."

"Me too." He flipped off the switch between my shoulder blades, and I don't know how, but I fell asleep.

excellent

CHAPTER 23

Grooming Aids Should Be Applied with Vigor

"Miss Corcoran, are you in there? I know it's early, but . . . duty calls."

"If you call me Miss Corcoran one more time, Magda . . ." I opened the door and swatted her with her *Scientific American*.

"How can you be mad at me when I am responsible for saving you from department-store-dress disaster?"

Magda advanced. I threw myself on the floor and grabbed the bedpost. "Exactly how are you going to do that?"

Pulling me by the leg, she said, "I'm friends with Bree and Bree likes to shop. She found a better dress for you."

"Oh, no. I'm not wearing one of her dresses. It wouldn't fit, for one thing." I flipped over and pointed to my upper regions, which, if they were a relief map, would fall somewhere in the middle of the Gobi Desert.

Magda pulled open my closet and dug in the back. It didn't matter that the pink dress had spent time in the laundry chute and, more recently, fallen off its hanger. It was standing up anyway. My baseball bat and my box of vintage Tigers cards—Dad's box, actually—had fallen on it, so when my sister held it up in front of her, it bent in crazy new directions.

It was like a dress having a bad hair day.

"A picture's worth a thousand words," Miss Know-It-All-Corcoran-the-Second said. "Just look at what Bree got, okay?"

"I'll look, but first I have to take a shower." I had a feeling old Mrs. Glennon would have a bloodhound's sniffer.

"Good point." Magda nodded. "Between the amount of covers you sleep under and the naturally moist environment in your arm—"

"I can't hear you!" My fingers plugging my ears, I ran toward the bathroom.

After showering and blow-drying my hair (and underneath my arms, just in case), I put on my hoodie and a pair of shorts and we walked over to the Bensons'. In the kitchen, Mrs. Benson looked up from stirring her coffee. "Cassidy. It's your big day!"

"Can I ask you a question, Mrs. Benson?"

"Shoot."

"How come you're always so cheerful?"

Cupping her hands around her mug, Mrs. Benson took a big gulp. "Well, one, I've had a decent amount of coffee. And, two, given a choice between happiness and sadness, it seems logical which one to choose, don't you think?"

"Is Magda here, Mom?" Bree called from upstairs. "Have you got Cassidy with you? She's going to love this."

"There's a cinnamon roll in the oven with your name on it if you try it on." Mrs. Benson pushed back my hood and said, "This *will* be a day to remember, Miss Cassidy."

I swallowed. That's what I was afraid of.

Glancing up the stairs, I told myself there wasn't much to lose. The only good thing about the dress in my closet was that it was so stiff, my elbows wouldn't bend to reach the table.

"Cover her eyes, Magda. I don't want Cassidy to see this until it's on." Bree stood guard in front of her bedroom door, holding out one of her stretchy headbands.

As Magda pulled it over my eyes, I pretended I was being abducted by pygmies who couldn't decide if they should eat me now or fatten me up for later.

Magda yanked off my hoodie. "You can leave your shorts on until I get this dress over your head."

I would have fought back, but the pygmies had their poison darts aimed at me. I held my arms up; it felt like Magda was putting my hoodie back on, only heavier.

"Now slip off your shorts."

"Has she changed? Can I come in?" Bree called out.

"Yep." I felt Magda's hands on my shoulders, turning me. Then she pulled off the headband and I was temporarily blinded by a lighted mirror, like the kind you see in a star's dressing room. Still, there I was, in a sky-blue sleeveless dress that felt as comfortable as my favorite pajamas. It went straight down, just like a nightshirt, until you got to the knees.

"Look at this." Bree put her hands on my hips and turned

me to the left and right. The bottom of the dress flared out in a circle.

"It's a little flounce. Adorable."

"Well, if this is legal, I'll wear it. But I have my doubts."

"Of course it's legal. It's a dress, isn't it? Look how it brings out the color of your beautiful blue eyes."

"But it's not ugly and uncomfortable."

"That was the brilliant thing about Coco Chanel. She believed in comfort. Still . . ." Twirling a piece of my hair around her finger, Bree went on, "You need shoes, and we're going to have to do something with this hair."

"Yes, we are," I agreed. "It's called a ponytail."

"Nope. A ponytail won't work. The dress is simple and angular, which means the hair has to be feminine."

"But I don't have feminine hair!"

Bree walked over to her dressing table and pulled a curling iron off a hook. "But you could."

Magda grabbed me from behind in a cross-armed surfboard. Curling irons excited my flight response. "She'll barely sit still for pumpkin pancakes, Bree. I'm afraid if you do that, Cassidy will wear burn marks on her forehead."

Bree didn't seem concerned. "Maybe. But I have a secret weapon. Mom! You're on!"

Mrs. Benson was obviously waiting for her cue. One quick knock on the door and she was in.

"Sit here, Cassidy," Bree said, patting a star-covered rolling stool. "Mom's got a story to tell you."

"I'd love to, but . . ." I started clawing my way out of Magda's hold. She was surprisingly strong for an egghead, but I was primed for takeoff. Mrs. Benson's stories could put me in a trance; I did not need any firing up about assassination attempts using cutlery when I was going to a luncheon where all I was allowed to do was pat my mouth with a napkin, take sips of water and pretend I found the weather fascinating.

"Oh, I think you need to hear this one, Miss Cassidy," Mrs. Benson said just as I'd reached the door. "It's about *Titanic* karma."

I used the intensity of my gaze to stare daggers at Magda. "Can't you keep even one family secret?"

"Don't look at me! I didn't say anything."

Jack!

Don't ask me why it took all the fight out of me that Jack had spilled the fact I had *Titanic* karma to the Bensons. I went over and sat on the stool with dismal posture, looking even more like the back-of-the-milk-carton girl than I had at Stetler's. *Even* in this dress that felt like a stretched-out T-shirt.

"Now, Cassidy, cheer up. This is a whopper of a tale. Swivel her around, Sabrina, so she doesn't have to look at herself while you work your magic."

"Turn me into a young lady, you mean?"

"That *will* require magic." Magda pushed in my stomach and pulled back on my shoulders. "Dining posture, Miss Corcoran."

I resolved to spend this time coming up with a baker's dozen plots to get revenge on my sister, but I didn't even get to one before Mrs. Benson launched into her story.

"This is the saga of Charles Joughin, chief baker on the *Titanic*. Charles was off-duty, sleeping in his bunk, when the fateful moment occurred and the *Titanic* ran smack into an iceberg. He jumped out of bed and reported to the kitchen, where he was told to take loaves of bread up to the lifeboats. After that, he helped other men load the lifeboats with women and children. As you know, Cassidy, the tragedy of the sinking was that there weren't enough lifeboats; the men held back as the women and children got on. Some of the women were frightened and had to be put on forcibly. Charles wrestled a couple of feisty girls in, too."

"Maybe they weren't afraid," I said. "Maybe they were willing to go down with the ship like the men." There's something about having people mess with your hair. I tried to fight the hypnotizing feeling of Bree's comb and the heat of her curling iron by blowing holes in Mrs. Benson's story.

She ignored me. "Even though he was assigned to lifeboat number ten, Charles held back when he saw that three other men had boarded at the direction of the ship's captain. That's when he went back to his cabin and had a drink. A stiff one."

"Was it whiskey? That's what pirates do when the ship's going down," I said. "They drink the captain's whiskey."

"I can't confirm it was whiskey, but it was most certainly alcohol. Once he'd got himself liquored up, he went back above deck and started throwing chairs over the side. He thought this might help the men who would soon be in the water . . . they could use them as flotation devices. While he was at it, Charles heard a terrible crash; he watched in horror as hundreds of people were flung into a heap on the deck below him."

Mrs. Benson took a sip from her water bottle. "The hull had cracked. The time was near. Charles tightened his life jacket and rode the ship down like he was taking an elevator to Neptune's basement."

Turning the stool in a one-eighty, Bree started pulling a comb through my hair on the other side.

"The water temperature was thirty-one degrees, just below freezing. Most people who died in the *Titanic* did not die from drowning. Every body that was recovered had a life jacket on and the water was as still as a pond.

"Charles didn't try to swim anywhere. He floated and treaded water. According to interviews he gave later, he said he barely felt the cold."

"Must have been the alcohol," I said. "Saint Bernards wear it around their neck, you know, when they're looking for people buried under the snow."

"Actually—" Magda started, but Mrs. Benson held up her hand.

"This is my story, Magda."

"Who wants a Tootsie Pop?" Bree asked, holding up the bag.

Not knowing when I'd have my next real meal, I raised my hand. "I'll take grape."

"Sorry. All I have is cherry."

"Fine. Cherry, then."

I unwrapped the Tootsie Pop and started sucking. "Go on," I said. I hate it when a good story gets interrupted—even for a Tootsie Pop.

"I'm not sure Charles is a good source for how long he floated, but once all the accounts were reconstructed, they figured he was in the water for nearly two hours."

"Tell the truth, Mama. Two hours? In freezing water?"

"At one point, he saw an overturned lifeboat in the distance with maybe twenty-five men huddled on top of it. He made his way slowly to the lifeboat, but there was no room for him to climb on. He was recognized by the cook, however, who took hold of his hand and held on to it so he didn't float away.

"About a half hour later, another lifeboat appeared out of the mist. They called out that they had room for more, but only ten. Since Charles was in the water, he began swimming over immediately and was hauled into the boat."

Mrs. Benson paused, tilting her head as she looked at me. "How much longer?" she asked Bree.

"Almost done."

"Soon the lifeboat was able to reach the RMS *Carpathia*, which had sailed over to rescue the survivors. When Charles Joughin was taken aboard, he was treated for swollen feet, but that's all."

"I don't understand why he didn't freeze to death," Magda said. "All things being equal, a body shouldn't be able to survive freezing temperatures more than fifteen or twenty minutes. The alcohol reason doesn't cut it."

My sister could be such a know-it-all pain! "You're telling me hundreds of Saint Bernards are running around the Swiss Alps with kegs of whiskey tied to their collars for no reason, Magda?"

"It makes you *feel* warm when you first drink it, but it doesn't keep your body warm. It dilates your blood vessels, moving blood closer to the surface of your skin. If you want to keep from freezing to death, you need blood flowing in the opposite direction."

Bree was brushing out my hair. She kept pushing my chin

back and forth and looking at me, frowning, and then brushing some more. I had just reached the chocolate part of my Tootsie Pop when she grabbed it out of my hands.

"All done," she said.

"Hey!"

"There is one explanation," Mrs. Benson said, leaning forward and tucking my hair behind my ears. She frowned, too, and put the hair back the way it was. "I can read your mind, Sabrina. Yes, we're going to need a headband."

Bree threw open her closet door. On the back, there were a bunch of plastic pockets with more colored headbands than you see in the hair-care aisle at the pharmacy. She yanked one out and came toward me.

"No saying no until you see the final result."

"Bree's right," Magda said. "With your hair in a headband, it won't fall in your soup, thus preventing at least one etiquette faux pas."

"Well, what's the explanation, then?" I asked as Bree scraped the headband over my temples.

"Against all odds, Charles Joughin survived two-plus hours with his body submerged in freezing water. The alcohol he drank did not protect him. The only explanation is that he had . . . *Titanic* karma."

Bree reached over my shoulder with something that looked like a pencil eraser and smeared it across my lips; then she turned the stool around.

"So . . . you're saying *Titanic* karma is *not* bad?"

"I'm saying it's all in the way you look at it. It wasn't bad for Charles Joughin."

Spinning the stool around so that I faced the mirror, Bree pinched my cheeks. "I knew you'd say no to lip gloss," she said. "I call this Cherry Toots."

"My tongue's red, too." I stuck it out to prove my point.

"We can brush that."

"Cassidy." Magda touched one of my many curls. "Just look at yourself."

I looked in the mirror at the girl with the long curly hair. In a headband. With red stain on her lips. She *might* have been my cousin.

"That is definitely not me."

"Yes it is," Mrs. Benson said. "Allow me to introduce you to Cassidy Corcoran at eleven-teen."

do not like ✗

CHAPTER 24

When You Find Something Undesirable in Your Food

Mrs. Bean dropped us off at the Egypt Valley Country Club, and we found Miss Melton-Mowry sitting in a chair on the patio.

Delton was already flustered. "How long have you been here, Miss Melton-Mowry? According to my iPhone, we are twenty minutes early."

"Whenever we have a major event like this, I like to come early to . . . strategize."

You'd think we were declaring war on China instead of eating lunch!

"You look very nice, Miss Corcoran. And you, Mr. Bean." Miss Melton-Mowry straightened Delton's bow tie. She was dressed in another skirt and blazer, only this outfit was yellow. It looked hot and stiff.

"I am thinking they will seat us at the table over there . . . under the oak tree."

"What makes you think that?"

"Because this is the only terrace with handicap access, and—"

"Do not tell me the old lady's in a wheelchair."

"She's not paralyzed, but her emphysema makes mobility an issue. And because of her breathing difficulties and the equipment, they'll want her in a less trafficked location."

I gripped Delton's elbow. "The equipment would include?"

"She needs oxygen. To help her breathe."

All of a sudden, I needed oxygen. I tried to find some in my belly, sticking it out as far as I could while looking over the golf course beyond the terrace. It was so green and smooth. It looked like a park, like one of those places you wouldn't mind sleeping rough.

Was it blistering hot already or was it just me? I hoped this jersey stuff could soak up the sweat.

"What is the matter, Cassidy? You're giving me a bruise! You're not afraid of oxygen, are you?"

Somewhere, I heard splashing. Possibly they had a pool here, and kids were doing what came natural on a hot day, something called swimming.

"I'm tempted to review, but I know if I've done my job correctly, we are ready." Miss Melton-Mowry pulled a mirror out of her purse and checked to make sure her face was in marching order. "We should be first in the lobby. Why don't we all visit the restroom and freshen up?"

As we walked toward the building, I pulled Delton aside. "I can't sit next to Mrs. Glennon," I whispered to him. "Because that's how I got myself into this mess, by cutting off my great-grandma's oxygen."

"You . . . tried to kill your great-grandmother?"

"No! It was an accident. Just like Miss Information was an accident." I took hold of Delton's lapels. "I have to graduate, Delton. Do whatever it takes. I'll . . . I'll owe you one."

"Does that mean we'll be friends? Next year? That you and Jack will let me sit with you at lunch? That the three of us will do a prank together?"

"Pinky-swear that your mother won't be in on it?"

"Pinky-swear."

We linked pinkies. "I'll consider it. Now, let's go get cleaned up."

"I am cleaned up."

"Well, clean your clean! I need private time."

I walked into the ladies' room and looked at myself in the mirror. Everybody kept saying how pretty I looked today, but I didn't look anything like Bree. I didn't even look like myself. I tried staring at myself until I could see double. That's when I realized that Janae was right. All these years I thought nobody could tell; I looked like a goofball.

Some fancy ladies came into the bathroom and stood in front of the mirror, fixing their hair. "Oh, you have to tell me where you got that dress. It's so retro. Perfect for summer."

"This old thing," I said, waving my hand in the direction of . . . me. Time to practice my la-di-da. "I picked it up last year in the south of France. It's a Coco Chanel."

"Beautiful craftsmanship," said Lady Number One. "You

don't see that anymore," added Lady Number Two, touching my sleeve. "I love the way the French finish their seams, don't you?"

"Hands off the goods, ladies. I'm trying to stay fresh here."

They laughed like I hadn't just warned them away from me. I watched Lady Number One pick up a bottle off the counter. "I love this fragrance," she said. "It reminds me of jasmine." She spritzed a little on her wrist and Lady Number Two held out hers for some spray. I waited until they'd left and sniffed it myself. Not too bad. I sprayed a little in my palms and patted my face.

As I left the bathroom, I got my first look at the etiquette judge. Miss Glennon wheeled her past the fountain in the lobby to the spot where Officer Weston and Miss Melton-Mowry were standing. Officer Weston was all dressed up in a suit and tie, looking handsome and probably smelling like, well, nothing, since that was what Miss Melton-Mowry preferred. Delton was pressed up against a potted palm. You'd think Mrs. Glennon was a saber-toothed tiger and not an old lady in a hat.

"It's showtime, Miss Corcoran," I said, pinching myself for good luck. Spine straight as a broom handle, I walked up to the old bat, stuck out my hand and said, "Charming lobby we're having. I love this décor, don't you?"

Mrs. Glennon's eyes got wide. For a second, I thought she was pulling *my* trick and looking at me cross-eyed. I stuck my hand out further, in case she was nearsighted, taking care not to touch the oxygen tube leading to her nose. "Miss Corcoran, at your service."

Then the old lady started sneezing to beat the band. She sneezed so hard her nose plug ended up in her lap.

"It's all right. No harm done." Miss Glennon grabbed my hand as she kneeled down and stuck the plug back in her grandmother's nose. "Grandmother is allergic to perfume. Do you mind washing it off?"

"Some fresh air will do us a world of good," Miss Melton-Mowry said. "Why don't we go out to the terrace and you can join us there, Miss Corcoran."

That's how I landed back in the bathroom, scrubbing my hands and thinking about what a phony Miss Melton-Mowry was. Fresh air, my eye. I could practically see her digging through her purse for my report card and failing me on first impressions.

What did I do wrong? I felt this overpowering anger at Mrs. Benson. For every Charles Joughin, there were at least a hundred people at the bottom of the ocean who thought *Titanic* karma was the worst possible kind to have.

There was a knock on the door. "Are there any ladies inside? Because there's been a report of a foul-smelling gas coming out of the ladies' room and we're here to investigate."

"Jack? What are you doing here? Where did you get that jacket?"

"This?" Jack tugged on his lapel. "I wore it to Bobby's wedding. Remember? I was an usher."

"You were in fourth grade. It looks ridiculous now."

"I couldn't zip the pants, so I just wore my shorts. Anyway, thought I'd come over and keep you company. This place really is swank. The men's room has mouthwash." Jack huffed big minty breaths at me before picking up the bottle of perfume.

"Don't touch that stuff! It's poison." I filled Jack in on my progress so far. "Jack, I don't know what to do! I'm hopeless at this stuff."

"Look at you, Cass. You're more nervous than a long-tailed cat in a room full of rocking chairs."

"Excuse me? Is that another Bree-ism?"

Jack scratched his palm, like he was trying to remember. "Maybe. What I mean to say is you're taking this too serious. It's just a game, Cass. Like Frisbee golf."

"We make up our own rules for Frisbee golf."

"True. But there are rules. Most kids follow them." By this time, Jack had discovered the mirror. He studied himself, using his fingers to comb his hair.

I whirled him around and grabbed his lapels. "Jack, I'm serious. I gotta do this right . . . not just to get out of class, but . . . I need to be a suck-up teacher's pet for *one hour,* so Miss Melton-Mowry can get the cush job!"

"You're gonna be fine, Cassidy. Remember that time we hid in the janitor's closet during lunch and recess? You were still for, like, forty minutes. And I'm here, aren't I? I've got your back."

Slipping behind me, Jack put his hands on my shoulders and pointed me in the direction of the patio. "Don't worry, Cassidy. We'll come out on top like we always do."

I started the long walk back to the table, going over the rules of fine dining in my head. My stomach felt so squeezy I couldn't even remember what *b* and *d* stood for. Hopefully, not Big Disaster!

It was just like Miss Melton-Mowry predicted. They wheeled Mrs. Glennon over to the table under the tree and gave her the view of the golf course. Miss Glennon sat on one side and Miss Melton-Mowry on the other. Officer Weston was next to Miss Glennon and Delton was next to Miss Melton-Mowry. As I came up to the table, Officer Weston jumped up to pull out my chair. Delton stood, pressing his blazer so it didn't touch the little bowl of red stuff that appeared to be our first course.

"I love gazpacho," Miss Glennon said with the kind of enthusiasm I reserved for a cheeseburger and fries.

"It looks like Andalusian gazpacho," Miss Melton-Smarty informed us.

"Looks to me like somebody got his guts blown out in the kitchen," I whispered to Delton.

"I'm sorry, Miss Corcoran." Mrs. Glennon was giving me the evil eye. "I'm a bit hard of hearing."

"The thing I love about gazpacho," I replied, turning it up a notch, "is that you don't have to worry about it getting cold."

She looked at me like I was up to something, but all she said was, "That is true."

I picked up my spoon and skimmed it over the top of my dish, netting mostly air.

Using the line *I* came up with in polite conversation in our practice session, Officer Weston began, "This heat is really getting to my roses."

Normally, his stealing my line would make me sore, but the poor guy looked worse than I did. There was a red ring around his neck where his collar dug in; a drop of sweat ran down his temple. You would have thought Honeybun was standing over his shoulder. He took a swipe of his soup, and a tiny drop of tomato juice ended up on his chin. Rough luck.

I watched Miss Melton-Mowry try to signal him by patting her napkin on her face. Delton was patting, too.

Old Mrs. Glennon seemed fixated on it.

I considered some Jim Leyland moves, but I knew that would get me a demerit; it was every man for himself out here. "This is so refreshing," I said. "I love a fresh-squeezed tomato, don't you?" I skimmed and sipped without making a sound—which wasn't hard, seeing as I wasn't really eating anything.

"Excuse me, ladies and gentlemen. Which way to the pool? I need to refresh myself." Delton nearly fell out of his chair when Jack appeared at his shoulder.

"You can't be thinking of swimming like that," Officer Weston said, taking in Jack's too-short suit jacket and shorts.

"Of course not. I sink like a stone. This is my suit for dangling my legs in the water." Jack hiked up his knee, so we could see even more of his hairy legs.

I stared at him cross-eyed, which was strictly necessary or else I would possibly have a giggling fit that could not be concealed by my wrist.

"Well, if you need any help, just holler," Officer Weston replied. "I'm fully versed in all emergency procedures, including rescu—"

"Young man . . ." Miss Melton-Mowry stood up.

"Yes, well . . . thank you," Jack said, giving me a thumbs-up before he made his getaway.

"You know him, don't you?" Officer Weston asked me under his breath. "This has to be an inside job."

Miss Glennon took advantage of the strange appearance of Jack to reach over and press her napkin into Officer Weston's hand. She touched her chin and hiked up her eyebrows. Even *I* couldn't mistake those signals. Both Delton and I sighed with relief as Officer Weston swiped his chin with her napkin before handing it back to her.

It was the last deep breath I would have for a while because as soon as I turned back to my plate, one of those creepy tree caterpillars dropped down from above and hung there, wriggling, right in front of my face.

It reminded me of the Houdini movie I watched where they had him underwater in a straitjacket! I bit my tongue and crossed my eyes. Again! Anything to keep the squirming green vision from being implanted in my brain and sliding into the home plate of my fear center.

"Miss Corcoran," Delton said. "Can you smell the roses at the edge of the patio? Taking a deep breath through your nose and inflating your diaphragm is the best way to enjoy the heady scent of roses, don't you think, Officer Weston?"

"Cassidy, are you okay?"

I tried to check in with my kneecaps, my ankles, my elbows, but they were all saying "Run away as fast as you can." I leaned as far back as the chair would allow.

Where is Jack when I need him?

Somewhere in the back of my head, I heard music, like drips of water from a fountain. I counted the drips. *Jack is dangling his toes in the pool,* I told myself. *Count the drips. He'll be back in a minute, but first . . . I suggest you breathe.*

I stopped the lean. It was a good thing, too, because one more inch and I'd be introducing the back of my head to the patio cement. I kept counting drips and took another deep breath, diving down with Houdini into the bottom of my belly and unlocking his handcuffs. Officer Weston's hand held the back of my chair while I took *another* deep breath.

Time to surface.

If I didn't rescue this worm from death-by-drowning in gazpacho, all hopes for passing the etiquette course and moving on with my life would go with it. I couldn't look it straight in its little wormy eye and I wasn't about to look at it double, so I squinted and pinched the thread it hung by.

"Is there something in your eye, Miss Corcoran?" Mrs. Glennon asked.

"No, I . . ." It was impossible to talk and save the worm at the same time. I turned in my chair and flung the little bugger into the rose bushes. "I . . . I was just admiring the landscaping, Mrs. Glennon. What charming roses we're having."

"And here's our next course," Miss Melton-Mowry announced, patting her forehead with her napkin. "Ah, look at this lovely salad."

I checked in with my body parts. Everything was still attached; after a few more deep breaths, my pulse returned to the normal range.

Straightening my shoulders, I returned to dining posture and considered the pile of green stuff in front of me. When you think about it, salad is easy to eat like a proper lady. Cherry tomatoes have the potential to explode, so I detoured around them and focused on sawing the slices of cucumber and leaves of lettuce into tiny pieces while Delton went on and on about the subjects he liked to study in school.

His description of his final project for fifth grade—a working model of a Boeing P-26 "Peashooter" that he donated afterward to the Third Coast Transportation Museum's traveling exhibition—took up most of the course. Miss Melton-Mowry had to give him a "My, that is detailed," and a "Thank you for sharing," and even a "Who knew there were so many parts to single-seat fighter planes," before I finally kicked him under the table; my jaws were seizing up from all the polite chewing.

I figured my turn was next, so I mentally prepared for the polite version of how hobos go days without bathing, sleep in haystacks and eat rail-kill stew out of rusty cans, when the waiter's arm reached in for my salad.

Now what? He left me holding my salad fork! This was so un-American. I didn't put my utensils at ten and four! Shouldn't he get a demerit for that?

What to do? I thought about quick sticking it on Delton's plate, but I might draw attention to myself.

I decided to float my hand under the table and set my fork on the chair. It was then I realized I was scooching over so I didn't get oil on my new dress.

What was happening to me?

Would a Knight of the Road worry about a little salad dressing? I looked around at my dining companions as a stinky piece of fish was placed in front of us. Of course, we had been instructed in the polite way to eat fish, but who wants to eat it? I was more interested in the polite way to push it around on my plate and then gorge on Tater Tots when I got home.

"And what about you, Miss Corcoran? What are your favorite subjects in school?"

"Why, thank you for asking, Mrs. Glennon. I would say it's a toss-up between recess and gym. We young people need to stay active. However, if you're more interested in my intellectual studies, I would say history. I find American history just after the Civil War to be my favorite."

"You mean the Reconstruction era and the rise of industrialization?" Delton Smarty-Pants cut in.

I turned the intensity of my gaze on him. He'd already had his turn. "Yes, Mr. Bean. In particular the Knights of the Open Road, otherwise known as hobos. Give me an adventure under the stars, a daring leap from a train trestle, and SSR just flies by."

"What is SSR?" Mrs. Glennon wanted to know.

"Sustained silent reading," I informed her, patting my lips with my napkin to get a break from pretending to eat fish.

"There are so many possibilities for a history major," Miss Glennon said. "Would you like to be a teacher? Maybe even a college professor?"

"You could work in a museum." Officer Weston was staring at his piece of fish like it was a puzzle. It had bones, of course, the kind that normal people would just use their fingers to pull out. But people like us—polite and destined to starve to death—had to pick out the bones with our knife and fork and the skills of a surgeon.

"Working in a museum would be satisfactory," I said. "Maybe Ripley's Believe It or Not."

I kept sneaking looks at Miss Melton-Mowry, trying to follow her lead. She would take a piece of fish the size of a peanut, put it in her mouth and chew it while smiling. It is difficult to chew and smile at the same time. I have tried this in front of the mirror. It doesn't even look good. It looks a little like you're in pain.

That's when I realized it. Sitting there with all my weight on one hip, trying to avoid a collision between my salad fork and my new dress *and* not breathe in the smell of poached fish, I realized that Miss Melton-Mowry was in pain. In fact, she hated this. And I didn't need a degree from the Cassidy Corcoran School of Espionage to tell.

At the same time, I noticed Officer Weston giving up on the polite way to dissect his fish; slipping his plate under the table, he yanked what was left of the skeleton right out and dropped it in his napkin. Miss Melton-Mowry was watching, too. In fact, she was watching so closely that she forgot the careful cuts and brought a big piece of fish with a glistening bone attached up to her mouth and stuck it all in.

Officer Weston seemed pleased with himself. He returned his plate to the table and set to work with his fork. "Delicious," he said. "For my part, I've always wanted to be a coach. If I weren't a community police officer, that is."

"What sport would you coach, Officer Weston?" Miss Glennon asked.

"Baseball. Hands down. I've been a Tigers fan since I was a little cub."

"Really? I'm a Tigers fan myself." After that, Officer Weston and Miss Glennon were off to the races. The big question for the Tigers, it seemed, at least according to Glennon and Weston, was how to make up for the loss of Prince Fielder? Was the new manager making a big mistake batting Martinez fourth instead of Cabrera?

I kept my eyes on Miss Melton-Mowry, wondering how she was going to eject the fish bone from her mouth, a subject that must not be covered until etiquette graduate school. But she didn't eject it. Her funny chewing smile ended. She even looked a little panicked—just for a moment—before she brought her napkin to her mouth.

Spit it out, lady!

Miss Melton-Mowry turned the intensity of her gaze on me and shook her head no. What was that supposed to mean? We didn't cover choking! Remembering our little talk, I sat back and tried to pretend that everything was fine as she pressed her napkin to her mouth again. *This is the moment she coughs it out.* But she didn't cough into her napkin. She made a soft wheezy noise instead.

I focused on my fish, sneaking looks around the table to see if anyone else had figured out what was what. Could it be that Miss Melton-Mowry would rather choke to death than break her own rules? Was it their shared fascination with the Tigers that kept anyone else from picking up on this?

"The thing with the Tigers is, you can go years with a drought. I mean, look at 2001 to 2004, and then they bust out with a streak of amazing hitters. Who do you think is better, Delton, Al Kaline or Miguel Cabrera?"

"My father would argue that if the older players had the same access to technological advances in training and pharmaceuticals, that would make the comparison more . . ."

Blah, blah, blah, Delton!

When Miss Melton-Mowry put her elbows on the table to steady herself, I knew we had escalated to Code Red.

Why didn't anyone else notice her elbows were on the table—the very first dining "never" she'd ever taught us? I tried to get Officer Weston's attention using my body language, gently inclining my head in her direction and opening my eyes a little wider.

"If you were a die-hard fan, you would know that Al Kaline has gone on record saying . . ."

My eyebrows could not get higher on my forehead unless I used a trampoline. My head couldn't bend any further. Not only did Miss Melton-Mowry have her *elbows* on the table; she was turning blue!

"Forgive me for interrupting, Officer Weston, but I must request that you stop nattering on about the Tigers and GIVE MISS MELTON-MOWRY THE HEIMLICH MANEUVER."

To emphasize my point, I lifted my end of the table, overturning all the water glasses and dousing my dining companions (something I later attributed to my hair-trigger adrenaline).

Officer Weston jumped up just as Miss Melton-Mowry went down. If only etiquette class went as fast as ejecting a fish bone. I tried to nab it—figuring there'd be a million ways I could hold Magda hostage with the promise of what digestive enzymes can do to fish-bone decomposition—but Officer Weston said they'd probably need it at the emergency room.

Of course, with my karma, we never made it to the one course even polite people have not been able to mess up—dessert!

finished

CHAPTER 25

An Especially Warm Invitation

It might not be a big deal to anyone else, but after all I'd been through with bugs, *I* thought it was a step forward that I could sit under our elderberry bush in complete darkness to listen in on what Jack was saying to Bree.

Mostly, it was things like "sure," "uh-huh," "I think . . . the red one."

Bree was rattling on about her latest fashion magazine. "The red one? Really? With that neckline?"

There was only one logical conclusion. Jack had lost his marbles.

"Cassidy, are you out there?" Dad called from the back

porch. "If so, would you mind investigating something in the front yard with me?"

It was just over a week since I couldn't keep calm in an emergency, resulting in Officer Weston saving Miss Melton-Mowry's life and getting a special pin for his uniform. At the ceremony, he made a nice speech about how my inability to follow directions helped save Miss Melton-Mowry's life.

"We'd have far fewer choking deaths in this country if diners were willing to cause the kind of ruckus Cassidy Corcoran can."

I think that was a compliment.

In Calamity Jane fashion, I might as well skip the boring bits about how I got "shouting at the top of her lungs" and "near-lethal first impression" removed from my permanent etiquette record. Our regular class ended, too, and we had a parents' reception to celebrate. With all the extra hours I'd put in, I outgestured Donna Parker and kept a group of health-conscious moms on the edge of their seats, talking about the pros and cons of the Corcoran family's new Yonanas machine. I even knew it was time to stop when Miss Melton-Mowry said, "Thank you for sharing the intricacies of banana transformation, Miss Corcoran."

It was Saturday night and Dad had promised a marshmallow roast in honor of my graduation from etiquette ~~prison~~ school, but we had to wait for Jack to be ready.

Since that didn't appear to be any time soon, I followed Dad to the front yard. One of the shop lights he uses in the garage was lying in the middle of the driveway, casting a strong beam on . . . a pair of arms reaching up from the ground.

"Either the Michigan Film Office is scouting locations for a remake of *Night of the Living Dead* or you've just been pranked."

I kneeled on the grass and examined the arms. There was no doubt about it—I'd know those slender wrists anywhere. Miss Information. Either she was buried under our lawn or someone had dismembered her.

Could it be? *Delton Bean!*

I pulled on one arm. It came out easily. Delton had wrapped a piece of florist's wire around the screw and inserted it into the lawn without damaging more than a blade or two of grass. I had to give him an 8.5 for technique. Still! I'd spent a bajillion hours in etiquette class for beheading her. How he thought he could dismember her and get away with it was beyond me.

"I know you're out there, Delton," I shouted into the darkness.

"I would imagine it's past Delton's bedtime," my dad said. "Jack?"

"Jack's busy, Dad. Plus, he didn't have access. No, this has Delton's fingerprints all over it. He's here somewhere, probably with his mom and they don't want me to know."

Dad unplugged the extension cord and everything went dark. "I've never thought of bonding with you over pranks. Can I have my shop light back now?"

I groped around for the other arm. "Sure." I set off down the driveway. "But I might need it later for interrogation purposes."

"And where do you think you're going, Miss Corcoran?"

"It's Saturday night, Dad. I'm going to search for the rest of Miss Information."

"Well, make sure you're back in thirty minutes. Your mother and I have a surprise for you."

I stopped. "A good surprise?"

"Yes, in fact. A good surprise."

When I got to Delton's house, I pushed the arms behind a row of flowerpots on the porch, just in case he was acting alone and Mrs. Bean did not know about this. Let the record show that Cassidy Corcoran is not a snitch. With the items in question stowed, I rang the doorbell.

"Oh, Cassidy. How nice to see you." Mrs. Bean looked over her shoulder, a little doubtful. "I think Delton's in his pj's, but I—"

"He can stay in his pajamas, Mrs. Bean, as long as you'll let him on the front porch. I need to ask him something."

"You're sure you don't want to come in?"

"No thank you."

Did that just come out of my mouth? Who says "no thank you" when just "no" would do?

It came as no surprise to me that Delton wore airplane pajamas.

"Cassidy. There's something I have to tell you," he said before I could get a word in edgewise.

"You're darn right there's something. I want you to explain—" I broke off, grabbing the arms from where I'd stowed them. "This! Where is the rest of Miss Information? I just got sprung from etiquette class, Delton, and if you—"

"Oh, that. That's easy. Miss Information belongs to me now. Miss Melton-Mowry gave her to me—well, to us—me and my mom, that is."

"And why would she do that?"

"Because she, well . . . she's retiring from teaching etiquette classes to focus on her videos."

I waved away a hungry mosquito with one of Miss Information's hands. "Not following, Delton."

"I told you my mom was in information systems. Well, she applied some SEO techniques to drive more Web traffic to Miss Melton-Mowry's website."

"Speak English, Delton."

"SEO stands for 'search engine optimization.' It's all about finding out how people search for what you want to sell and matching those key phrases with your Web content. After she did that, Mom set up Miss Melton-Mowry's video channel and her website with a commission-driven advertising company that placed ads to appeal to her audience. The real money comes with finding items related to etiquette for sale online and linking to them on your site. The clickables there are up to eighty cents per. Cloth napkins were a huge hit."

"Okay, whatever. I'm getting eaten alive here. Cut to the chase."

"She made four hundred dollars in the first week. Mom thinks if she focuses on generating quality original content, she can double that. It's a lot easier than trying to teach kids in the classroom. Plus, she wouldn't have to travel so much."

"But wouldn't she . . . want Miss Information for the videos?"

"No. She's too hard to bend . . . I'm afraid she doesn't translate well to the screen."

"Where's the rest of her, then, Delton? Why'd you take her apart?"

"I . . . be right back." Delton went into the house and returned with a set of car keys. We walked over to the car parked in the driveway. I peered in the windows.

"Back here," he said, and popped the trunk. There, in the trunk of Mrs. Bean's car, lay the pieces of Miss Information.

"We had to dismantle her to fit," Delton said. "Neither Mom nor I was certain that Dad would endorse this plan."

"What plan?" I looked at poor Miss Information, whose head and legs were piled on top of her torso.

"Miss Melton-Mowry didn't know how to thank Mom for all the work she's done; when she told her she was going to sell a bunch of her stuff to pay us, I suggested we take Miss Information in trade, Cassidy. You have to admit, these body parts could make some pretty good pranks."

Delton had a point. "The one on my lawn was sweet."

"And you probably want to up your game . . . seeing as we are heading into middle school."

"Wait? How did I get pulled into this?"

"I asked for Miss Information for us—you, me, Jack. Miss Melton-Mowry liked the idea. She said if it wasn't for your lack of composure, she wouldn't be with us today."

I considered what it might mean to go in on pranks with Delton Bean in middle school. Then I was hit by a vision of her toes (which I'd get Bree to cover in pink nail polish) sticking out of a locker. . . .

"To further prove myself . . . as a prankster, I sent your friend, Miss Olivia Dunn, a package."

"You what? How did you crack that code?"

"It took me a while. It was an interesting variation on the PigPen cipher, which uses fragments of a grid to signify letters or numbers. I wrote her back for you."

"Seriously? What did she say in her letter? What did you say?"

"I can show you the letter if you like. She reported on various camp activities . . . it's an all-girls camp, so there was some skinny-dipping, putting baking soda in the cook's chili; she finally mastered the double flip but doubts her parents will allow her to do it on the slopes until she's a legal adult and no longer relies on them financially. . . . She left several instructions for what you should send to satisfy her sweet tooth."

"I bet she did."

"In keeping with her . . . and *your* mercurial style, I wrote her back using a Caesar cipher. There are twenty-five possibilities. Usually you give the code reader a clue, but to make it extra frustrating, I 'accidentally' tore the letter there so it's impossible to tell. It will probably take her all summer to go through the possibilities."

"What did you say?"

"I took one of my mother's old candy boxes and filled it with peanut shells. On the note, I wrote: 'Dear Olivia, I prefer cracking peanuts at a Tigers game to cracking code during my summer vacation. Hope you're having loads of fun flipping and skinny-dipping. Have to run! Am jumping a train this p.m. Cassidy.'"

"She thought she was getting chocolates and the box was full of peanut shells? And you sent it all in impossible-to-read code?"

"It seemed in character with one of your pranks. As well as the phrase 'loads of.' That's not a phrase I typically use."

"Delton, normally I would congratulate you . . . it's the perfect prank. But . . . but . . ." I stopped talking; I was picturing

Livvy all excited to open her box of chocolates from me, only to find . . . garbage and an impossible-to-read code.

For a moment, I was there with her, watching it happen and feeling her disappointment. "You didn't put any chocolates in at all?"

"I didn't. I . . . didn't think that would be in character." Delton put his hand on my shoulder. "Cassidy, are you all right?"

I shrugged it off. "'Course I am."

"Good, because that's not what I wanted to tell you earlier. I wanted to say that . . ."

I knew I was in trouble when Delton assumed his dining posture.

"Well, I never realized that making pranks with you would be so much fun. That, and discovering you were an actual girl at the luncheon." Delton cleared his throat. "The next logical question would be to ask you if you would—"

"Delton!" I clapped Miss Information's hand over his mouth. "Don't ruin this perfectly good gift of code-cracking and body parts with a subject that's not fit for polite conversation!"

I tossed the arms into the trunk and slammed it shut. "Now go inside and go to bed. I gotta go home."

But I didn't go home right away. Instead, I sat on the curb outside Delton's house trying to figure out what was happening to me—on the inside. Why didn't Delton's prank make me want to hug myself tight to keep from bursting out laughing?

I put my hands on my stomach and felt around for my organs.

They felt . . . complicated.

CHAPTER 26

When at a Loss for Words

I could smell the smoke from the fire pit as I came up the driveway. Mom and Dad, Magda and Jack were all there, sitting on the sawed-off tree stumps Mr. Taylor had nabbed from a housing development and leveled into the perfect stools.

"Cass, come help us test-drive this new product I'm considering for the baking aisle," Dad called out.

"These are amazing." Jack pulled a perfectly crisp marshmallow off a skewer. "They're made of surgical steel so they cook the marshmallow from the inside out."

"And the ceramic handles keep you from burning your hands." Mom held out the bundle for me to choose. "I vote yes."

Handing me the marshmallow bag, Jack asked, "So . . . how's ole Delton?"

"Fine." I was about to ask "How's old Bree?" but instead I shut it, preferring to listen to the fire crackle and turn my skewer—slowly. Our family takes a lot of pride in the way we roast marshmallows—toasty golden, that's our motto.

Pulling his cell phone out of his pocket, Dad looked at the screen and said, "There's someone here to see you, Miss Corcoran. It's about your etiquette class."

"Not her . . . no, Dad. That cannot be my good surprise."

"I'm afraid it is." Mom propped her skewer against the edge of the fire pit and went into the house. As she led Miss Melton-Mowry into the backyard, Dad explained, "You see, there's a part two to your inheritance from Great-Grandma Reed."

"Hello, Cassidy. I bet you're surprised to see me."

I let my skewer dip into the fire, ruining what promised to be a perfectly toasted marshmallow. Was it the sight of Miss Melton-Mowry in a pair of pants or her taking a seat on a tree stump and selecting a skewer that just did me in?

"I am." Which was all I had at the moment for polite conversation.

Jack handed me another marshmallow; I popped it into my mouth and chewed it raw.

"Your parents have given me the distinct pleasure of informing you of the second part of your inheritance. But first, maybe you can instruct me in the proper way to roast a marshmallow. I have very little experience in this area."

I held out my hand for Miss Melton-Mowry's skewer as nightmarish thoughts of etiquette stay-away camp filled my mind. "You can touch as many marshmallows as you want before you choose," I heard myself say. "They get roasted, so it burns off any germs."

"I see."

Handing the skewer back to Miss Melton-Mowry, I watched as she leaned forward and stuck it into the fire.

"No, no." I grabbed it back without saying "excuse me." "That's too close to the flames—you'll burn it. Oh, and it's okay to grab someone's skewer if they're about to scorch a perfectly good marshmallow."

"Here, I'll show you, Miss Melton-Mowry." Jack took the skewer and demonstrated his patented twirl, exactly eight inches above the source of heat, which always changed because flames have a way of bouncing around. It was quite a performance.

"This is more complicated than it seems. Forgive me, but . . . aren't you the young man who visited our table at the country club?" Miss Melton-Mowry asked Jack. "Of course you are." She reached into her purse and pulled out an envelope. "This is your fellow Knight of the Road, isn't it, Cassidy?"

"But how—"

"Maybe you should read the letter, Miss Melton-Mowry," Jack said. "Especially since it has to do with what I've been saving up for all summer."

"You?" I forgot my manners again and pointed at Jack. "You're in on this, too?"

Putting on a pair of reading glasses, Miss Melton-Mowry pulled a single sheet of paper out of the envelope, which she held out to me so I could see what was printed on the front: "To the parents of Cassidy Eleanor Corcoran, to be read and passed on to her etiquette instructor."

"Your mother gave me this letter on the first day of class, when she explained your situation," she said. "To prevent any special treatment of one of my students, I did not read it until our session was over."

She turned in her seat so the fire gave her enough light to read.

To Cassidy's etiquette instructor, please read this to my great-granddaughter if—and only if—she can successfully complete your course.

Dear Cassidy,

Something important happened during your last visit. It wasn't that you nearly killed me or that you destroyed some of my precious possessions. It was how upset you got seeing that poor earwig struggle to free itself from the spider's web. I knew then that you were the child who'd inherited my genes and that someday, when you grew up, the drive to stand up for the voiceless would kick in.

But truly, you were the most undisciplined child I had ever met! How to get all that energy going in the right direction and harness it for good—like saving the rain forest or protecting Bengal tigers from being hunted to extinction? I knew it would nearly kill you to take politeness lessons, but I firmly believed that if you could live through them you might see there's an upside to self-control. You cannot always travel on the My-way Highway, Miss Corcoran. You need discipline.

If you are reading this, it means you successfully completed your etiquette lessons. Congratulations. A fine

effort should be rewarded, and so, in addition, I bestow on
you three tickets to the National Hobo Convention in Britt,
Iowa, plus meals and lodging; that and two first-class train
tickets to transport you and your father as far down the
line as you can get. If your fellow Knight of the Road wants
to accompany you, he'll have to pay for the train himself.

As you travel along the rails of life, Cassidy, remember
that things are not always what they appear to be. I hope
that you will now stop cursing me and enjoy your trip back
in time.

With love,
Great-Grandma Reed

"So . . ." Instead of pointing my skewer at Jack and pretending we were about to duel, I simply said, "Mr. Taylor, is it true
that we're going to the National Hobo Convention?"

"Sure we are. Isn't it great?"

"Yes, it's great! Really?" I was having trouble taking it in—
given my karma and all, I was sure there must be a hitch—but
the whole family was nodding at me. "Wow. This is loads better than dead-body camp!"

"Cassidy, can't you just be happy?" Magda impaled the
ground with her skewer. "Why do you have to keep making
my camp sound so ghoulish?"

I was about to shoot back "Because it's fun to drive you
crazy." But that was not polite and there sat Miss Melton-
Mowry.

Having her around was a real blow to my comedy routines.

"I'm sorry, Magda. I know that the mystery of decomposition is very important to you, and I will try . . ." Ugh. I

couldn't bring myself to be any nicer to my sister, so I turned to Miss Melton-Mowry. "Delton says you're going to make more videos."

"Yes, that's the plan. I have some free time now that our session is over."

"You're still working with Officer Weston, aren't you? Until the big reunion?"

"I thought so, too. Miss Honeycutt had an impressive list for us to cover—cocktail nibbles, holiday punch bowls, invitations to dance—but yesterday Officer Weston called to inform me that he'd decided he was polite enough. He said that saving me at the luncheon reminded him that life is short and that maybe he needed to rethink his priorities."

Jack handed a perfectly browned marshmallow to Miss Melton-Mowry, who stared at it, clearly wondering what to do next.

"Why, thank you, Jack. Speaking of Officer Weston," she continued, "I thought it might be nice to hold a little reunion in a week or so. I was thinking of inviting him, along with you and—"

"I might be busy," I said. Even lying in my Indian sweat lodge was more important than being back in the Melton-Mowry School of Poise and Purpose.

"You, Mr. Bean and . . . Miss Glennon."

I thought about it for a minute. "Would you let her bring Feathers?" I asked. "I happened to learn during polite conversation that Officer Weston is very curious about long-tailed rodents."

"For a private event, I would consider making an exception to the no-dander rule."

"I'll have to check my calendar, but I might be able to work you in. If I'm not Frisbee golfing, that is."

Mom was giving me a look that, for the record, was hard to read in firelight. But I think I got it. "Thank you for the invitation, Miss Melton-Mowry," I said.

Dad took the skewer out of Miss Melton-Mowry's hand. "I think we have the fixings for s'mores in the house, Miss Melton-Mowry. I will be happy to share the etiquette of eating one if you'll follow me. Come on, Mags. Let's leave these two to their plans," he said. Taking Mom's hand, Dad pulled her up.

"Congratulations, sweetie." Mom kissed the top of my head. "See? Your karma isn't so bad after all."

I waited until I'd heard the screen door shut before I said, "You knew all this time and you didn't tell me?"

"I was sworn to secrecy!" Jack protested. "Your dad made me spit-swear."

"So . . . that's really what you've been saving up for?"

Jack reached into his back pocket and pulled out a wallet.

"You have a wallet now, too?"

"I wanted one for these." He fanned a wad of tickets in front of me. "All the way to Osceola, Minnesota. We'll have to take a bus to Britt from there."

"Or hitchhike."

"Not sure your dad will be on board for hitchhiking. Want me to make you a marshmallow?"

"Maybe just one more." I lay back on the grass; it was a perfectly clear night and you could see the Big Dipper and the Little Dipper and a million more stars I didn't know the names of.

"Jack?" Pushing myself up on my elbows, I asked him, "Is that really what you want to spend your money on? You're not just doing it . . . for me, are you?"

"Are you kidding me? This will be sweet. Your great-grandma even picked your dad to go with us. We'll get way more train snacks with him."

"True. Maybe you *are* the same Jack I knew last summer. So now you've got the tickets, will you stop doing odd jobs for the Bensons?"

"Nope."

"Because that's how you get to hang around with Bree," I said, even though I knew it took me dangerously close to ruining another perfect summer night.

Jack removed the marshmallow from his skewer and handed it to me. "You might as well know, Cass. I asked Bree to be my girlfriend. . . ."

Fortunately, a mouthful of marshmallow kept me from answering right away.

"But she said no . . . she said . . . I already had one."

I swallowed. "There's another one? Geez, how many lawns can you mow in one day?"

"She meant you, Cass."

"Jack Taylor!" I got to my feet and tackled him, ending up on his stomach with his arms pinned to his sides. He didn't even fight back. "Don't ever say anything like that again."

"She said all this wrestling that we do . . . how we finish each other's sentences . . . how we . . . watch out for each other; it's what guys and girls do when they—"

"Don't say it. I'll spit in your face! I swear I will."

"What do you want me to say, then? 'Uncle'?"

"Don't say that, either." I rolled off Jack and lay on my back in the grass. "Let's think for a minute."

We crossed our legs and arms, trying to think our way out of this mess.

It was me who broke the silence. "You never say 'uncle.' If you do now, that means you've changed; I don't want you to change."

"But we have changed, Cassidy. You're eleven-teen and I'm . . . I'm almost twelve-and-a-half-teen."

I didn't have a comeback for that. Stargazing can come in handy when you're at a loss for words. "There must be something that stays the same. Forever."

"'Course there is. Stars don't change. At least not for a million years. The Grand River. You and me."

"You and me?"

Jack reached over, grabbed my hand and held it, giving me the perfect opportunity to twist his wrist, bend his arm back and put him in a reverse chinlock.

But I didn't do it.

"You heard me. You and me." He squeezed my hand, but not too hard.

"Jack-Cass Inc."

About the Author

SUE STAUFFACHER has been etiquette-challenged most of her life, but her family lets her eat with them anyway. Sue's novels for young readers include *Harry Sue* and *Donuthead*, which *Kirkus Reviews* called "touching, funny, and gloriously human" in a starred review. Young readers will also enjoy her picture books about plucky real-life heroines, including *Tillie the Terrible Swede* and *Nothing but Trouble*, which won the NAACP Image Award for Outstanding Literary Work for Children. Sue lives in Grand Rapids, Michigan, with her family and various pets. To learn more about Sue and her books, visit her at suestauffacher.com.